THE SEA ON FIRE

Also by Howard Cunnell

MARINE BOY

Howard Cunnell

THE SEA ON FIRE

PICADOR

First published 2012 by Picador
an imprint of Pan Macmillan, a division of Macmillan Publishers Limited
Pan Macmillan, 20 New Wharf Road, London N1 9RR
Basingstoke and Oxford
Associated companies throughout the world
www.panmacmillan.com

ISBN 978-1-4472-0240-0

1 3 5 7 9 8 6 4 2

A CIP catalogue record for this book is available from the British Library.

Printed and bound by CPI Group (UK) Ltd, Croydon, CR0 4YY

Visit www.picador.com to read more about all our books
and to buy them. You will also find features, author interviews and
news of any author events, and you can sign up for e-newsletters
so that you're always first to hear about our new releases.

for Gillian and Adjoa Cunnell

'He supposed he'd had it coming, for his desultory ways. For that failure of perception which had allowed him to conceive of the extended party as a suitable response to life's trials. He had meant no harm. He had failed to compensate, was all.'

Kem Nunn ~ The Dogs of Winter

'The danger of civilisation, of course, is that you will piss away your life on nonsense.'

Jim Harrison ~ The Beast God Forgot to Invent

'Yo ho ho and a bottle of rum
Hoist the mainsail – here I come
Ain't no room on board for the insincere
You're my witness
I'm your mutineer'

Warren Zevon ~ Mutineer

THE SEA ON FIRE

Garland Rain has a golden cast in his grey right eye.

'You still have the sun in your eye,' my daughters tell him whenever he comes to see us in London. He jets in from somewhere hot without telling anyone but me, stays for a night or two in our house in Brixton, and then jets right out again. Where does he go? I don't ask.

'You know you're welcome here any time, Garl,' I say, 'but if you care for us, don't tell me where you're going. If I don't know, I can't say. I'm thinking about my family now. My children.'

'That's good, Kim,' he says, 'that's how it should be. It's all about proving your love.'

I know that's the right thing for me to say to Garland, but he talked about this one place long enough when we were travelling together to get the name into my head: Raja Ampat, the islands of the Four Kings in the Coral Triangle, West Papua, Indonesia. The best wall diving in the world and more besides, Garland said to me once. You've got to see it, Kim. Proper inner space. Big pelagics and clean reefs. The schools of fish are so huge there that they block out the sunlight for minutes at a time.

So deep down I believe I know where he is, that he finally got there, but then I have to think that maybe he just put the name out there for me to pick up. Because he doesn't back me to take a beating even after all we've been through together. I can't blame him. It's like getting a free flow at forty metres down and watching the air you need to live disappearing fast in mercury-coloured bubbles up to the surface. You don't know how you'll behave until something like that happens, but you can look inside your heart and take a good guess. I just have to hope nobody comes here looking for us. That it's all been forgotten.

Suzy, the baby, comes up close to Garland. She sucks her thumb and plays with her belly button. She climbs Garland to stand in his lap. Garland is fudge-coloured, enormous. His brown feet are monumental, his home-made flip-flops big as canoes. Suzy licks his shoulder. She's not really showing off. After all she's known him all her life.

'You taste like salt,' she says.

'Everybody does,' Garland says.

Their brown African noses touch. Suzy, Ghanaian from her mother. Garland, white South African. Suzy holds onto Garland by his long, sun-bleached hair like she's holding the snowy mane of a Palomino horse she's going to ride. With Garland's hair bunched in her little fists, Suzy stares into the eye with the golden cast for a long time. Her mother and I wonder what continents, what worlds she sees. When her thick dark eyelashes tickle Garland's face, he laughs.

'Sing the meteor song,' Suzy says.

'Maybe in a little bit, Suze,' Garland replies.

Jay sits in her mother's lap staring with wide, black, manga eyes. Jay wishes she was a boy, and sits chewing her fingers, consumed by what she wants to be but isn't, wondering if she is the only girl who feels this way. She's waiting for her little sister to do or say something she thinks is funny. Jay knows that if she laughs we will all join in – my daughter has a sweet giggle that you love to hear – and she will feel herself reconnected to the world by the shared laughter of our family. Afterwards she will go back to worrying and chewing in her mother's lap.

Holding Jay, Araba transmits love to her through hands that are never still, sending subtler messages than the declarative hand signals Garland and I once used to communicate underwater. Araba rubs Jay's back, she smooths her short black hair. These gestures recognize Jay's sense of herself as alien. It's going to be all right baby, Araba's hands promise, there are other girls that feel the same. They are waiting for you, and I will help you find them. Jay, her frayed fingers momentarily out of her mouth, leans into her mother's strong hands.

Araba's hair is an Angela Davis explosion, as if my wife should be carrying a rifle and wearing a black leather jacket, not a soft red winceyette house dress faded to coral pink. The way she looks at Garland I can't tell what she's thinking, and I have learned that there is no future in assigning Araba motives she will never claim or recognize as her own. Still though, she's not smiling.

5

'I know you don't really like Garland,' I said when I called from work to tell her that he was coming.

'You still don't understand. It's not that I don't like him, I do. It's what happens to you when you're with him I don't like.'

I want my wife to believe that the terms of my long association with Garland Rain have changed for ever, but I can't pretend I don't know what she means. Araba thinks I'm just as restless as Garland, but I'd say 'he's out there and I'm not', so that should tell her something. Still, there's no denying that Garland will always have a hold on me. We've shared so many head- and heart-changing visions underwater, it truly is a wonder I'm not sitting next to him when he jets back to wherever he's going.

I can remember a stand of ancient and vast Gorgonian sea fans, coloured pinky gold, flaring out from a reef wall at right angles to catch plankton in the current, ninety feet down. Or thousands and thousands of tiny, beach-fire-bright anthia fish disappearing into hidey-holes in the coral as Garland and I swam to them through a shimmering thermocline, the shining fish reappearing in great expelled showers of coloured sparks as we looked back. Swimming one morning inside a giant, shape-shifting cloud of silver fish that suddenly detonated in a starburst under the hunting charge of a gang of barracudas and bonitos. On a shallow reef dive a fork-tailed dugong, back-lit by sunlight, head down and feeding in the sea grass, fully eight feet long and hovering above the billows of sand it made like a radiant golden dirigible above the clouds. Most of all, I remember a glimmering thresher shark edged in light made by countless luminous marine algae. My wetsuited body and the bodies of my companions fringed by the same illuminations, the sea on fire.

Sights that if my wife would ever put her head under the water to look would certainly confirm for her the existence of God. Instead, the things I saw promoted in me the maddening realization that there were endless variations of such wonders, that were both of an everyday brilliance and at the same time unaccountable and lunar strange. What was hard was accommodating the obvious truth that I would not live long enough to see even a fraction of them. Maybe it's just that underwater you are always aware of how little time you have left down there: the finite and ever-decreasing number of breaths you carry with you in a twelve-litre steel tank are recorded and measured on your air gauge. As the needle passes from black numerals to red, you approach the end of your time in the blue world.

It's the same up here of course, we're all running out of air, every second that passes, even if we've constructed a way of life that's intended to distract us from ever thinking about the only thing that really matters. If you do think about it – the closeness of death – how wonderful everything appears! The swirling grooves in the wood of the table I sit at, with Araba at rest in the warming sun, her face to heaven. My daughters' smiles. These things are equally the same magic details of my life that too often go by unnoticed.

One of the kids, Jay, will say: 'I wish I could fly, Daddy-Waddy.' It's likely we'll be in Brockwell Park on a Saturday morning, standing on a rise near the empty basketball courts and looking down at the tropical blue field of the open-air pool. Bright green, ring-necked parakeets – jungle birds some-how transplanted to the city – fly above us, screeching from treetop to treetop. I will be dazed, no doubt, by the accumula-tion of another week at work – swinging a sledgehammer, carrying timber, running a heavy drill into brick and concrete – and Friday night's beers. Looking north, we can see London's gaudy wheel, her towers and skyscrapers, through and above the trees. 'Delivered from gravity and buoyancy I flew around in space,' Jacques Cousteau said after his first dive with the aqualung that Emil Gagnan had built to his design in 1943.

'You fly underwater,' I'll say to Jay, 'you'll see,' and imme-diately I am daydreaming about warm remembered seas when I should be listening to my daughter. I remember star-jumping with Garland down through endless blue water, free-falling through thick clouds of what to me were undifferentiated diatoms and protozoa, gliding down to the masts of a wreck which appeared out of the forest of the reef much like the towers that Jay and I can see ahead through the trees, but sunk and gone beneath the waves.

In 1936 at Le Mourillon, near Toulon, Cousteau, his eyes protected by Fernez goggles, had looked below the Mediter-ranean's surface for the first time. He had been meaning only to swim, and wore the goggles to protect his eyes from the stinging salt. 'Sometimes we are lucky enough to know that our lives have been changed,' he wrote. Astonished by wild gardens of silver algae and unknown fishes swimming in crys-tal water, Cousteau began his journey of exploration. 'Standing up to breathe I saw a trolley-bus, people, electric street-lights. I put my eyes under again and civilization vanished with one last bow. I was in a jungle never seen by those who floated on the opaque roof.'

Because she knows and loves me, every time Garland surfaces back in our lives Araba fears that I will be with him when he leaves, in flight once more from the family she has done so much to make and hold together. She believes my running away is made more likely because Garland and I have secrets that we keep from her. It's a fact that every time I see him I am reminded that the life I live now, with Araba and our daughters, could fall in at any time. Araba might take a phone call that's meant for me, somebody other than Garland could decide to get on a plane and come calling at my door. You've heard how people who want to hide something often choose water – rivers and seas are where we put the things we want to stay lost for ever. And years later the tell-tale thing – often a body of course: a rival, a faithless lover, sometimes a child – comes rising up from where it has refused to stay. I can't speak for Garland, but I'm always waiting for the things we put there to come up out of the water.

But that's not the real reason why I might still run. Once before, I'd left behind a surface world I thought was rotten and looked for refuge under the water, only to find corruption there too, and a greater, final refuge in Araba's love and the love of my children. On good days that's all clear. At bad times, when the bills pile up and Araba and I fight, it's impossible to forget that I was once a waterman – a free voyager in inner space – and here it's a struggle just to put my feet on the floor in the morning. So that's why I'd run and where I'd run. Back to those warm places where the sun came up each morning with what was for me a full and holy brightness, and illuminated the sea with the golden light I wanted to live in for ever. Under the brilliant surface of the water I could hide from a world I couldn't believe in. Each dive a ritual challenge to the murderous insubstantiality in myself that I have otherwise never been able to get rid of for long enough to live well.

For now, I am with my daughter Suzy. Her hair is in riot too, but lion-coloured, not peat-dark like Araba's.

'The sun's behind a cloud,' Suzy says, staring into Garland's eye.

Garland says, 'Is the sun coming out or going in, Suze?'

She looks at him for a long time. Like all of us, Garland's face helps tell the story of the life he's lived. It's an outdoors face, as tough and as weathered as any of his Dutch-Calvinist pioneer ancestors, but rubbed smooth like a beach stone from all his time underwater.

We wait for Suzy to answer, she's thinking about it. Is Garland bringing her family sunshine or grey clouds? My daughter turns her tawny head to me. Her voice is grave, inevitable, a perfect copy of the way that she has heard grown-ups pitch their voices to tell one another bad news. Trying hard to hide her secret delight at being the centre of attention.

'The sun's going in, Daddy,' Suzy says this time.

Everybody's sad, but Suzy gets to decide.

WATERMEN

When I first met Garland he was playing an mbira and singing a song about an asteroid hitting the earth. This was in late November, by a driftwood beach fire down in Al-Quseir, on the Red Sea, years ago now. I had been qualified as a dive guide for less than two months. Every day then was like the birthday that finally turns out the way you hoped it would. In those days there weren't many places to stay in Al-Quseir, and there were not as many divers as at Sharm or Dahab further north, and these were things I liked about the place. That's changed, of course, just like Garland said it would. There's now a hotel where Garland's camp was, and the last I heard the little beach at Mangrove Bay that we used for morning shore dives was a building site, but back then there wasn't much there at all. Hans Hass, the first man to dive and photograph the Red Sea, had said that before he got there he'd learned everything he knew about the region from the journals of an Austrian naturalist named Klunzinger, who had worked as a quarantine medical officer at Al-Quseir from 1866 to, I think, 1875. So the place had that connection with Hass too.

13

In my camp on the beach, I'd wake up to the building heat. As the sun rose, I'd make thick strong coffee on my fire and watch the sea turn from gunmetal grey to a shining lightness. I had worked as a labourer in England for years to pay for the diving courses I needed to qualify as a guide. Those first weeks in Al-Quseir I used to sit on the beach as the heat began to lean hard on my head and chest and work its way inside me. I believed that I had managed to escape the fate that every teacher or social worker I'd ever met had assigned to me and seemed to think I should be happy with.

I was twenty-five then. Why did I invest so much hope in what lay beneath the surface of the blue water? Is it too neat to say that like my daughter Jay, I have always felt as though I come from another planet, and that when I first put my head underwater I thought, There it is? Maybe. I spent my boyhood in a small seaside town on the south coast of England. I'd guess that had something to do with how I felt – growing up in a three-sided world with the fourth open to light and water that went away into the distance for ever. Until I was sixteen, I loved the summers. I would spend all day on the beach, swimming and looking at the water, wondering what was out there beyond the horizon. I read a book about surfing once, where the writer had said how it was hard to imagine death when you danced across the water with a smile on your face and the sun in your hair. That's how the summers were in our town. But there was trouble too. My brother Scott and I were wild, with a too-young mum and no dad.

There must be boys who don't miss a father so badly that the absence is transformed into a kind of interior malignancy you can't get rid of except temporarily, with strong drugs and acts of destruction. Despite the differences between us, Scott wasn't one of those boys, and neither was I. Of course I didn't know that's what it was. You only start to figure these things out when you're older. Back then, I was a liar and a thief, and I got sent to a bunch of places they send boys like me to when they don't know what else to do with us. Scott's three years older, and he was, it seemed to me, everything I wasn't: tough, brave and honest. My wife says that I blame myself for our dad not being there, because he'd left just before I was born, and so I would find ways to hurt myself. I'd cut words and marks into my skin, or let myself be caught stealing a new knife.

Scott was so angry, he burned with it – although if you asked him if he remembered Dad he'd say he didn't. You could see the anger in his shining eyes and his high cheekbones that went brick-red when he was getting ready to fight, but he didn't hate himself. He had a compact certainty that came naturally to him, but that was precious to me because it seemed so far out of reach, and I loved him and wanted to be like him more than anything.

The last place they sent me to was a Methodist-run school with barred windows looking out over the South Downs and the silver sea. I spent my time there gazing through the bars at the open horizon, and thinking about the difference between what I had and what I wanted, and when I got out, at sixteen, in the summer when the real trouble started, I came home to a town that was suddenly full of gangs: Punks and Teds, Rockabillies and Bikers. Scott had been a punk before I went away – punk was made for boys like us – but now he was the leader of a gang of skinheads who were the toughest kids in town. Scott's cropped hair was lightened to gold and his skin was deeply tanned by the southern sun. Like me, Scott's gang would follow him everywhere – we all wanted something to belong to – and we found ourselves in a fateful war with a group of rich young Persians. That's what they called themselves then. Nobody I knew remembered a time when there weren't Persians in our town, and with the help of a reclusive biker called Dug, they controlled the trade in hash and acid, speed and downers. But Scott wanted to change things, he wanted to get past Dug and the Persians and take over. It was a bloody summer that changed everything.

When it was over, Scott went to prison and I ran away, leaving behind a handful of friends getting high on the cheap heroin that began to flood down from the north. There were some years lost to drink and drugs and more violence. I got tattooed from top to bottom with protective mantras and blessings, ships sailing homeward, tropical flowers and nautical stars. Discovering diving when I was twenty-one, it was as though I found myself returned to the summers when I was a boy, with no foreknowledge of harm.

Diving also encouraged me to avoid any demands to grow up or settle down, which was good, because I wasn't ready – not after what had happened and maybe not at all. This would cause its own problems later, when I met Araba and she wanted me to do just that – although, because she knew my story, Araba showed more patience than perhaps I deserved.

Being underwater helped me understand that the surface world I mostly lived in was not the only reality, any more than the way that world was ordered, the death sentence of work and consumption, was either natural or inevitable. When I first reached Egypt all those years ago, it was as though I had finally made it across the border from some huge, cold dark-zone into a dream world, where every day the sunlight made rainbows in the moving water. Emphatically, I was on the run. From the pure poison of the only kind of life I believed I could expect in England, but also from a rottenness that had slowly flowered inside me. At last I felt that I had got away. I would live in the sun for ever, and let it burn out the corruption inside me. Like Cousteau and Hans Hass I would dive with manta rays and sharks, and welcome the reality of all the monsters of the deep. I counted on them to defeat the other monsters I often saw when I closed my eyes and tried to sleep. The people who made rules to try and govern my life couldn't follow me down into the blue. But if I would like to believe that these different worlds – the onshore inland world where I am still often frightened, and the blue underwater world where I can fly – remain separate, then I know now that's not true. Like Cousteau, I was delivered from gravity in inner space, but not from my character or my past.

I found a job working as a guide off an old Nile steamer that was moored to a little cracked wooden pier and operated as a guest house for divers who were looking for something out of the way. Something less crowded than the famous sites at Abu Nahas, where it was not unusual to see fifteen or twenty dive boats all anchored over the Cousteau-discovered wreck of the *Thistlegorm*.

The steamer was owned by an aristocratically mannered

Austrian called Liselle. She was in her sixties, I'd guess. She had a lemon-coloured crew cut and was deeply tan, with thick patterns of freckles that made her brown skin look tooled. She employed a handful of Bedouins who cooked, pumped the air tanks and made running repairs to the ancient Beauchat regulators and buoyancy jackets which made up most of the dive gear. Liselle barked at the men who worked for her in a fluent, rough sounding Bedouin Arabic.

The dive guide I was going to replace was a Swede named Lars, who was around forty or so, big-nosed and rangy, his brown skin marked by cancerous patches – the result of a life lived in the sun. Lars was headed to Mozambique, to Maputo, where the diving had recently opened up. In the days before he left, he took me through the local sites, shore diving along the coast at Maklouf, Mangrove Bay, and El Kaf, which we reached in rickety jeeps that the Bedouins drove through the dunes in bone-shuddering races against one another. Onshore winds were pretty constant. Most often you went into the water from a break or a small canyon in the reef, swimming along the wall of corals into what current there was and drifting back. When you're in the water two or three hours a day you fall into a kind of dream life. And that, of course, was exactly what I wanted. I was counting on this dream world becoming my new reality, so that what I'd left behind would become as unfamiliar as the happiness I was feeling now still seemed.

After I had rinsed off the sets of dive kit and hung them to dry at the end of each day, Lars would mix our sun-downers as Liselle smoked the first of many Nat Sherman Fantasias, fancy coloured cigarettes with a gold leaf filter.

'She has them sent here,' Lars told me, 'thousands at a time.'

My berth on the steamer was down below and it was hot and cramped, airless even with the little porthole open, and loud at night with the rackety sound of the ancient compressor pumping tanks. Plus, Liselle always wanted to sit up drinking gin and bitters and talking about the old days in Egypt when things were, of course, not only different but better. It was always late before I could get to my bunk and you're up early in this game. So after a couple of weeks of not much sleep, I left my dive kit with the other stowed gear up on the bow deck and pitched a tent on the beach.

A day or two before Lars headed north to fly out from Sharm, we were driving back to the steamer after a pretty dive at Maklouf where I had seen my first little reef shark. The party of four German divers we had guided were up ahead, buzzing after seeing the shark. Lars had taken the second jeep out himself. Through the sunglasses we wore against the whipped-up sand, the evening's redness bled into the sea, into Lars's melanin brown hand on the wheel and his free arm on the open window frame of the jeep, into the ruby dunes, into the still-warm air and the bucking sand spouts we passed through. Lars shouted over the sound of the jeep's engine and the roaring wind we made.

'Don't hang around too long after I've gone, Kim. There's no future with the steamer. The wild diving is finished here. For sure, you could make a good living guiding for one of the hotels that are going to be built on this beach, but I don't think that's what you want. I've told Liselle over and over to sell up and move on, but she wants to stay. She says she's been here too long to move, and between us, she doesn't need to make money. I need to get out. A man shouldn't get used to living off a woman.'

I looked at Lars. Liselle handed me worn US dollars at the end of every week. I thought it was all right to be diving every day and getting paid for it. In the lenses of Lars's sunglasses I saw two of me. What Lars meant, I think, is that Liselle would pay us both to stay whether or not any divers came.

'I will miss her, very much. We've been together nearly eight years and, I must admit, I entertained romantic thoughts about her before I even met her. I really came here because of who she was.'

'Who is she?'

'I thought you knew. I thought that's why you were here. I couldn't think of any other reason, unless you're running away from something? Liselle dived with Hans and Lotte Hass in the fifties. On one of their first expeditions to the Red Sea. Can you imagine what it must have been like back then, when nobody had dived here? Can you picture the reefs? How unspoilt and beautiful they must have been. My God. Well, you've read the book *Manta – Teufel Im Roten Mer*: that was the first trip here, in 1949 I think, when Hans was completely on his own. What does he say about the coral fish? Something about the Almighty testing His whole palette on them. As you know, after that first trip Hans and Lotte made many more safaris here and Liselle met and dived with them.'

Lotte Hass was the first woman to dive the Red Sea. I had read the book Lars mentioned. In English it had been called

Under the Red Sea. I'd also read Hass's first book, *Diving to Adventure,* published in England in 1952, a year before Cousteau's *Silent World.* Hass and Cousteau are the most influential figures in the history and development of modern diving. Both men would become environmentalists, increasingly convinced of the need to protect the oceans, but in their early books the dominant images were of a sea where men hunted fish and killed sea monsters who would otherwise kill them – a wild unknown territory to be conquered. When I showed my kids the film of *The Silent World,* the sea was so often red with blood that Jay had nightmares and made me promise not to kill any animals when I went diving.

'Of course, Liselle was a pioneer too,' Lars said. 'Very few women were diving then. Lotte was the best-known, and that American girl, Zale Parry. Liselle, I suppose, was fortunate – she didn't need to make a media career from diving and she wasn't interested, although she had the looks. So nobody knows about her. Fifteen years ago, one of the magazines published a story about her with lots of old photos. Dive mask pushed up in her wet blonde hair, drops of seawater on her brown skin, that kind of thing. I have a copy of it somewhere, I must show you, reading it was what made me want to come out here and find her. The thing is, Liselle fell in love with the Red Sea and stayed. Nobody knows more about this part of the world – everything I know about it I learned from her. But the life she has lived here is finished and the builders are coming. She's already had offers from developers for the steamer. I asked her to come to Maputo with me, but she says it's too late for her to start somewhere new.'

That night the giant old headman, Abdul-Hadi, built a fire on the beach and cooked the snappers he had caught that afternoon on a hand line. I sat on a Pepsi-Cola crate. Lars and Liselle sat in picnic chairs. I asked Liselle about Hans and Lottie Hass. She waited for Lars to light her cigarette before talking.

'They were so beautiful, both of them, they looked like movie stars,' Liselle said, and seen through the smoke her face seemed to become lovely, and for a moment I could see her when she too had been young and beautiful. 'I think the fact that they travelled and dived together was good for their marriage. Of course, he always said that she insisted on coming with him. That she learned to dive and took underwater pictures in the Danube to prove she'd be useful to him. But I just think they were in love, and anyway, he'd have been mad to leave her behind. She was such a lovely girl, all these blonde ringlets. And with the sun on her she was unmatched. Show Kim the picture.'

Abdul-Hadi took out a small photograph from a worn, thin wallet and handed it to me. Recognizably, the photograph showed Hans and Lotte, fresh from the water, their bodies and faces sun-kissed, bright smiles in dark faces that were vibrant with youth and adventure, even if the photo was brown with age. Hass was bearded, his thick, sun-lightened, wet hair swept back, and smiling widely. Inhale and exhale hoses ran up over his shoulders into his air bag. Below the air bag the small oxygen cylinder was attached. He was holding up a large, indeterminate fish. Lotte wore the same dive rig, with her single-lens mask pushed up into her hair. Standing beside her, and lovely enough to be a sister, was the young Liselle.

Behind all three divers, and towering possessively over them, was a white-robed Abdul-Hadi, his youth returned.

After Lars left for Maputo, Liselle took down the faded dream catchers and wind chimes that danced above her sun-blistered cabin door. She seemed stricken. Some mornings she took off in one of the jeeps and you wouldn't see her until it was time for her sun-downer. She ran out of Fantasia Lights and had to smoke rough Egyptian cigarettes. Day and night she walked all over the steamer muttering to herself. I guess I thought it was funny, a story to tell somewhere else down the line. I didn't have the sense to know that I was looking at someone whose heart had been broken.

If we had divers – and most days we didn't – Abdul-Hadi and I would map out the day's two dives; where we dived was dependent on wind and predicted currents, but also on whether we had enough fuel to get there. Divers in the Red Sea wanted clean reefs with good visibility, but of course most people also wanted to see the wrecks and the big pelagics – the oceanic whitetips, the hammerheads and thresher sharks – and we never went far out enough to see those. The tourists were mostly Germans and Austrians who wanted to hear Liselle's stories about Hans and Lotte Hass, but there weren't enough of them. Six divers would be a busy week. That's when I realized that this new life was real. In not much more than a month I went from believing I had found paradise to thinking I might be able to get something better. I quizzed the divers who passed through and thought about making a move.

≈ ≈ ≈

I'd heard stories about some wild divers who had taken over a half-finished and abandoned resort complex a mile or so up the beach, and one night I went along to see for myself. I walked for a while until I could see lights and a little column of smoke rising in the sky beyond the canted dunes.

There were two floors of white boxy rooms with small balconies arranged in a horseshoe around a pool that had no water in it. The floor of the pool had little hills of sand in the corners and piles of empty bottles of Castle and Steinlager beer. Lights were showing in a couple of the rooms and faded wetsuits hung over some of the balconies. Through the lighted window of an empty room I could see a small, well-used submarine compressor and silver tanks lined up for pumping. In the lee of the half-circle of rooms there was a battered pick-up truck with a tarpaulin covering the engine against the sand and salt. A half-dozen tanks sat in the truck's flatbed, mostly twelve-litre steel cylinders, but also a couple of fifteens rigged up as a twin-set. I wouldn't have liked to carry anything that big on my back, and it made me wonder about the man who did.

Men, some with long waving hair, some carrying red-light torches or wearing silver can headphones, moved in and out of the light made by the fire in an oil drum, like the strange creatures you see on a night dive. This was, I later realized, my first sighting of what was to become my tribe – the people who were like me. I had thought myself alone up to this point, so this was a thunderous realization. Some had travelled south from Dahab, others were guides who were passing through to jobs along the coast. Tanned, bearded, self-contained, they looked like men who had made the same kind of base camp on many other lunar shores. Staging posts for voyages to inner space. The sea was their home. I knew that they were looking for pure water; that they'd move to the next rumoured place, dreaming of an underwater paradise where the diving would be of a virgin majesty previously unencountered. This was the quiet determination of us all.

By a driftwood fire, a man bigger and darker than the rest was playing an mbira and singing. The wooden bowl of the thumb piano looked tiny in his huge hands. He had a pair of sunglasses pushed up into his snowy hair. He was wearing an ancient, sun-faded denim shirt cut off at the shoulders, and old rugby shorts. His large feet were stuck into oversized, home-made, rope-soled flip-flops. His big head and huge shoulders were lit up by the beach-fire light as he sang:

Deep down in their graves,
the dinosaurs smile.
No, there ain't been nothin' like this
for a while.
From one end to the other,
it measures a mile.

It's 1997 XF11,
and it's comin' around the bend.
Your plastic is worthless.
You're credit ain't shit.
There'll be no place to use it,
when this sucker hits.

So try to remember,
I know that it's hard,

but 1997 XF11
won't take your Discover,
your Visa or Gold MasterCard.

For a while it'll look like
a star or a comet,
but it's a big badass rock
with our name written on it.

Garland's singing voice was plaintive, surprisingly high for a man his size, and I was affected in a way that I didn't understand. It turns out that there really is an asteroid called 1997 XF11, but it isn't going to smash into the earth, although that's the story that went around when it was discovered. It will pass within six hundred thousand miles of us on 26 October 2028, which is a lot closer than you might think. So it was kind of a silly song, about something that isn't going to happen. At least not this time, but the song still hit home. For some reason the words reminded me of a story an American astronaut had told about coming back from the moon and seeing the earth as a tiny blue pixel, just visible, in infinite black space. How insignificant and fragile and, of course, how precious.

The astronaut had said that after this vision he had given up the story of God as an insufficient explanation for the world, believing instead that the chance existence of our planet and our own fleeting lives on it were the greater miracles. 'That's right,' Garland said when I told him, 'the earth's our only boat, and look what we're doing: punching holes in it. It's like Cousteau said: we depend upon water and air to live, and we've turned them into global garbage cans.'

While I couldn't help but agree with Garland when he got onto the subject of what we had done to the planet, I was most often overwhelmed by the immensity of the damage caused. Which meant that when Garland brought further horrors to my attention, I didn't want to hear him, not at first. What can you say when somebody tells you there's a continent-sized island of plastic rubbish floating in the Pacific Ocean? I wanted to close my head to that kind of talk and drink a cold beer or go diving.

It sounds strange, given the subject matter but, when I think about it now, what's funny about the song is the evidence it suggested of the singer's light-heartedness. I didn't see a lot of that in the years after I got to know him. Garland has many qualities, but the ability to look on the funny side is not foremost among them.

A tall man with a pointed face and pointed ears like a fox, and red hair sun-lightened to copper and hanging past his waist, gave a little whoop and holler and shouted, 'That's it, Garland, that's great man!'

He looked at me with eyes made yellow by the firelight.

'Hey, Garland,' he said. 'Who's this?'

The big man stopped singing and looked at me across the driftwood fire.

'Check the shirt, Rowdy,' he said, and smiled at me. 'He's one of us, so give him a beer.'

I was wearing a cave-diving T-shirt, which a friend had brought back for me from Ginnie Springs in Florida. I'd worn it on purpose, but as soon as I walked into the camp I wished I hadn't played that game. I hadn't been to Florida and I wasn't a cave diver. Cave diving scared me, to put it plainly. I didn't want anything over my head but water when I was diving. It was dark in the caves and I was scared of the dark and had been for a long time.

Rowdy got a bottle of beer from a black plastic dustbin half-filled with seawater. Wiping his hands dry on his plain black T-shirt, he opened the beer with his lighter and handed me the bottle. With every movement he made, his long, penny-coloured hair waved like sea grass in the tide. His arms were slim and tan, corded with veins and muscle, and the hairs on his arms and legs had been burnt yellow by the sun.

'You a cave diver?' he said. 'Good on yer. You blokes are hardcore.'

He took a beer for himself, and held out his bottle to touch mine.

'Not really,' I said.

The long-haired Australian pulled his bottle back.

'You're wearing the shirt though.'

'I just grabbed it on the way over here,' I said, 'A mate of mine brought it back for me.'

'Shit,' the yellow-eyed man said, 'next thing you'll be telling me those tats aren't real. Hey, Garl,' he called, walking away, 'I'm going to pump the rest of those tanks.'

'All right. Hey, do me a favour? Get some of the blokes to clear up the rubbish in the pool.'

Rowdy waved his hand to indicate he'd heard, and then he turned back to Garland, as if remembering something he'd meant to say.

'Have you heard from Tyler yet?' he said.

'What did I tell you about that?' Garland said, an edge to his voice that I would have done well to pay more attention to. Garland owned a familiarity with command and would resist any challenge to his self-appointed status as top man.

'You don't need to keep asking me. I haven't checked my post for a day or two. I'll get into Hurghada soon, maybe, and do that. I'll tell you when I know something.'

Even in the unreliable beach-fire light I saw Rowdy's face redden. He walked away into the darkness without saying anything.

The big man waved me over.

'Don't worry about Rowdy,' he said. 'He's pretty full on and he can seem rough when you first meet him, but he's OK.'

'He's right, though. I shouldn't have worn the shirt.'

'Maybe not if you haven't been there, but I wouldn't beat yourself up over it. What's important is that you learn from mistakes like that.'

He stuck out a big gnarly hand that was both rough and smooth, like a large pumice stone.

'Garland Rain,' he said.

'I'm Kim,' I said.

Straightaway I was grateful to him. Years later I was talking to a surfer girl with a nose ring and getting up myself in a bar in Hana, Maui, when Garland mentioned the shirt again, and that was only, I thought at the time, because he wanted the girl for himself.

'How'sit, Kim – good to meet you. You are a diver, though? I got that much right?'

'Yes.'

'Looking for work?'

I told him about the steamer, about wanting to move on. I said that diving was all that I wanted to do. Garland nodded.

'I can see you've got the fever for it,' he said, 'and I don't want to burst your bubble, but this place will be dived out in a couple of years. Maybe less. I know that's hard to hear. I guess you think you've rocked up in heaven, but somebody's going to come and finish building this place soon, and they'll build more like it up along here and you'll wake up one morning and there'll be a Hard Rock or a Burger King or a Dunkin' Donuts where that big dune is right there. The sea will be thick with boats and overrun with people who dive one week a year. They'll trash the reefs and frighten off the life like every other place somebody found and couldn't keep quiet about. The thing to do is keep ahead of them. Go to work for small opera-tors, and try and educate people about protecting the water and the life in it along the way. Do that before the reefs are gone. Some reports I've read reckon it's already too late, that in less than fifty years we'll lose them all. If the reefs go, that's the way the world will go. Trouble is, it's hard to find anybody who gives a shit, you know?'

'Yeah,' I said, 'you're right.'

I looked at the fire and drank some beer.

Garland was hoping to get out to Indonesia, where conser-vation and environmentalist groups were doing good work trying to protect the Coral Triangle. Forty per cent of the reefs and mangroves there had already gone just in his lifetime, he said, as a result of acidification, rising water temperature and pollution. For Garland it wasn't just a question of getting out there: when he went he wanted to be gone for good, and for that he needed more money than he could raise by diving. Garland said that he was trying to save money so that he could get out to a place called Raja Ampat and maybe buy a share in an eco-friendly dive centre. You couldn't make much money as a dive guide, I'd never had any illusions about that, and looking round the camp, with its makeshift vibe, I had the feeling that Garland's dream was still far off.

Garland became an almost mythical figure for me, and it's hard to distinguish between what I believe about him and what I think I know. His biography is so uncertain as to be, for all practical purposes, untrustworthy. At times I wonder if I give him the qualities I do so that he can serve as an example of how to live my life. I would once have said that because I travelled with him for years I knew him as well as anyone, but now I know that there is at least one person who knows him better. About his family I know nothing except that, like me, he had grown up not knowing his father. He didn't tell me about the circumstances. Whether his father had ever been around, or had left, or died when Garland was small. He was responding to something I'd said: 'Oh yeah?' I remember him saying. 'Me too.'

It was not something Garland ever felt the need to talk about. Not having a father was something he seemed to accept as a given – like being blond or having a cast in his eye – whereas I had obsessed about it for years and years. Garland's view was that I may as well have spent my time obsessing about why there were no more dinosaurs. They were just gone, and had been for a long time. It wasn't as though there was anything anybody could do about it. When he said that it was like a light going on inside me. I'd never considered that I could choose how I felt about things. Not that I really changed, but after I met Garland I was sometimes able to switch off the voice inside my head that was constantly telling me I was shit.

As close as we became, I guess I should know more than I do about Garland, but he is not the kind of man who encourages intimacy. As you can imagine, there were plenty of star-struck diver girls throwing themselves at Garland when we were travelling together, like that girl with the nose ring in Hana, but I don't remember anybody that ever meant anything to him. Despite his long hair, ever present flip-flops and occasional hippy-speak, when it came to the women he loved Garland was reticent to the point of saying nothing at all.

What I do know is that he is part of a white tribe for whom rugby is second in importance only to race, and that when he was a boy growing up in the little beach town of Salt Rock, just north of Durban, Garland had been a brilliant player. His match-changing performances for junior representative teams were still talked about, if not by him, then by people who had seen him play – and when he was just a boy Garland had played before crowds of thousands. And some of those who saw him still talk about what might have been, about the great international career that never materialized.

What seems to have happened is that after his two years national service in the army, Garland walked away from all organization and back to the coast, to Salt Rock. Why, I don't know. This was a year or two before Nelson Mandela was released from prison, and the army was still fighting a bush war with the ANC. Maybe the things Garland saw or did were the reason for the long silences and periods of introspection, that sometimes dented his grey eyes, and hid the golden cast that shone there.

I hear Garland went to work as a beach lifeguard, grew his hair long and spent all his spare time diving the coastline of South Africa's abundant eastern seaboard. There he was a witness to the annual migration of millions of sardines, travelling north in shoals that are so huge – up to fifteen kilometres long and forty metres deep – that they are visible by satellite. These shoals are attended by thousands of predators, by birds, dolphins, sharks and whales.

'You get in the middle of something like that, Kim,' Garland told me, 'I mean, you're in the water with all that life and death, it makes you understand your own insignificance.'

To most people, my wife included, Garland is a man defined by his physical qualities. And to look like he did – the exemplar of a golden waterman: blond, tanned and massive – would feel like a gift for most of us, but sometimes I imagined that other people's concentration on what his body could do saddened him, as it had when he'd played rugby. The fact is, as an athlete – and I played with and against him in hundreds of beach football games – and specifically as a waterman, he was superlative. I only ever met one person who was his equal underwater, a man who, physically, was the complete opposite of Garland, and who abused his body so cavalierly that I had to believe that his almost supernatural ability in the water was a freakish gift, and not the result of the kind of concentrated application to diving that Garland showed.

But Garland was also a source. That first night in Al-Quseir he talked about diving history, and showed me how far back that history went. I'd always thought it started with Hass and Cousteau, but Garland told me that way back in Homer there were stories about men free-diving a hundred feet for sponges and mother of pearl. In Pliny, he said, you could read about divers who used air hoses, while Aristotle wrote about diving bells.

'When did you read Homer?' I asked him.

'Why, does it surprise you?' he said.

'No, mate, I read a lot too. I was just asking.'

'I read him in the army,' Garland said. 'I had big ideas about myself then.'

If all this makes Garland sound too good to be true, he was also sometimes given to brooding and anger. This meant that he was hard on those divers who did not respect the ocean, who didn't care or wouldn't learn. Garland's mantra was: touch nothing underwater. I once saw him publicly dig out an inexperienced diver who had lost control of her buoyancy and grabbed on to part of a reef to slow her involuntary ascent. Garland had seen her break off a piece of hard coral and he was livid. I thought maybe he would be better off talking to the girl quietly, rather than making her cry in front of her mates. But Garland believed most people had no business being in the water in the first place. He was especially critical of instructors and training agencies that certified people as being fit to dive before they had properly mastered neutral buoyancy. For him the ability to put yourself where you needed to be in the water was the first requirement. What Garland cared about was the trashed reef – the coral the girl had broken would be dead for a hundred years. So there was anger in him, and violence too. But I more or less turned a blind eye to that side of him, until it was too late.

≈ ≈ ≈

When Garland packed up and moved south to the Yemen, I went with him. There was a massive falling out with Rowdy before we went. It was none of my business and so I stayed out of it. Rowdy left and I didn't see him again for years. Garland and I found work wherever we went. In the Yemen or Mexico, Borneo or St Kilda, on land or underwater; I'd look round and there he'd be, always by my side, the relative brightness of that golden cast in his eye the only reliable index to his mood.

Living, as we did, at the shore, in makeshift beach camps in groves of windblown palms, or neoprene-smelling rooms at the back of dive centres, even sometimes in balconied guest-house rooms overlooking the ocean, was to live in that marginal place between known and unknown worlds. Between a hard-edged, solid-surfaced world, with its locked doors everywhere, its no entry and stop signs, and the open water, the wild, free territory of flight and possibility. When Cousteau talked about civilization vanishing when we dived, I always thought he meant that was a good thing. Either way, when you dive on shipwrecks you realize that civilizations are impermanent, just like everything else.

At the beach we seemed to live and move in an accompanying and permanent haze of golden light. Maybe it was just that we were always outside and chasing the summer. The kind of light, when I think about it these days, which I remember from my boyhood. Aqueous light, of course, beach light, and the variegated colours and radiance of sunrise and sunset in the tropics. The sky and the shore transformed by an intense but evanescent blood-orange or crimson light that overwhelmed me then and overwhelms me now. It's no use to say that I don't remember the violet sunsets over the South China Sea, because I do. If I shut my eyes I can see it now, sweeping down and softening the beach and the palms and the stoned sunset watchers in a cushioning purple haze.

In those first years diving with Garland, when I was still young, it was as though I had walked through a secret door into the kind of enchanted world that filled the storybooks I had lost myself in when I was a kid – before the violence that had engulfed me when I was sixteen. And the sea was full of even more fairytale animals than you find in books: unicorn fish, spotted eagle rays flying like spaceships, the great trunk-like bodies of moray eels secretly curled in the broken-down holds of derelict ships. And just like in the storybooks, the enchanted world was one where I had special powers. I could fly, but only there, above fantastic coral gardens, or searching through the wrecks in the muted underwater cathedral light.

These were the years when Garland and I became friends and dive partners. The sea challenged us every day. You can't forget that you can die if you make the wrong decisions underwater. In our work we needed to be able to trust and rely on one another. Finding that we could – that each of us was trust-worthy and reliable – meant that the connection between us quickly grew strong. For whatever reason, I commanded an easy grace underwater that did not go unnoticed. Certainly not by Garland, who ever since our first dive together – a sunrise dive at Maklouf the day after we had first met – had called me a natural, and had made me feel good in a way I can still remember, even with all these years gone by. Garland worked hard to master those skills that came so naturally to me, which meant that he owned those skills more truly than I did. His brilliance in the water was backed up by knowledge – the scientific understanding of why not just your body but your consciousness behaves as it does at depth – that I had once sweated to learn for my diving exams, but could never retain in my mind.

How I loved those bright early mornings when we went down to the sea to dive. We lived naturally, as animals or little kids do. I didn't read a newspaper or watch television in years. As much as I was able, I lived entirely in present time. In the mornings Garland and I talked mostly about the weather. Standing barefoot on wet sand we would ask how much wind there was and where it was coming from. We reviewed the tide tables, and reminded each other what time slack water was. We speculated on the likelihood or otherwise of good visibility. What I always hoped for – and got rarely enough for each occurrence to shine in the memory – was stillness, an apparent suspension of the weather. Mornings when there was no wind and the water was flat calm, so that, as they skimmed easily across the glassine water to the dive site, the light inflatable boats we most often dived from in those days would seem to be the only movement in the still and golden light of the day.

More than any other place I can remember, that was what it was like on Nyali beach in Mombasa, Kenya, where the quickly lightening and warming morning air was always fragrant with salt, hibiscus flowers and acacia trees. Garland and I lived there for eight months one year, taking tourists from the hotels diving. I always promised myself that one day I'd go back.

We would leave the beach super early, before anybody else was up, not the women who sold sandalwood carvings of jungle animals, or the men who tried to sign up tourists for safaris or trips in glass-bottomed boats. Later there would be jet-skiers roaring across the water, and three swaybacked horses decked out like Arabian chargers giving kids rides along the shore, but the beach would still be empty when we left for dive sites up and down the coast. Wading out to the little Zodiac inflatable with our kitbags, our feet in the warm shallows would puff up white sand in slowly rising little clouds that turned the water milky. You could feel the outgoing tide pulling at you.

Hovering in the warm and lush water of the Indian Ocean, I remember most often a soft stillness. Aware of the effect each of my inhalations and exhalations had on my position in the water, I would, for once, not hear the ordinarily deafening sound of my own breathing. Instead, ten or so metres down, with sunlight blossoming above me in the shallows, I would find myself surrounded by an overwhelming silence, broken only by the obscure clicks and whistles that you hear on every dive. Seeing long chains of expanding silver bubbles rising to the irradiated water at the surface, I'd look and there would be Garland, sitting motionless, like a meditating Buddha in the water. OK signs flashing between us as we watched a great band of barracudas, lead-dark with the sun above them, cruise in a slow loop over the crown of the reef. Not conscious of the weight I carried – not my body, the twelve-litre steel tank on my back, or the four pounds of lead around my waist – I'd reach out, pushing against the water with my hands and fins, sensitive to more than the water's wetness, to its density and pressure, its swells and currents. Away from the ground, it's freedom that you feel. Like a bird coasting on the gentlest of morning skies. Signalling my divers to follow me, I'd just point my head down and go. In a trance I'd fly over the impossible architecture of the reef – the minarets and domes, high-rise towers and deep tunnels – and examine its uncountable citizens, from tiny, candy-striped nudibranchs to a solitary and giant indigo Napoleon wrasse, as dazzling reef fish quivered in the blue water like animated spring flowers.

In Mombasa there was an open-air place called the Lookout Bar, high up on the bluff above Nyali beach, where you could sit and watch the lowering sun dance in the long breakers of the Indian Ocean. Most afternoons after work we'd head up there to take in the view and drink some cold Tusker beer. Garland wasn't completely straight-edged, though more often than not he disappeared after a couple of beers, but I loved to get high almost as much as I loved to dive. And it's true that the places where we lived and worked – coastal towns and villages that came with picture-postcard, palm fringed, white sand beaches and blue seas – shaped their economies to meet the needs of ever increasing numbers of wealthy western visitors. Which meant, apart from anything else, that there were always drugs. At the Lookout you got Germans who were in Kenya for the safaris, divers from all over, and Nairobi businessmen in shiny suits and pointy shoes, who always had party girls with them. In that crowd I became well known for being up for whatever plans materialized – plans to drink more beer, to get higher, to head into Mombasa to keep the party going – even if, in the morning, I could seldom remember the names of the people I had partied with the night before. There was always a moment in the night when the drink and drugs seemed to align and allow me what I always took to be a true insight, a moment of clarity and understanding about how the world really was. I counted on those cloud-parting visions, chased after them with cold beer and strong grass, and cocaine when I could get it.

I had escaped from everybody's attempts to fuck me and use me and impose their will on me. From the commute and the mortgage. All that shit that you just walk blindly into unless you're smart or lucky or both. Late at night I'd swing in my hammock under a tropical sky filled with shooting stars, and there was me and there was *all that shit out there*, and I would secretly thrill at how great a distance I had managed to put between all that shit and me.

I was among like-minded people of course. People who had washed up on these shores for reasons as complex as mine, or maybe just because they loved the sun. I can't remember his name, but there was a tall, gap-toothed Aussie snowboard instructor with dirty feet, who looked at me across a table full of empty Tusker bottles in the Lookout one night and said: 'You know this one? "Any man who puts their hand on me to govern me, is a usurper and a bloody tyrant and I declare him my enemy."' The Aussie said, 'I live by those words, mate, bloody live by 'em. I do the boarding season up in Banff, and then I take off, go wherever I bloody feel like. I see your tats, reckon I'll get that tatted on me, whaddya reckon?'

'Who said it?' I asked.

'Fucked if I know, mate, does it matter? Let's get a couple more Tuskers, that stuff's the bloody go.'

Because I was young, I was always more or less ready for work in the morning. I felt fine as soon as my head was underwater. It was a long time before Garland voiced his disapproval. It was a lot longer before I could see the harm I was causing clearly enough to trace with certainty the arc of what would become my burnout.

≈ ≈ ≈

Every year or so I'd wash up back in south London for the summer, just to have a base. Sometimes Garland came with me, other times he went on to different places on his own. During those summers I worked as a lifeguard at an open-air swimming pool in Brixton. Sandy Wolfe-Mason, the pool's owner, was a diver and a friend of mine. He always kept a job open for me. Sandy was around fifty, tall and willowy with watery blue eyes and an aristocratic voice and manner that he used to keep most people at an emotional distance. With the people he loved, he couldn't do enough. For Sandy, who was divorced, love was constancy's outcome, and thus hard earned. He had spent twenty years in military intelligence before, as he said, 'giving in to his hippy nature' and taking over the old pool. On summer days, Sandy would look out on the busy water from behind a battered, dog-chewed pair of Arnette sunglasses. Most often he wore ancient linen trousers and a succession of Sun & Sea Hawaiian shirts, so, unless you included the long, straw-coloured hair that he wore in what might be taken for a Samurai's topknot, there were few clues in Sandy's appearance to his martial past. Not until you factored in his ability to watch the water for hours at a time, and remembered that his survival in Berlin or Armagh had most often depended upon a protean talent for disguise. I'd met him in Hawaii, on a boat going out to dive Molokini Reef. He was one of those resourceful, modest blokes you want to be friends with. Sandy the Gent, as Garland called him, valued loyalty and honesty above everything else. Seven and a bit years ago Sandy introduced me to Araba and her nine-year-old daughter Lee. Then pop pop, we had the babies and that was the three girls – Lee, Jay and Suzy. Jay was, strictly speaking, my adopted daughter. Araba was a couple of months pregnant when I met her. The baby wasn't planned but she was going to keep it. She told me straightaway. I convinced myself it made no difference to me, and not long after we had Suzy, Araba and I were married. We spent our honeymoon at Sandy's white-washed cottage near the Cuckmere River Valley. I tried to keep a wife and a family while travelling all over.

Why would I want to get married when I had worked so

hard for my freedom? Certainly I think Garland was bewildered by my decision at first. Growing up without a dad, I don't think it's a real surprise that I ended up with the kind of family I did. I guess deep down I always wanted to have kids, but I hadn't really thought about what that meant. Now, I don't need to be told that being a dad and wanting to be free are contradictory desires, but everybody needs to find out things for themselves. I did think that what I thought of as Araba's exotic appearance – her dressed hair, the ranks of chiming bracelets on her arms – might correspond to an interior wildness that matched my own. I thought she might come with me, in other words. I thought she might want to learn to dive. I soon discovered that Araba had no interest in diving or travelling, and she was as grounded as I was free-floating and irresponsible. By then it was too late. I think she was the first real grown-up I'd met. Maybe because she was so young when she had Lee. Araba's appearance was exotic only to me – not to the community she belonged to or the continent she came out of.

That was the first of many things I needed to learn about Araba – and I wanted to learn because our story was the oldest of old stories. I fell in love with her the minute I saw her, before Sandy introduced us, when she came into the Lido after church one Sunday morning, looking for Lee, and I could no more resist her than I could ignore the call of the sea. I always wanted to have the smell of her on my skin.

Araba is short – her head comes up to my chest – with a boyish upper body and a slim waist flaring out to full African hips, over strong legs and flat feet that seem to be forever planted on solid ground. The day I met her she'd changed into a halter top decorated with sunflowers, and faded blue shorts belonging to an uncle who had played football for Sweden. Her jewelled and decorated arms were both slender and sculpted with muscle, and her brown skin was darkened further, made blushed and shining by the sun.

She had locks then, and they were tied back so that the sun-lightened tips touched her narrow shoulders. It seemed to me then, and still does, that Araba owned an interior luminosity that suggested a hard-earned certainty about herself and how she saw the world. Certainly her shining eyes sought me out, in a way that was both interrogative and welcoming. Araba is no pushover, but she has a smiling way of looking at me – a look full of tenderness and understanding and sometimes even admiration – that makes me feel more than I am.

Inevitably though, I began to travel less. Before Araba, I was away for maybe nine months of every year. By the time Suzy was born, it was less than half that. I was in love enough to give up that much. I thought it was a fair arrangement, to leave Araba alone with Lee and the babies while I trucked off to Borneo or wherever. Araba loved me enough to say nothing at first, and if she was unhappy, I didn't want to hear it. I thought I was the one making sacrifices. After all, Garland was still out there all the time.

It was my belief that Araba disliked Garland from the start. When my father-in-law, Kwame Mensah, was still a young man, he had left Ghana for South Africa. In Ghana, Kwame had written articles for the *Daily Graphic* that were critical of Kwame Nkrumah's new independent government. The story

Araba told me was that pressure had been put on her father to leave the country. He went to Europe first. This was in the fifties. After ten years, around the time of Sharpeville, Kwame felt compelled to go to South Africa, where he immediately joined the struggle against apartheid.

Kwame spent some years in prison, and when Garland talked, I believe my wife heard, before anything else, a man talking in the accent of her father's torturers and jailers. Kwame eventually went back to Europe. He lived in Stockholm for a time, where he met his Swedish wife, my mother-in law Benedikta, and where Araba was born. The family came to England when Araba was very small, and settled in Wotton-Under-Edge in Gloucestershire. Araba had come to Brixton when she was a seventeen-year-old punk. In Brixton, she said, people looked like her and not at her, and that had made all the difference.

Garland was over for a visit once and the three of us were out somewhere.

'What's the difference between a white cow and a black cow?' Garland said.

Araba made a face.

'White cow says moo, black cow says moo, man.'

The way Garland spoke it came out *'bleck caa'*.

'When was the last time you heard me say "man", Garland?' Araba said.

Garland was surprised that Araba was angry with him. Garland made jokes so rarely, I honestly think he was trying to make a friendly connection with Araba. I sometimes thought he didn't care about people at all, their fights to live and so on.

As far as I could make out, he had left the struggles of the peopled world behind when he left the army and headed for the coast. Nothing that happened on the dry surfaces of the earth seemed to upset him, not bombs nor wars – nothing. He thought that story was already over.

Garland's politics were concentrated on the sea, and in practical and moral terms, the destruction of the coral reefs meant the end of the world to him. That's where most, if not all, of his anger came from. So it was unusual to see him try and make a connection with Araba, somebody who was not a diver and so was not tuned into how he saw things. My own surprise that Araba was upset about the joke was, when I thought about it later, confirmation I shouldn't have needed that my marriage was as much a journey of discovery as any diving safari to the remote and lovely offshore reefs of the world.

≈ ≈ ≈

In the summer before Garland and I returned to the Red Sea, I was doing some lifeguarding, a bit of pool teaching two nights a week, and when one of the bigger dive schools needed an extra instructor I was also spending the weekends up at the National Diving Centre in the midlands. This was a freshwater quarry called Stoney Cove, where I spent long days and nights running people through their qualifying dives in cold, dark water. I'd spent a month in the early spring guiding with Garland on the island of Ponza in the Tyrrhenian Sea, but I'd been home since then, and although I wasn't planning to go away, the feeling that I needed to was building again.

We lived in rent-controlled housing, but I still wasn't bringing home enough money to feed my family. I made fifty pounds each night for the pool teaching, and could earn a couple of hundred for the teaching at Stoney, but I might only work one weekend a month. Sandy gave me as many hours lifeguarding as he could, but it was a bad year for sun, and so the hours I got still didn't pay enough. When I did get a few quid together, I sometimes drank in a pub called the Effra Tavern, on the corner of Kellett and Rattray Roads in Brixton. The Effra stands on a hidden London river of the same name that empties into the Thames at Vauxhall, and if you believe the stories it's a river that King Canute once sailed on. I didn't even try and turn back the tide of drink that came my way in that place. I didn't want to admit that my old free life had ended, and that if I wanted to get it back I would have to smash up my family. Here it was, summer in England, and I was spending too much time looking out the pub window at the August rain, dreaming of all the places I had been. I should have been at home telling stories to my children.

When Araba and I first got together we made out like kids on the settee every night. Then she began working as a fund-raiser for a Christian charity, and at night she studied for a lay reader course, or went to Parochial Church Council meetings, or visited one of the old women she knew from church who lived alone and wanted somebody to pray with. She never seemed to have any time to just hang out and drink a cold beer. The kids ran loudly around the house, and Araba and I fought all the time. The religion she embraced so joyfully, that gave her face such radiance when she prayed or sang her hymns, I held responsible for the subjugation and destruction of the Polynesian people and islands where I sometimes fantasized I might belong.

On the day Garland and I were due to leave for the Red Sea, Araba and I were walking in Brockwell Park trying to ignore the rain.

'What are we going to do?' she said.

Araba walked directly ahead with her feet flat on the ground, and when she spoke her almond-shaped, honey-coloured eyes looked me straight in the face. She was wearing a burnt-orange and yellow kente head scarf, but the striking colours seemed pale against the brightness of the crucifix that she wore next to her dark skin.

'What do you mean?'

She put her cool hand on my face.

'I don't think you want to be with us. Do you know how much money we owe? I can't sleep because I'm so worried about money, and you don't care or think about it or even notice. I'm doing everything. I need more from you. You're not lifeguarding now the pool's closed and I need more money than you get from diving. I need you to help with the kids.'

Back at the house, Lee looked at our faces and said 'Gosh', the way she did when Araba and I fought, drawing the word out so that it seemed to mean everything at once. Disappointment but not surprise; anger that we were together if we were just going to argue and upset her and her little sisters. She went into her room, slamming the door. I got a beer from the fridge, Araba made herself some herbal tea. Jay had a broken amphora that I'd brought home from the Mediterranean on the table and was trying to glue the pieces together. Suzy was bashing away at the mbira which Garland had given her and singing the meteor song:

> *We could live like God's children,*
> *we could come from the heart.*
> *We could all pull together,*
> *instead of apart*
>
> *Who knows*
> *for a while it could*
> *seem heaven on earth.*
> *It's just an idea,*
> *tell me what is it worth?*
>
> *To unplug the telly,*
> *and get out of the car*
> *And if you need help,*
> *just look up at the stars*
>
> *They seem a great distance,*
> *but we know they're not far,*
> *cause 1997 XF11 is a comin'*
> *around the bend.*

Jay held up two amphora pieces by the side of her head so that they looked like ceramic ears.

'When's the meteor going to get here?' Suzy said

'The meteor's not coming here, baby,' Araba said.

'But Daddy says it will.'

'It's just one of Daddy and Garland's stories. Daddy doesn't mean it.'

Later that night Araba said, 'He's here.'

I got out of bed and pulled on a pair of shorts.

Garland and I had signed to an agency that found work for dive guides. A lot of the time it was last-minute stuff, and a couple of days earlier Garland had called to say he had got us a three-week safari in the southern Red Sea. Araba and I had argued about it, but I was going.

Araba sat up in bed and watched me get ready. The lamplight shone behind her head and made the thick black curls of her hair glow redly. I always kept a dive bag packed and ready to go. I sat on the bed to put my boots on, Araba pulled me to her and held me. I held her and breathed her in, pushing my face into her thick hair.

'I can't promise I'll be here for you when you come back this time,' she said.

'This is what I do,' I said.

'It's what you do now,' she said. 'The girls need someone who's going to be around. I do too.'

When I didn't say anything she said, 'I mean it.'

'I love you,' I said.

'I know you do,' Araba said, 'but I need more from you now.'

'You told me we needed money. I'll be earning.'

'Oh Kim, the money's not enough, not when I've paid for somebody to look after the kids.'

'I could be sitting here on my arse and earning nothing. It's work.'

'It's not enough.'

'I've got to go. I'll be back before you know it.'

Araba held on.

'I've got to go, sweetheart.'

Good luck Tibetan charms – an ohm cut out from a coin, two protective little sugar-white skulls – tinkled on the ignition key-ring of the cab Garland picked me up in. Garland sat in the front.

'Put your kit on the back seat,' he said, 'the boot's rammed with my gear.'

I sat behind the driver. A dark unshaven man with black circles under his eyes. He had a picture of a woman and two children blue-tacked to his dashboard. There was a hanger by my window with a supermarket uniform on it. Garland turned round to look at me.

'Everything all right?'

I rubbed my face.

'Mate, you know how it is.'

'I know you think that you're following your heart,' Araba had said, 'but you know your heart is here with us.'

'I know.'

'You say that but you're still going.'

'Yes.'

She pushed me away. 'It's not just you that wants to be free,' she said. 'I'm sorry for what happened to you but that was a long time ago. You can't keep hiding behind it. You need to meet your responsibilities, and you can't keep living with us unless you pay the bills.'

'How would it be if it was you?' I said, suddenly furious. 'What if the things that happened to me had happened to you?

And I told you to stop hiding behind it, and just forget about it. How would that be?'

'Oh Kim,' Araba said.

'What?' I shouted, 'Oh Kim, what?'

When Araba didn't say anything I said, 'I can't not go, but I'll be back in three weeks.'

'That might not be good enough,' Araba said.

'That's the best I can do. I've got to go. I'm going to kiss the kids now,' I said.

'Did you say goodbye to Lee?'

'Yes.'

'All right,' Araba said. She wouldn't look at me.

'All right,' I said.

Jay and Suzy were sleeping the way only little kids can, submerged deep in the dreamworld of flying, or being chased by monsters. Jay was five and a bit then and Suzy was four. In the top bunk Jay slept with her Buzz Lightyear duvet cover thrown off, and one foot hanging over the side. Suzy sucked her thumb. Her hair was dark and wet with sweat at the roots, her cheeks looked flushed. Suzy's head was hot and I opened the window. I climbed up the ladder to kiss Jay goodbye. I kissed her and, still with her eyes closed, she reached up and pulled me close.

'Daddeeee,' she said.

Suzy, out of sight, said, 'Dadda,' in a sleepy voice.

'You awake, Suze,' I said.

'Yeah,' she said.

'Come up here then.'

Suzy's head, her hair all bushed out and wild, appeared at

the top of the ladder. She started to climb up on her sister's bed.

'Can you manage, Suze?' I said.

'Yeah,' Suzy said, her voice made small by the physical effort. When she made it up onto the bed, I sat with my back against the wall, Jay hanging onto my neck and pretending to be asleep, Suzy in my lap.

'You know I've got to go away for a bit,' I told them.

Jay squeezed my neck tighter.

'Where are you going, Dadda?' Suzy whispered.

'I'm going to a place where there are lots of sharks and dolphins, but I'll be back before you know it.'

'No you won't, Dadda,' Suzy said. 'You always say that and it always seems long to me.'

'I know, Suze,' I said, and hugged her. 'I'm sorry.'

'Will you bring me a present?'

'Of course, honey. What do you want?'

'A sharky.'

'OK,' I said. I gently tickled Jay under the arms.

'What about you, Jay?' I said.

Jay kept her eyes tightly closed.

'I don't want you to go,' she said.

'I know, baby.'

I sat there holding my girls. A car horn sounded.

'OK, I've got to go, babies.'

'Nooooo,' Jay said, and opened her eyes.

'I've got to, sweetie.'

I unlocked Jay's arms from around my neck and got her to

lie down. I carried Suzy down the ladder and put her into bed. I felt their eyes on me.

'Bye,' I said softly.

'Bye, Daddy,' they whispered back.

I left the house. It was dark outside. Garland was waiting in the car. I wiped my face. The Tibetan charms promised good luck. The driver pulled away, the photograph of his family where he could always see it. I thought of my wife and children awake in the house, thinking of me, and I said goodbye to all that love.

SHANG-TU

Garland looked out the open bus window at a huge hoarding that read 'Buy Your Dream Home in the Sun'. 'No chance,' he said. We were driving on a new-build, four-lane motorway to the marina. It was dusk, but the air coming in the window was thick with heat.

'What's that?' I said.

I had been miles away, thinking about marriage. About all the things that we bring to a relationship that gain a weight as time passes. Sitting next to a fidgeting and uncomfortable Garland Rain on the flight out to Hurghada, it seemed to me that Araba and I could talk for ever, but the different things we told each other we needed to make us happy, suggested we would never have a good marriage. I believed that we both knew this, and that we also hoped we could find some so far undiscovered common ground to build our family on. It was not lost on me that when I was home I was forever thinking about places in the sun, but now it was Araba who filled my mind. I was homesick for her, and this homesickness was as inevitable as my need to get away.

Araba doesn't know this, but whenever I went on a trip I always dug out of the wash and packed a T-shirt she had recently worn, that had her scent, and sometimes I would sleep holding onto it. The difficulties we had living together had nothing to do with love, and everything to do with the unresolved conflict in my heart. Maybe I just needed to think differently about what love meant. How far you would go, how much of yourself you would give up, for love.

'I said, not a chance. Look at this place,' Garland said.

Hurghada had changed since Garland and I had seen it last. On the outskirts of town the bus lights had illuminated a shadowy landscape of half-built apartment blocks, surrounded by an incredible tide of rubbish and litter. Downtown was booming, flooded with lights and people looking addled and sunburned, blasted by the day's heat and the night's cocktails, reeling from one gaudily lit storefront to another. Outside the bars and the four-floor malls, hawkers called the tourists in. They crowded outside Moby Dick's, Tropical Murphy's Irish Pub, The Ministry of Sound. Drum and Bass clashed with the Egyptian dance music pounding out of every taxi, reverberating against the pastel walls of the buildings that were lit up brighter than day by strobes and floodlights. On the illuminated walls, clubs and parties were advertised: Little Buddha's Full Moon Party, The Calypso Pub, Hedkandi. Soldiers guarding the entrance to the marina stood in front of a sign that said: 'The Adventure Never Ends.'

On the plane Garland had told me what he knew about the job partly, I guess, to take his mind off how much he hated flying. The seats were always much too small for him, and he was so big that his head brushed the ceiling when he stood up. The experience, I would guess, was almost the exact opposite of the freedom he found underwater.

'The guy I talked to said his name was Casey. He told me the *Shang-Tu*'s a new build,' Garland said. 'This is the first time she'll be going out. We're taking her down to the islands.'

'The Brothers?' I said.

'Yep, the Brothers, and maybe Daedalus and Zabarghad.'

'They're taking her all the way down there first time out?'

'So he said.'

The Southern Red Sea begins at Safaga and extends to Sudan. In the middle of that region are the island groups of the Brothers, Daedalus and Zabarghad. Of these, the Brothers were the northernmost, but still 150 kilometres from Hurghada – which meant a sailing time of eight hours.

Diving in the Red Sea was popularized by Hans Hass's book *Under the Red Sea*, by Cousteau's *The Silent World*, and by Eugenie Clark's articles and David Doubilet's photographs in *National Geographic*. It was sustained by the success of PADI – the Professional Association of Diving Instructors – in making the sport more accessible. After the Sinai was returned to the Egyptians in 1982, dive tourism really boomed. There was a huge hotel building programme, together with increasing numbers of dive centres and the development of live-aboards. Chasing the tourist dollar, Sharm El Sheikh and Hurghada became what we now saw – a tacky hybrid of western seaside town and Arabian bazaar – while the sites within a day's boat ride out of these towns, such as the famous wreck reefs of Abu Nahas, had all become hopelessly over-dived. So some divers turned their backs on the mess they had created, and went looking further south for new and unspoiled sites.

Thirty years ago, as few as fifty divers a year visited the Brothers. One eighties pioneer was Eric Hanauer, a writer and photographer who had named the islands after the figures in George Orwell's book. Hanauer described sailing to the islands in a thirty-foot wooden fishing boat powered by a two-litre diesel engine, with mattresses, tank compressor, and water jugs tied to the deck. Once people like Hanauer had showed the way, however, others followed, and from the mid-to-late nineties the Egyptian government had denied divers access to the islands, partly because of the cost and inconvenience to the Egyptian navy of rescuing sub-standard dive boats that broke down so far away from the nearest port, but also because the government wanted to protect the islands from harm caused by diving, in particular from the damage caused by boats anchoring on the reefs. The Hurghada Environmental Protective and Conservation Association was formed to install and service permanent mooring buoys on dive sites including the Brothers Islands. The sites were reopened to dive operators in 1999, subject to a fee, and their boats meeting tough entry requirements.

From the water, you might easily miss the two islands but for the British built, Victorian lighthouse standing thirty metres high on Big Brother. The islands sit about a kilometre apart, and are a pair of steep-sided cones made from volcanic eruptions. They are small – Big Brother is only about 400 metres long and 100 wide – and isolated more or less midway between Egypt and Saudi Arabia. The water surrounding them is notorious for fast and unpredictable currents. The deep plunging walls of the reefs are characterized by dense fields of hard and soft corals of all colours, and by great shoals of reef fish – anthias, sweepers, glassfish. Larger marine animals, barracudas, jacks and tuna, turtles and groupers are present in big numbers, too.

What the islands are best known for, apart from the two wrecks – the *Numidia* and the *Aida* – on Big Brother, and the forest of giant Gorgonian sea fans on Little Brother, are the numbers of sharks you can, if you're lucky, expect to see there. Not just reef sharks and oceanic whitetips, but scalloped hammerheads and even thresher sharks. For my money, the fast currents, big sharks, and sheer drop-offs mean that these two small islands offer some of the best wall diving anywhere in the world, but because of the isolation and the currents, to dive them safely you have to know what you're doing. There have been plenty of accidents over the years.

When the bus stopped inside the marina the doors sucked open and a small bug-eyed white man got on carrying an open can of Sakara beer. He was smoking, and except when he was in the water I never saw him when he wasn't. There was a dirty luminosity to his skin, like the bad part of town at night, and you could smell old sweat on him. He was wearing an unwashed, candy-striped Reebok tennis shirt with the collar up, football shorts and off-white Reebok tennis shoes with no socks. He had a little pot belly, a grown-out crew cut that showed grey, and odd long hairs on his face that he must have missed when he was shaving.

'I'm Casey,' he said. 'The boat's down at the end of the harbour. You can go straight down.'

'I thought we'd have a sit down and a talk,' Garland said, 'get the paperwork out of the way.'

Garland wanted to see a contract. He wanted things to be done correctly. He wanted Casey to show us around the boat and meet the skipper. He wanted to know that we had permits to travel to the islands, and he wanted to see the certification cards and the logbooks that would tell us whether the divers on board were all experienced enough to dive there. Casey looked out the bus window, and made a kind of low 'unh' noise in his throat. I came to recognize that sound as a signal of his unhappiness. I heard it so often over the coming weeks I would expect it whenever I spoke to him, as if for him unhappiness was a condition that at some point in his life had become permanent. Plainly, he was spooked, and gave off a persecuted, beaten-dog vibe. I wondered if it was Garland, looming over him, with his hair loose and wild, the cast in his eye seeming to blaze and telling you, if you were paying attention, that he was just this side of being pissed off. But then it was clear that Casey wasn't paying attention, not to us. Whatever was eating him was a story that we'd walked into halfway through.

'There's no time now,' he said, looking past us down the road. 'I'm supposed to be in town. I'll see you blokes later, or in the morning. We'll go through everything then. We're heading for the Brothers, but you know that. Go on down. Jody'll show you around.'

Without waiting for Garland to protest or say anything else at all, and still carrying his beer and smoking, Casey got off the bus and walked out of our sight past two soldiers in dusty black fatigues who were patrolling the harbour in the moonlight.

Casey had a thin, unconvincing voice to begin with, and both the volume and clarity of his words diminished as he came to the end of whatever he was saying. As if by this dissociative tic Casey could avoid responsibility for what he said. After all, you couldn't be asked to stand by your words if nobody was quite sure what they heard. Casey's voice reinforced the sense of oddness inspired by his appearance. Casey didn't look or talk or carry himself in any way at all like a man who owned a brand-new dive boat.

'What do you make of that?' I said.

Garland was looking after Casey as he walked away.

'Who did he say? Jody?' I said.

Garland nodded.

'You know anybody called Jody?'

'Nope.'

'Is that a boy or a girl even, do you think?'

'Mate, I've just said I don't know.'

Garland and I got off the bus and carried our gear down to the wooden pier to where a dozen or more live-aboards were moored. Garland stomped along the marina's boardwalk, not speaking, humping his gear as if he wanted to throw it at someone. Dance music rumbled from the town. Boat lights illuminated the littered and dirty harbour water. Posses of sickly green, blind-looking fish were rising out of the dark water to eat the rubbish. A pair of ragged and hungry mongrel dogs swept past our legs like fast moving shadows. But otherwise the marina seemed deserted. I shifted my kitbag to my other shoulder. My T-shirt stuck to my back but I didn't mind. I could feel that old free feeling coming back. At the far end of the pier we found *Shang-Tu*, the new boat shining white under the harbour lights, like a three-tiered wedding cake before the guests arrive.

≈ ≈ ≈

Jody turned out to be a girl, and she lay stretched out on her stomach on the floor of the over-lit saloon, smoking a joint and watching *Point Break* too loud on a laptop. She was hugging a couple of big saffron-coloured brocade cushions. On the screen a suntanned kid sold Keanu Reeves a longboard and told him that surfing was 'a source'. The film seemed to play on every dive boat I'd ever been on. Keanu played Johnny Utah, an undercover FBI agent investigating a series of bank robberies by a gang calling themselves the Ex-Presidents. Utah's partner, played by Gary Busey, believes that the Ex-Presidents are surfers, robbing banks to fund their endless summer. To get close to the gang Utah needs to learn to surf. 'It'll change your life,' the kid selling Keanu the board says, the voice distorted by the volume, 'swear to God.' I've seen the film at least a dozen times, but I still couldn't tell if the kid in the surf shop was a boy or a girl.

Jody was fair, with bright green eyes and a sunburned broken nose, and she was beginning to tan in her legs and face. Her figure was boyishly slender, and she was wearing very tight coral-coloured Fat Face shorts and a baby blue fleece. She had a red hibiscus flower in her shoulder-length, woolly, locksed-up hair. She was all of nineteen, I thought, and when she sees Garland she's going to flip.

In the forward half of the saloon there was a big dining

table, a serving counter, and a small door into the galley. Built into the corner was a hot water station with packets of tea and instant coffee, and cups in racks, and little plastic pots of UHT milk. Dive computers and cameras were plugged in and charging, lights blinking red and green, on an extension board on the floor. The stairs going down to the berths were in this part of the saloon. In the other half of the saloon, where Jody lay on the floor, there was a long three-sided couch and a glass table etched with a picture of a three-masted schooner. On the table, but not on the coasters that were placed there, were two dirty glasses and half a dozen knocked over, empty cans of Sakara beer.

A glass sliding door opened out onto the kit-up area and a small dive deck. A young crewman slowly wiped the glass and tried not to look at Jody on the floor. In racks above benches set into the middle of the kit-up area there were tanks with little strips of silver gaffer tape across their O-rings to show that they were pumped full of air and ready to use. Under the benches there were plastic trays for keeping kit in, and above the benches, dark wetsuits had been hung up and pairs of black neoprene legs swung back and forth as the moored boat rocked gently on the harbour water.

Jody was kicking her slim, toffee-coloured legs behind her as she watched the movie, her feet scissoring and making the silver-plate charms of her ankle bracelets ring against one another. She looked up as Garland came through the glass door behind me, and her legs and her feet stopped moving and the tinkling of her ankle bracelets came to a gradual stop.

'Shit,' she said, 'it's Bodhi.'

I don't think that Garland knew she was referring to the man Patrick Swayze plays in *Point Break*, the surfer and leader of the Ex-Presidents whose name was Bodhi, short for Bodhisattva. Garland did look like him, although he was bigger and blonder. Garland might get it if you asked him to remember watching the film with me on the beach at San Augustinillo, on Mexico's Pacific coast. Which we did, the film projected onto a white sheet staked in the sand, the soundtrack blasting over the ever-repeated rushing noise of the waves breaking on the beach. But you'd have to remind him; he just wasn't interested in anything that wasn't real. I don't imagine he ever gave a thought to how much, or how little, he was like Swayze's surfing Bodhisattva. From the Sanskrit, Araba had told me after we had watched the film one night. One whose being, or *sattva*, is *bodhi*, or enlightened, but who from compassion postpones entering nirvana in order to help suffering souls.

'It's a funny name,' my wife said, 'to give to a character who robs banks, gets his brother killed, kidnaps his ex-girlfriend and holds her hostage just so that he can go surfing all year round, don't you think?'

I hadn't answered. Swayze's resemblance to Garland was not lost on her, and she was letting me know that no matter how many times I watched the movie, taking Patrick Swayze's character as a model of how to live was never going to be a good idea. More than once Araba had sat through *Point Break* as the night-time winter rain drummed down outside our little house, and no doubt she resented the way I seemed to lean towards the bright screen, feeding like a starving man on the

Californian sunlight, the endless parties, the golden beaches and the never-ending blue water.

'So are you the guys we've been waiting for?' Jody asked. 'Can we go now you're here?'

'You want to go?' Garland said, and smiled at her. 'Where do you want to go?'

'Where do you think? The islands. I'm going spare. I need to get wet. Diving's a source,' she said, mimicking the stoner certainty of the Californian girl-boy from the movie. 'It'll change your life, swear to God.' She laughed.

Garland said, 'I'm thinking we'll get underway in the morning, but I need to talk to the skipper, and Casey when he comes back from town. What's Casey said to you about what's happening?'

'Nothing, except to say we're waiting for you guys, and that you were supposed to arrive sometime tonight, and here you are. I doubt you'll be up by the time old Casey gets back, though. Not if he's on it with Teddy.'

'On it?' Garland said.

'You know,' Jody said, and put one freckled and painted finger against the side of her nose and sniffed.

When she did that I shivered and the small hairs on the backs of my hands rose the way they did underwater, when thousands of tiny bubbles congregated between them. Garland looked at me but didn't say anything. He looked around the saloon and grunted. He picked up a small smeared mirror that was on one arm of the couch, and looked at me again. He put the mirror back and looked at our worn and faded kitbags as though he wanted to take them back off the boat.

'You known these guys long?' Garland said. He'd stopped walking around the saloon and sat on the couch.

She looked at the joint, shook herself, lit the joint and took a big pull, hoovering back the smoke. She got smoke in her eye, and she looked up at me with that eye closed.

'I'm Teddy's PA.'

'Who's Teddy?' Garland said.

'You don't know Teddy King?' she said, as if to say, you don't know the stars come out at night? You don't know you were born?

'This is all his: the boat, the dive shop back home, the video business, and a whole bunch of other stuff.'

'I thought the boat was Casey's,' Garland said.

'Nope, Casey works for Teddy, like me.'

The story was that Casey had been working as an instructor in Malta when Teddy and a friend had been there on business. The friend was a diver, who persuaded Teddy to learn.

'Teddy took lessons with Casey and loved it, being under-water, with how big he is and everything. So, Teddy being Teddy, he brings Casey back to London and puts up the money for a dive shop, sticks Casey in it to run it, and I get lessons, and here we all are. So it's lucky Rowdy got Teddy into it in the first place.'

Garland looked at me.

'Rowdy?' he said to Jody. 'Aussie? Tall, long red hair, cross all the time?'

'He's got short hair now, but yeah, it sounds like him,' Jody said, 'You'll see him soon enough, he's on the boat. Why, do you know him?'

'Yep,' said Garland, 'I knew him years ago.'

Garland bit his lip. I didn't know what had happened between them, but it wasn't just for Garland's sake that I wasn't happy about being on the same boat as Rowdy.

A young crewman in a Red Sea Divers fleece and blue shorts came in to the saloon carrying two cans of Sakara and two glasses on a tray. He handed us each a cold wet can and a glass. He put the empty glasses and cans on his tray, set the tray on the floor, and wiped the table clean of the smeary rings left behind. When he'd finished, Garland carefully put his can and glass on coasters. I did the same. The boy watched us. Garland thanked the boy in Arabic.

The film ran on. Jody had turned the volume down but not by much, and our voices clashed with those on the screen. Once or twice Garland had looked as if he was going to tell Jody to shut it off, but he didn't. A different girl-boy, the one he ends up sleeping with, was dragging Johnny Utah out of the water and telling him he had no business being out there if he couldn't surf. The girl is Bodhi's ex-girlfriend, and later Johnny will get her to teach him to surf by claiming his parents died in a crash like hers did.

I drank some beer and watched the film for a little bit because my favourite scene was coming up: the one where the girl is by her car in the dunes, and shimmies out of her bikini and into her cut-offs before driving away. It was my favourite mostly because the girl and the scene reminded me of growing up at the beach in a way that made it seem like yesterday. Beach girls in falling light, getting into their cut-offs and T-shirts after a day in the sun and sea. I loved how quick the girl was to change, none of this taking hours getting ready. Sun and salt on her skin, wet hair, no make-up. I couldn't help but notice that Jody had that look about her too, small breasts, a face made boyish by her broken nose. An action girl, the kind that made the best divers. With blokes there was always too much proving something to themselves.

When Jody caught me looking at her I felt myself redden. She smiled and said, 'What's your wife's name?'

'Why?'

'I'm just curious. If I was your wife, I wouldn't let you out of my sight.'

'Araba,' I said.

'Araba?'

'It's an African name, my wife's half Ghanaian and half Swedish. It means born on a Tuesday.'

'Your wife doesn't dive, then?'

'What makes you think that?'

'Well, because, look, I don't mean anything by this, but how many black divers do you know?'

I was willing to bet that around the world there were plenty of black divers, and would put money on most of the crew of the *Shang-Tu* being as good in the water as I was. But no one in my family, not Araba, nor her father or brother had ever been interested. It's also true that if most divers who travel on live-aboards are white, then a lot of the best diving in the world is in countries where the people are black or brown. Jody wasn't talking about any of this. She said, 'black people don't dive' the way you hear people say, 'black people can't swim because their bones are too heavy', the kind of nonsense idea white people in England take inside themselves from the day they're born. But the best swimmer I ever knew was a Zambian named Victor Malwa, a lifeguard I worked with one summer, who was the first Sub-Saharan African to swim the English Channel.

Jody lit the joint again. She bugged me, or maybe I was just tired. At the same time I couldn't keep my eyes off her. I was tripping from not sleeping. Often when I was that wiped out I would lose whatever small amount of self-possession I had managed to accumulate over the years. I would lose my manners, to be frank. At such times and in such arguments I was not beyond using my wife's blackness, and the fact of our kids, as a means of claiming some – some what? Some unearned authority? That I didn't do so this time had less to do with control than with how Jody, filled to the brim, I shouldn't wonder, with more stupid and harmful ideas, was packed into her tight coral shorts. How young she was. How she seemed to be coming on to me. How the compact shape of her pressed against her baby blue fleece.

'If Teddy catches me smoking weed he'll go mad,' she said, holding up the joint. 'He doesn't seem to care what anybody else gets up to, just me. Don't tell him, all right?'

She pulled an aerosol of Citrus Magic out from under the brocade cushions and lay on her back and squirted a little of the air freshener straight above her. I recognized the brand as the one Araba bought from the whole-foods shop on Atlantic Road in Brixton. My mind flashed on Araba and home, as the smell of grapefruit that was nothing like the smell of grapefruit blossomed around me.

'Shit!' Jody said. 'It's gone in my eyes! Get me some water!'

I wetted a tissue from a box on the glass table and wiped Jody's eye. The stuff cost over £8 for a little aerosol, I guess because it was supposed to be natural and you paid more to feel better about yourself. Why not just open a window?

Back at FBI headquarters Johnny Utah was using the girl's licence plate number to get information about her, something he could use to get an in with her.

'Can you show us where we're going to sleep, Jody?' I said.

'I like it when you say my name,' she said. 'I like your tattoos. They're groovy.'

Jody gave the room another squirt. She held her arms up. When I pulled her up, she stood close to me. In bare feet she came up to my chest. She reached for Garland. She swung our hands and said, 'Come on handsome boys, let's go downstairs.'

She took us below. There were rooms to either side of a narrow corridor. The overhead light was red and unsteady. A door opened as we passed and a dark-haired couple poked their heads out.

'Hello, Jody,' the woman said, 'any news?'

They looked like brother and sister. Both had short black hair, very white, capped teeth, and looked like they spent a lot of time in a gym. They were both wearing black running vests and shorts. Diving would be one of a number of expensive sports they would have taken up, I guessed. They were the sort of people who would never lose the sufficient amount of self-consciousness to really embrace the water. They would be gear-heads – for them the point of diving would be to overcome the challenge of not wanting to dive in the first place.

Standing in the doorway I could feel the heat coming from their room and I wondered why they were spending their evening below. I thought they might be the kind of couple who went everywhere together and never socialized with anybody else. Maybe their idea of socializing didn't involve cocaine and lager.

'Hey, Susan. This is Garland and Kim, they're the guides. And this is Susan and Tony. So I guess that's news, right, Susan? And it looks like we'll be getting underway in the morning.'

Susan looked at Garland and said, 'Is that right?'

Suddenly Garland smiled radiantly. He was good with clients. 'Should be,' he said, 'Can't see any reason why we wouldn't.'

At the end of the corridor Jody showed us into a two-bunk cabin. Garland threw his dry bag on the bottom bunk.

Jody said, 'Those two are the only people on this boat paying full-price. Tony and Susan. He doesn't say anything, but she always wants to know what's happening.'

'How do you mean they're the only people paying?' I said.

'Teddy partly put this trip together as a thank you for the people who work for him. It's the kind of thing Teddy does.'

'Partly?'

'Yeah, well, Teddy's smart. He says the trip's a thank you but he invited a journalist and a photographer he knows from *Banker* to write about the diving.'

'The sex and football magazine?' I said.

She nodded. 'Yeah, can you believe it? He's paid for them to come out for three whole weeks. Teddy wants to sell trips, eventually he wants a whole bunch of dive boats, so if he gets a feature in *Banker* that can only be good, right? That's what this is really all about, business. They get a free diving holiday, free kit, and Teddy gets to sell dive trips.'

Banker was one of the first of what became known as Lads' Magazines. I could see how a trip on a live-aboard could service *Banker*'s view of the world as a playground – the site of a never ending party for thrill-seeking white boys with nothing in their heads but a sense of entitlement. That we were being employed by a man who wanted to bring more and more of these people out to a place as pure as the Brothers would bug the hell out of Garland. I wasn't too happy about it either, but I was more used to these people than Garland. At heart, a lot were just wild boys who resisted anybody telling them what to do. I wasn't too far off being like them. All we wanted was to escape a life of circumscription and wage slavery, and get out into the world to see what was there.

The trouble was that this attitude most often led to selfish and destructive behaviour. The thing was to try and learn something from the places you went to and the people you met along the way. That might sound obvious, but what I've found is that plenty of people have no interest in those kinds of exchanges. All they're out for is a good time, and stuff anybody else. I wondered what kind we had on board.

Jody opened a door to a small bathroom, showing us the toilet and the little bin where you put the used paper.

'Somebody empties the bin every day but it can get a bit stinky in here. Still, you're big tough divers, you know the score. You want to chill,' she said, 'then unpack? I'm going back upstairs for a beer. Will I see you up there?'

Jody stared hard at me. She made her eyes go big and tried not to laugh. The cabin was too small with Garland in it. I didn't have the energy to listen to whatever it was he was working up to say after Jody left us alone. I didn't want to go from Araba owning everything I did to Garland doing the same. Through the tiny porthole the harbour water sparkled under the lights of the dive boats. There was rubbish in the water but it still looked pretty. Garland sat on the bunk and started taking things out of his dry bag.

'That sounds good,' I said, 'I could drink another beer. You coming back up, Garl?'

Garland looked at me with the ceiling light haloing his head, his face dark with the light all behind him. The light was full on Jody. I was so tired I felt like I was in two countries at once, but when I looked at Jody I could feel the excitement beat in me.

'We need to talk about tomorrow, Kim. What we're going to do. Plan the dives.'

'Well, come up with me now,' I said, knowing that he wanted to talk to me alone, 'and we'll talk. Or we'll get up early. My head's buzzing. I'm going up for a cold beer and a look at the stars and then I'm going to bed. I'll most probably sleep up on deck, like usual. If I see the skipper before I crash, or if Casey comes back, I'll call you.'

'Do you like to sleep outside?' Jody said. 'Me too. I'll show you a good place.'

I could feel Garland's look on me but I kept my eyes turned

away from him. Garland could be relentless. All the questions could wait. I'd been around enough to know the score, and from what I had seen and heard so far nobody was going to be up and around too early in the morning. And that suited me. If this lot were as far into the dope and drink as it seemed, nobody would hold us to a schedule. I'd worked on party boats before and while it was always hard on deck there was often less pressure on you as a dive guide. That people weren't up at sunrise meant that often you could do the best dive of the day with no one else in the water.

Plans could wait. Part of me wanted to carve out a little time and space for myself. I wanted to drink a cold beer in the warm homecoming night and look at the stars and know that I was really back in Egypt. I told myself there would be no harm in sharing a beer and a joint with a pretty girl who didn't know anything about me, with whom I could pretend to be anybody I wanted.

'I'm going up,' Jody said, standing with one hand on the door frame, the other on her hip. She was fringed in dim red light from the hallway. 'And I'm getting beers out of the fridge.'

'We're in the harbour,' Garland said when Jody had gone, 'you won't be able to see the stars for all the lights.'

It was, I thought, entirely in Garland's character to say something like that.

'Mate,' I said, 'Work starts tomorrow, unless I missed something.'

Garland snorted again. Like I say, I can lose my manners and my discipline when I'm tired.

'Look, Garl,' I said, 'I just need to put an end to the journey.

Come up. Anything you think needs figuring out will be easier over a beer.'

Garland pulled more stuff out of his bag.

'Have you spoke to Araba and your kids?' he said.

'You know I haven't. I need to borrow your mobile to call them.'

'You want it now?' He'd pulled the phone out from his bag and was offering it to me. 'It's got juice.'

I was halfway out the door. I could smell Jody's after-sun in the passageway.

'No, mate,' I said, 'it's too late.'

≈ ≈ ≈

Jody was back hugging the brocade cushions. There were two unopened and sweating cans of Sakara where the empty ones had been.

'Hey,' she said, 'there you are. You alone? Good.'

She patted a saffron cushion. 'Sit.'

She opened a beer and poured slowly, so that it didn't foam, into a tall glass held at a tilt. She handed me the glass. It was cold.

'Here,' she said. She watched me drink it down. When I put the glass on the table she smiled. 'Better?' she said.

'Yes. You look like you've done that before.'

'You too,' she said. 'I've done a lot of things before.' She picked up my glass and poured some more beer into it and put the glass down on a coaster.

'So, he's the boss?'

'Who, Garland?' I said, and looked at her.

Her white hair had not quite settled into locks. It was still woolly. Maybe she didn't know how to treat her hair the way Araba did. Individual wiry little hairs stood free, and were illuminated by the light that framed her head, like filaments made incandescent by a living current pulsing through her.

'Yep,' I said, feeling light-headed, 'Garl's the chief.'

'Do you mind?'

'What's to mind? Garland's a legend. I mean he has some trouble switching off when he's working. He's like—'

I stopped. I was about to say that Garland was like my wife.

'Like what?' she said.

'No, nothing, I was just saying Garland's good, nearly all the time. He can take things a bit seriously that's all. He's a bit relentless.'

'Not like you?'

'No. I can switch off for sure.'

'I'm glad he's not here, he scares me.'

Jody reached into the buttoned pocket of her baby blue fleece and pulled out another joint.

'Come on,' she said. 'You said you wanted to sit out. Bring your beer.'

She went through the sliding doors that went out onto the kitting-up deck. The lights were still on in downtown Hurghada, and I could hear thumping Drum and Bass. Jody swayed up the stairs to the sun deck, ankle bracelets tinkling, as I followed with my nose close to her backside. I wanted to pull her shorts down. Her legs smelled strongly of after-sun and I wanted to kiss them.

'Up here,' she whispered when we reached the sun deck, and we went up more stairs to the flybridge. There was a sleeping bag rolled up on the deck.

'I sleep there,' Jody said, and unrolled the bag so that we could sit on it. *Shang-Tu* rocked gently and pulled on her moorings.

I looked up, and sure enough, the stars were almost invisible. Jody and I shared the joint and I rolled another one. We told each other our stories. After a while I put my arms around her, and she cuddled into me, and we sat like that for I don't know how long. I can't say that I really knew what I was doing. Certainly I never thought about consequences. We slept still holding each other. I woke to loud voices. The boat moved as people came aboard.

'Shit!' Jody said.

'What?' I said, and raised up. Jody pushed my head back down.

'It's Teddy and everybody. He'll go mad if he finds me up here with you. Get down, get in the bag.'

'Why?'

'Don't talk, just get down.'

Heavy feet were banging on the stairs. Somebody stood on the top step and breathed hard. After he got his breath back he said, 'Jody? Jo-o-o-o-o-o-d-e-e-e-e-e-e. You asleep? Jody? You asleep?'

His breath rumbled some more. Then the ladder shuddered again as he went down the stairs.

A different voice said, 'She asleep, Ted?'

'Like a baby. Fuck, I love her. Did I ever tell you that, Aussie?'

'Only a million times, Ted.'

It was Rowdy all right. I recognized his voice.

'Well, I'm telling you again, so don't be fucking smart. Get it out.'

'All right, Ted. Hang on. Where's Casey?'

'Don't give any to that cunt.'

'I wasn't going to, that's why I want to know where he is. There you go, mate, get it into yer.'

'Nice one.'

'Bobby, Bobby! How ya battling, mate? Have a bit of this. Do yourself a favour and get out from under for once in your fucking life. Stop feeling sorry for your fucking self. That's it, mate, that'll cheer you up.'

I wondered when Rowdy had fallen into the cocaine, and whether it was before or after hooking up with Teddy King. It wasn't a situation Garland was going to enjoy.

'Oi Oi, here he is,' said Teddy. 'Case, Case – where's my fucking beer? You just got yourself one? Rowdy, you always said he was a cunt and you were right. What sort of cunt gets a beer for himself and nobody else.'

Casey said, 'The kind of cunt who's sick of everybody getting on his back. Who's got the gear?'

'You have, Case, last we heard,' Teddy said. 'Ain't that right, Rowdy?'

'That's what we heard, Teddy, yes, mate. Casey's holding all the gear.'

'I haven't got any gear.'

Rowdy said, 'Then you're fucked mate, because you're not getting any of mine.'

Bobby said, 'Here, Case, I chopped one out for you.'

'Bobby, Bobby, Bobby,' Teddy said.

A new voice, drunker and more expensively educated than the rest, said, 'Here, have you seen my impression of an octopus? This is really fucking brilliant.'

There was laughing and cries of outrage and Teddy said, 'That is the most fucking disgusting thing I've ever seen in my fucking life. Bobby! Bob! Throw the cunt over the side. Do one of your stunts on him. Fuck. I'm going to have to have another line after that. Fucking put your bollocks away, mate. Tristan, can't you control him? Oh fuck look, he's only taking a picture of it!'

There was more laughter, but when Teddy spoke again his voice owned a harder edge.

'Don't you point that at me,' he said. 'You take a picture of anything but your octopus bollocks and I'll throw the fucking camera over the side, and you as well. You'll take pictures of us when I tell you it's time to take pictures. Otherwise keep the fucking thing away from me. Do you know how much money I've sunk into this boat? You're being paid to make me look good. Make me look bad and you will fucking regret it.'

'Christ,' I whispered into Jody's ear, 'are they like this all the time?'

Jody said, 'They'll be at it all night. Come here, I'll make you forget about them.'

≈ ≈ ≈

I opened my eyes to a white sky, and there was white, locksed-up hair on the head of the bare white girl who was sleeping curled into me. I shut my eyes and thought: when I open them again it'll be dark because the heavy velvet curtains will be closed to the morning light, and Araba's locks will be black again and she'll be black again. But when I opened my eyes the sky and the girl and her hair were still white and I remembered. Something had woken me. We were underway. There was something digging in my back – the plastic hibiscus flower that I thought had been real when I first saw it in Jody's hair.

Sometime in the night I'd worked out that Jody reminded me of a girl I used to know when I was a kid. The same fairness, the same boyish figure, the same electric-green eyes. The resemblance was so strong that, under a bruise-coloured night sky, and falling half in and out of sleep with Jody's breath hot on my face, I couldn't help but be taken back to a part of my past I was always trying and failing to forget.

Her name was Dawn, and when we first met she was twelve and I was fourteen. She was a tiny, super-tough punk then, but when I got out of that place on the Downs, when I was sixteen, she was one of Scott's new gang, a fierce skinhead boot-girl with a bleach blonde feathercut, huge, kohl-lined green eyes and bleached, skin-tight Levis and monkey boots. I was her first proper boyfriend. We carved our initials on each other's arms.

Dawn's father was Dug, the ex-Hells Angel who controlled the supply of drugs in our town. The Persians sold in the wealthy areas in the west, and the skinheads had the poorer territories east of the Pier, but it was Dug who sold them the stuff in the first place. He lived with Dawn in three unpainted rooms above a garage where he did custom repair work on motorcycles, and when I think about him, which I still do too much, he is always dirty in my mind. His forearms were most often so thick with grease and dirt that I couldn't see the winged Death's Heads I knew were tattooed there. There were other tattoos buried under the dirt on his hands. On the left between the thumb and index finger he had '13', and in the same place on the right he had '1%'. The '13' was for marijuana – M the 13th letter in the alphabet – and '1%' meant that he belonged to the 1% who didn't fit in and didn't care.

Dug mostly wore dirty blue overalls and no shirt, and steel toe-capped boots whose heels made sparks as he crossed his yard. He had long black curly hair, a greasy black beard and black eyes with irises so compressed they seemed crushed. His low brow was deeply lined and overhanging, and his nose had been bashed in more than once. He had 'AFFA' – Angels Forever Forever Angels – tattooed on the left side of his neck. Back then, his muddy coloured shoulders humped with muscle, his voice a low rumble, he had seemed like a giant to me – now I reckon I must be a head bigger than he ever was. Dawn was the only person he cared about, and he had a fierce love for his daughter. After her mum took off it was just the two of them. Dawn told me that in the summers when she was little he took her to biker festivals like the Bulldog Bash. She loved riding with her dad. She'd hug his back as he pushed the big bike past a hundred miles an hour, and scream happily as her dad leaned so far into the curves she could feel the heat coming from the road. All she felt was safe, she said. Dug did everything to keep me away from her. I was a beach bum – a tan pretty boy in cut-off jeans, flip-flops, and red hair down past my shoulders. I looked more like a girl than his daughter did.

My brother Scott wanted me to use Dawn to find out which side her dad was favouring in the war between the skinheads and the Persians. Dawn found out about it and we split up. When the big fight finally happened between the two gangs, by mistake I beat up and badly hurt a kid who had nothing to do with the Persians. Scott raged at me for always screwing up, and hit me, and because I was mad at my brother and mad at Dawn but mostly mad at myself, I ran to Dug's compound and tried to burn it down. He caught me in the alley behind his yard, beat me unconscious and dragged me inside, and it was three days and nights before I escaped.

Who really knows why things happen? I'm not saying I slept with Jody because she reminded me of the first girl I loved. I try not to think about Dawn too much, to be honest, because all that happens when I do is remember what her dad did to me. The time when I was a prisoner is one that, as you might expect, returns to me most often in the dark. So perhaps the familiar nightmare woke me first, as it has done more times than I can count, and finding myself holding tight to Jody it came to me how fair and slender she was, like Dawn. And did Teddy's crazy-man voice, drugged and ominous in the dark, subconsciously remind me of Dug? Maybe. Then again it could just have been that I was back in Egypt once again. What happened to me when I was sixteen was what had led me to Egypt, and Garland Rain, in the first place after all.

Clearly, too, there was a connection between my sleeping with Jody and how things were left between Araba and me in London. Did I believe that the way I lived my life out of sight of home held no consequences for the family I left behind? I must have. Had I thought of my children before I took Jody in my arms? Not enough to stop me putting my hands under the waistband of her soft shorts that were the same colour as my wife's favourite house dress, and pulling them down past young legs that were, no matter how tan they became, always palely unfamiliar next to my hand.

The truth is, Jody was young and she was hot, and she was into what I was into; and the place I had come from and had trouble calling home was so far away it began to seem, as my days in the sun and nights in her arms accumulated, not to be there at all.

On that first morning I struggled out of her sleeping bag, stood up and started looking for the heavy dive watch I had taken off in the night because the cold glass face and metal bezel had made Jody jump when it touched against her heated skin.

'Fuck,' I said.

'What?'

'Fuck fuck fuck. What time is it?'

'Early.' She lifted the sleeping bag so that I could see her. 'Come here,' she said. I could smell us. I could taste her on my mouth.

'I've got to go to work. Fuck, Garland's going to kill me.'

The early morning sun spangled the water and hurt my eyes. Ahead of us a flotilla of day boats were racing, rushing to get onto the closer dive sites before each other. Off the stern I could still see the pink, blue, yellow and terracotta buildings of Hurghada marina, and the exposed frames of dozens more unfinished buildings. One concrete, windowless minareted building might have been a mosque or, come to that, a shopping centre or yet another hotel. All these buildings diminished until they became shapes, and then slowly disappeared, until only the red coast remained visible.

The crew were praying together on the sun deck. When I first came to the Red Sea it was rare to see the crew praying in public together. Now it was a common sight. Garland had told me once that I needed to understand that the dive guide lives and works between worlds. He didn't just mean in the obvious sense of the difference between the undersea world and dry land, but between the paying divers and the working crew. The dive guide is somebody who needs to live between cultures.

Relations between these two groups are obviously different on every boat. I've found that many divers seem not to notice the crew at all, especially when that crew is black, and will go the whole trip never learning the names of the people who are in control, for the short time they are aboard, of the world they are living in. I thought the least you could do was to learn the name of the person who collects your dirty toilet paper every morning, but you'd be amazed how many people didn't bother.

It's also true that people who can afford to dive on liveaboards in remote places in the world are most often well-off, and that's always true when it comes to how much money they have compared to the people who service them. Garland had taught me how important my relationship with every member of any crew was. Your reputation, and with it your ability to work, was based on what these men said about you – how you were in and out of the water. Five minutes after the first dive the crew will have decided whether you are any good or not. Garland said that I had to be extra careful because of my tattoos. In a lot of countries we worked in, including Egypt, being as heavily tattooed as I was meant that you were taken for a criminal and an outcast unless you could prove otherwise.

For a good crew you needed a top-class skipper, engineer, cook and small boat handler. A good skipper can make your life as a guide a whole lot easier, but if he doesn't like you, watch out because you might find that he'll start telling you he can't take you to the dive sites you want to go to. He'll tell you the tides or the currents are wrong. Maybe there'll be a problem with the engine or the compressor that the engineer can't fix, and you'll find yourself stuck where you don't want to be. So you needed to be the kind of person a crew was happy to work with.

I knew that every crewman would already know that the new guide had slept with the blonde girl. It might make me look like a big man to the readers of *Banker*, but I doubted that the crew of praying men, who did not see their families for weeks or months at a time, would think much of me. Especially if they knew I had a wife and daughters at home.

So when Garland's white head showed and he thumped up the ladder to the flybridge, I knew why he was angry. It wasn't just because he disapproved. It was because I had made our lives a whole lot more difficult. When Garland appeared, Jody held the sleeping bag up to cover herself.

'Get dressed,' he said to her.

Jody disappeared into the sleeping bag and wriggled around in there. She came out dressed and red in the face. She started down the ladder. I watched her go. She stuck her tongue out at me, and rolled her eyes. I wanted to smile but didn't.

I had taken great pride from my friendship with Garland. When I doubted myself as a waterman, the man I partnered with supplied my bona fides. As far as our community was concerned I needed no other. If Garland said you were sound, then you were. Now we couldn't look at each other. It was a hard realization to bear that when he spoke to me, all the years we had spent together, the equal and familiar professional relationship I believed we had built on our friendship, Garland's respect for me that I had worked for and coveted, more than I should have, all that seemed to be gone from his voice. We were not yet out of sight of land, but Garland looked and sounded like a man who already believed that the success of our trip to the islands, and our safe return home, was his responsibility alone. He could depend on nobody but himself.

'Get below,' he said, staring at the water. 'Get some coffee into you or do whatever it is you need to do to be ready for work and get back up here. You've got ten minutes.'

≈ ≈ ≈

Shang-Tu's crew were still praying in the photographic light of early morning. Near by and paying them no attention were three other men, white divers, sitting on the banquette that ran around the sun deck. Of these, two were men I didn't recognize. One was a fit-looking man in his early thirties, wearing tight green swimmers, mirrored aviator shades, a red wool hat, and a silver medal of St Jude, the patron saint of lost causes and desperate situations, on a delicate silver chain around his neck. His long, knotty, horse face, pitted with deep acne scars, gave away nothing of what he was thinking. He was rubbing baby oil on his smooth brown stomach in the early morning sunshine.

The story Jody had whispered to me, as we lay under the Arabian sky, was that Bobby Ballet had lived in La Rochelle for years, where he made an all-right living as a dancer and stuntman, until his body couldn't take the hard dance floors any more, and the stunt work slowly dried up. Bobby had put by a bit of money, and started to look around for something else. He had run into Casey and Teddy King on a dive trip to Mauritius. Somehow, sitting by the Indian Ocean and partying through the long hot nights, Teddy had persuaded Bobby to put all the money he had saved into his dive shop. Bobby was left with the idea that he was coming in as a partner, but three years later he was still working all hours in the shop and hadn't seen any return on his money. I suppose Bobby knew deep down that he had lost every penny. It must have been a hard truth to accommodate. I thought that Bobby had every reason to hate Teddy King, and to want to do him harm, but to look at him in his shades and Cousteau hat, sunning himself in the early morning, you wouldn't think Bobby was troubled by anything at all.

'Something's going on,' Jody told me. 'Behind those shades Bobby's got a black eye, and he didn't have that when he got on the boat. It's all mucho suspicio,' she said, and kissed me on the ear.

Rowdy sat near Bobby. He had cut back his copper-coloured hair and grown a chopped red moustache but I recognized him straightaway. His slim arms were still corded with muscle, the hair on them still burning yellow, but it was the angry vibe he fired off that made me sure it was him. Rowdy had always been tightly wound in the short time I had known him. Now – whether because of the cocaine he had evidently become fond of since I'd seen him last, or for some other reason – an angry, molten energy vibrated from him. He pushed a freckled hand through his flaming hair and tried and failed to smooth down his electric-looking moustache. He was wearing an orange Quiksilver fleece, black trackies and orange-lensed Arnettes.

'Hey,' he said, 'I know you. You're that bloody English fraud from Al-Quseir. You still running around after that two-faced bastard?'

When I didn't answer, Rowdy said, 'Oh shit, he's not on the fucking boat is he?'

The man sitting between Rowdy and Bobby Ballet and towering above them was as fat and as grand as an old-time wrestler. Teddy King was wearing a pair of navy football shorts and nothing else, suggesting that his size was all right with him, gut hanging down to his dimpled knees or not, and what were you going to do about it? He was shockingly pale next to Bobby. The great expanse of him was the colour of chewed gum: the doughy and rolling folds of skin, the elephant-sized legs stippled with what looked like broken blood vessels, the pendulous chins that gave him the nickname – Teddy Ten Chins – that Jody told me nobody dared say in front of him.

I tried not to stare – straightaway I recognized that the power he radiated fed partly on others' disgust for how he looked. I took in the scene as quickly as I could – the three white men ignoring the small squad of brown men praying on their hands and knees not six feet from them, the bright morning sea spangling all around, and moved to go below. Teddy's cornflower-blue eyes shot into me and a crazy thing happened. I felt a perceptible gravitational tug, as though Teddy were sucking me into his world in the way that when you're hovering in the water by a reef wall that falls thousands of metres, you can sometimes feel yourself being called down to the black depths.

'Who the fuck are you?' he said as I disappeared, turning my back and going down the ladder to the saloon and the dive deck. Teddy had no problem cursing me over the bowed heads of praying men.

'Oi! Where's he going?' Teddy said.

'I guess Teddy's kind of my guardian angel,' Jody had told me in the night. 'I mean, I know how he really feels about me.'

'How does he feel?'

'He loves me, I suppose.'

Jody told me enough about Teddy that the thought of him finding out I had slept with her made me sweat in my shorts. He had been brought up on Canvey Island, and he had that 'make it happen and take no prisoners' attitude that made him one of those blokes money sticks to, although I think he was motivated by more than just the accumulation of a fortune. I could imagine him as a fat kid being turned away from some fancy pants nightclub in town, just because he didn't look right, and Teddy promising to come back and buy the place out, and later he does. He had that getting-his-own-back vibe. Exactly what he owned and how much he was worth were things he kept to himself, but I had a vision of Teddy growing bigger and bigger as his fortune grew. I saw him looming gigantically above cities, stomping on skyscrapers, thousands dead under his feet.

Teddy had a big car and an office in Soho, where, Jody said, he spent all his time on the phone. She was working as a cycle courier when she met him – she was seventeen and a runaway in the city. 'I'll tell you about that when I know you better,' she said. She had a package for him. Teddy was on the phone and he told whoever was on the other end that he'd call back. It was a hot day and Jody was wearing lycra shorts and a white vest. Her face was flushed and her skin was slick. Teddy put the phone on the hook and immediately it started ringing.

'He was staring at me,' Jody said. '"Work for me," Teddy said, "I'll pay you three times what you're getting now." I said, "Doing what?" Teddy pointed at the ringing phone. "Start with that," he said.

'He's never really tried anything on with me,' Jody went on. 'He says things, and he can get out of line with me when he's wasted, but really he's more like my protector. He pays me well, and he takes me places like this, and he keeps all the bad boys like you away from me.'

I reckoned it was more complicated than that. A girl like Jody would never let on that she was conscious of the power she held over men like Teddy and me, or the different fantasies she would promote and fulfil for each of us. And if she wasn't aware of the effect she had, that just made her more dangerous and more in danger. From what she'd told me about him, I didn't think Teddy was the kind of man who put money into something, even a girl, without expecting some return.

'So what, you're not allowed to have boyfriends? If he can't have you no one can, is that it?'

'Hey,' she said, her breath sweet and hot on my face, 'just because we're here like this doesn't mean you can talk to me that way. You don't know anything about it. Teddy's been good to me. I have boyfriends, I just try not to hurt him by rubbing his face in it.'

'So, why me?'

'I don't know, maybe it's the heat, maybe it makes me feel a bit reckless. Who knows? Plus, we're on a boat.'

'So?'

'Come on, you know. We're away from all the rules. There's nobody to tell us what we can and can't do. And when I saw you I wanted you straightaway. You've got that look on your face that I bet all the girls go for.'

'What look?'

'Like you're searching for something.'

'Why is that good?' I said to Jody, as we lay skin to hot skin in her sleeping bag.

'Because a girl might think that she could be what it was you were looking for. That's a pretty romantic idea.'

'How old are you?'

'Twenty. Why? Were you worried I was younger – or hoping I was?'

'I didn't know that people your age still went in for romance.'

'I guess I'm old-fashioned,' Jody said. 'I'm interested in dark and mysterious men who need saving.'

'You think I need saving?' I said.

'You know you do,' Jody said, 'you wouldn't be here otherwise. Now close your eyes.'

≈ ≈ ≈

I went through the sliding glass doors into the saloon, shutting out Rowdy and Teddy's laughter, made myself a cup of coffee at the hot water station, grabbed a bottle of water, and started down the narrow steps to the cabin. I dropped the cup and spilt hot coffee all over my feet.

Garland's bed was neatly made, army style. He'd left his phone out with a note that said, 'Call your wife and children.' I wasn't very good at talking on the phone, either to Araba or the kids, though there was a need to hear my wife's voice. But we were out of signal range now we were underway. And besides, what could I say? 'Baby, I cheated on you. I want to come home, will that be OK?' I looked at the phone and crumpled up the note.

My dry bag was still unpacked where I'd thrown it on the

94

top bunk. I dug around in there and found my toothbrush and some calendula cream, and went into the small bathroom where Garland's washbag was already hanging up. I washed my feet and put some calendula on them where the coffee had burned them. Araba was into homeopathic remedies and made me pack arnica and calendula whenever I travelled. I washed my face and brushed my teeth and grabbed a clean T-shirt, a pair of sunnys and a tube of Ambre Solaire, and went out of the cabin and up through the saloon to the dive deck to sort my kit out.

There was a crewman at the compressor pumping tanks. A slim, black-haired boy, no more than eighteen, with salt marks on the brown skin of his big feet and legs, and salt rings on his shorts and on the sun-faded Iron Maiden shirt he had got from God knows where. He smiled when he saw me, and tried not to stare at my tattoos. I wondered whether the whiteness of my skin promoted a reflex action in his face, or whether he was just a nice kid. *Shang-Tu*'s movement through the water created a kind of local wind trapped in the kit-up area that only the two of us experienced, and together with the noise of the compressor and the engine it was impossible to talk. I smiled hello and shouted my name then reached over the rack of steel dive tanks to shake hands – the cylinders held in place by braces placed down the centre of the back-to-back benches where the divers kitted up.

'Kim!' I shouted.

'Suhail!' he shouted back, and then said something I couldn't hear or understand.

He was a Bedouin, the Arabic he spoke had a rougher

sound than Egyptian Arabic. There were many Bedouins working on dive boats. An equivalent nomadism to take the place of the culture they had lost to development and tourism. Suhail took a digital camera out of his shorts and took my photo and looked at the result.

'Very nice!' he shouted, and showed me my photo.

I was red eyed and looking both hangdog and surprised, as if Suhail had snapped me immediately after sneaking out of Jody's arms.

'Look,' he said, and showed me a picture of a young woman holding a baby. Suhail pointed to himself and I gave him the thumbs-up. I dug out my dive bag and found an empty space on the back-to-back benches next to Garland's set-up. I pointed at a tank with a strip of silver tape covering the O-ring, and made the diver's OK sign at Suhail, thumb and index finger circled.

'Yes, OK!' Suhail shouted. 'Cool cool, full-up, go ahead.'

I set my kit up. For tropical diving I was using an old, back-inflating Zeagle Ranger buoyancy jacket with an integrated weight system – which meant that I carried the lead I needed in pockets in the jacket rather than on a belt around my waist: in an emergency the weight could be dumped by pulling on a ripcord. I peeled off the gaffer tape from the tank and fitted the first stage of my Scubapro regulator to the O-ring – making sure the O-ring was clean and free of scratches. I turned the tank on to check for leaks, and then I sat on the bench and got into the kit. I breathed through the primary and back-up second stages, checking the air flow and making sure that the needle on the contents gauge didn't fluctuate abnormally –

this would indicate a bad fill, maybe some carbon monoxide might have got into the tank. I put air in the jacket and tested the dump valve, and I adjusted my straps. I hadn't dived in the tropical set-up for a good while and I wanted everything to fit right.

When I was satisfied, I got out of the kit and put it back in the rack on the bench. There was a bungee to wrap around the pillar valve of the tank and hold everything in place. Suhail made the OK sign at me and grinned. 'OK! OK!' he shouted, and I made the sign back at him. I pulled out my Cressi full-foot fins and clear mask and put them in the plastic crate under the bench seat. I hung up my black O'Neill wetsuit.

Up on the flybridge a middle-aged man, with curly black hair that may have been dyed, and a thick but neat black moustache, was sitting in a weather-beaten chair steering the boat with his dark brown, salt-stained feet. He was smoking a cigarette and drinking a glass of tea, and his eyes were lined with kohl against the sun's glare. On the sun-faded wooden instrument panel there was an ashtray full of butts placed and held steady by a couple of switches. Garland and Casey were sitting there looking unhappy.

'This is Nawfal, the skipper,' Garland said.

Nawfal hit me with an appraising look that could have meant anything but didn't, I thought, radiate any kind of approval. I reached over and shook hands. My hand disappeared inside his. Letting go, he turned back to the wheel.

Garland said, 'Teddy wants to head straight for the Brothers.'

'We're not stopping at Little Giftun?'

I'd taken it for granted that we'd head to one of the reefs close by Hurghada for shakedown dives. A shakedown is a shallow, unchallenging dive where you can sort out any kinks in your gear. For me and Garland, a shakedown was a chance to see how the divers we would be guiding performed in the water. Some divers, it goes without saying, are better than others, but even some technically good divers need an eye kept on them. Overconfident divers often dive too deep, or pay no attention to the briefing before the dive, or to the guide or anybody else once they are in the water. My feeling was that we had a few of those on board. And then there were others who would lack experience and confidence, and who would need you to look after them, help them with their kit, remind them to check their air.

From what Jody had told me, Tony and Susan had spent next to no time in the water. Casey had taken them through their first diving course, and then sold them the trip to the islands. They'd never dived in the ocean before, and had no business diving at the Brothers. They were only qualified to dive to eighteen metres, but Casey had got round that by signing them up for an advanced course that he planned to take them through on this trip. It was borderline legal, almost certainly a decision taken for financial reasons, and not at all wise. And then there were the people from *Banker*. Could they, when it came to it, really dive? To judge their ability and make plans for the Brothers, Garland and I needed to see the divers in the water. The Giftun Islands east of Hurghada were the best bet. On the southern side of the smaller island was a lagoon where you would be sheltered from any northerly winds. There was a nice reef wall east of the mooring point. A good spot for an easy shakedown.

Smoking, Casey made the 'unh' sound in the back of his throat.

'Mate, none of you have dived the Brothers before,' I said. 'That's right, isn't it? I mean, that's why me and Garland are here. Tony and Susan have never dived outside of the UK. Neither have the journalists. We should definitely do a shake-down. You know you're asking for trouble otherwise.'

'Yeah, well, like I told Garland, we're not going to. Teddy just wants to get there, so that's what's going to happen.'

He went below, his head in a bubble of smoke.

'Garland,' I said, 'shit, what was that? No shakedown?'

Garland was wearing a black and white patterned futah – a kind of Yemeni sarong – wrapped around his waist, and a dazzling white v-neck T-shirt. His blond curls shone in the bright morning. Other than underwater, on the open sea in the sunshine was the best place to see him. Except now he seemed deeply pissed off, and not just with me.

I looked down from the flybridge to the sun deck. Rowdy and Teddy and Bobby Ballet had been joined by Casey, although only Bobby was talking to him, and by two other skinny, pale and unfit-looking men I hadn't seen before but who I knew must be from *Banker*. Tony and Susan sat by themselves in the opposite corner. There was no sign of Jody. Rowdy and Teddy sent up huge clouds of pot smoke.

'Why are you agreeing to this?' I asked Garland. 'We're in charge of the diving, aren't we? You could make them do a shakedown – tell them they wouldn't be able to dive otherwise.'

'I could do that,' Garland said, 'but I think I'm going to have to be careful where and when I fight my battles. I don't know if word's got out about what you were up to last night, but I can't risk a scene.'

'Mate,' I said.

Garland held up his hand.

'I don't want to hear it,' he said. 'I don't want to hear about how things are with you and Araba. You know it doesn't matter if you're single or married, or whether I think it's all right for you to cheat on Araba, the rule is we don't sleep with the clients.'

He was right, so I couldn't argue.

'What do you want to do about the shakedowns?' I said.

'I'll make the best of it,' he said. 'We'll just take it easy when we get to the Brothers. Small groups. You and me will take care of the novices. And no wrecks for the first day or two until people are dived up, just reefs.'

'Have you spoke to Rowdy?'

Garland shrugged.

'What happened?' I said.

'He told me to keep away from him.'

'What's he so pissed off about after all this time?'

'Mate, it's nothing you need to know. Not your business.'

It was my business if I was going to be on a boat with them both for the next three weeks, I thought, but I knew better than to push Garland. He wasn't going to tell me. I did think of saying, 'Mate, how about you staying out of my business if I stay out of yours?'

'Yalla!' Nawfal shouted suddenly, turning to smile at us through kohl-lined eyes. 'Let's go! The Brothers! The cream of the milk of the cow!'

So we passed by the Giftun Islands, where Rob Palmer had died, and we didn't stop. Rob Palmer was perhaps the most gifted English diver of his generation. A master cave diver, a technical diving pioneer and teacher. In 1982 Palmer had made a 2,700 feet dive through the Blue Holes of Andros Island off the Bahamas, but he didn't come back from what should have been a straightforward wall dive off Giftun Island in the spring of 1997.

There had been a lot of stories told about his death, and I won't pretend to know everything that happened. I'd heard Palmer was wearing borrowed gear as his own had been lost in transit from England. He was diving on air, using two independent twelve-litre steel cylinders, and a stage bottle of 50/50 Nitrox for a planned decompression stop.

The friends who dived with him reported seeing Palmer falling fast through the water. Whether he was alive then, nobody knows. Two buddy pairs tried to stop his descent and pull him back. For their own safety, the first pair stopped at seventy-five metres, and the second at ninety-five. Ninety-five metres: that's like flying down to the street from the top of Big Ben.

As Palmer's body was not recovered, what caused his uncontrolled descent, and how exactly he died, remains unknown. Was he dead before he started falling? Whenever

I thought about Palmer I remembered something he said that I think was really about the consequences of getting into the water unprepared, not fully concentrated on what you're doing. About how the underwater world will always be, for us, an alien environment. So, plan your dive, and dive your plan, or bad stuff will happen to you. I thought about it again as we passed the Giftun Islands.

'You get away with it,' Palmer had said, 'until you don't get away with it.'

≈ ≈ ≈

After the rose light of afternoon gave way to the ruby-edged darkness of night on the Red Sea, another session, or the next go-round of the same continuous party, got underway. I went up to see if I could find Jody but there was no sign of her. On the sun deck Teddy King was wearing a floor-length hooded violet robe, the robe embroidered with gold stitching at the hem, the lower folds and embroidery and Teddy's pavement-coloured feet weakly illuminated by the marker lights that were set at intervals at the deck's perimeter. The rest of him vertically darkening, his massive shoulders and small head a dark cut-out against the star-lit horizon. Teddy was surrounded by barefoot people all arranged to either side and before him in the strange half-light – not just Rowdy and Casey and Bobby Ballet, but the two pale and wired-looking journalists in tracksuits sitting at Teddy's feet – so that it was impossible, in that light and under those storybook Arabian stars, not to read into the frozen tableau the idea of Teddy as their tribal leader.

Shang-Tu rose and fell on long swells. We were out of sight of land, our own nation. What was to be decided in the days ahead, I realized, were the government and laws of this new country. One of the men in a fresh-out-of-the-packet white Adidas tracksuit with a pale-blue trim – I found out later that as a matter of honour all the gear the boys from *Banker* had brought with them was comped or blagged – knelt to take Teddy's photograph. In the flash of light I saw that Teddy was staring at me from under the hood of his robe – the hood, again, gilded and royal. His picture taken, Teddy's voice – stoned, trying for benign, trying for intimacy – came to me from out of the restored darkness.

'Here he is,' he said, 'the scrotey. What have you done with my bird? I haven't seen her all day.'

I didn't answer. I hadn't seen Jody since I'd climbed out of her sleeping bag.

'These blokes are writing a story about me,' Teddy said. 'Maybe they'll put you in it, so you want to watch how you go on. The streaky-looking one is Tristan, he's the writer. That's Johnny, he takes photographs when he's not taking the piss. I've paid for them to be out here, so they're going to write what I tell them. Ain't that right, boys?'

'That's right, Teddy,' Johnny said, in the posh voice I recognized from the night before.

Teddy said, 'Cunt doesn't think I know he's taking the piss.'

Johnny snapped Teddy again, and then swivelled on his pipe-cleaner legs to take a photograph of me. Instinctively I raised my hand to my face.

'Come over here,' Teddy said, 'sit by me.'

There was no room by him. The place where he'd told me to sit was filled by Casey. Teddy looked at Casey who was brooding, smoking. 'Move up, you cunt,' Teddy said to him. 'Better still, go and get us a beer.'

With his head framed in clouds of smoke and his eyes bulging in the gloom, Casey looked like a frog sat in a pan of warming water. Would he jump before the water got too hot, or would he fail to notice the heat increasing and get boiled alive? For the minute he didn't move and neither did I.

'I don't know why we need guides myself, but silly bollocks here reckons we wouldn't be allowed to leave Hurghada without them.' He gave Casey a kick. 'That's what you said, right?'

Casey mumbled something nobody could hear.

'What?' Teddy shouted. 'Fucking speak up, nobody can hear you.'

'I said that's just the way it is, Ted,' Casey said. 'It's just how things are here. You can't go to the Brothers without permits or guides.'

'Just how things are,' Teddy said. 'Fucking shitters in this country, the lot of them. Bribe-taking lazy cunts. I hear you got a thing about blacks,' he said to me, 'is that right?'

Rowdy snickered. Johnny kept snapping away – so that we seemed to be attended by localized flashes of lightning. I wondered when Jody had talked to Teddy about me and under what circumstances. I wondered if she was keeping out of my way or Teddy's.

'What?'

'Blacks, fucking blacks. Keep up. Your wife's black, that's what I heard. What's that about, then? I don't get on with them myself, thick, robbing, lazy cunts most of them. What about you, Rowdy?'

'What's that, Ted?'

'Blacks. What do you think of blacks?'

'The wogs at home are stupid bastards, mate.'

'They all robbers and cunts?'

'Pretty much.'

'There you go,' Teddy said. 'What's long and hard on a black man?'

'I don't know, mate, what?' Rowdy said.

'School. Ha ha.'

Only Rowdy laughed. Casey smoked, looking if anything even more downcast but relieved for once, I thought, not to be the object of Teddy's sharp attention. Clearly Teddy King exercised control over everybody on board – except maybe Bobby. It was hard to tell, in the concealing darkness and with the sunglasses he always wore, but Bobby Ballet looked tranced out in the corner banquette seat he sat in – like he was tripping, his mind walking in some personal inner world, or maybe he was astral projecting, who could tell with Bobby? His body was completely still, like he could be dead, left behind waiting for his mind to return. Johnny had his camera on me.

Shang-Tu steamed towards the islands, following the snow-thick stars of the Milky Way. The slow, deep swells of the Red Sea were evenly spaced, and I kept my balance by stepping forward and back on the slowly undulating deck. Maybe it was just that I was more at home in one place than the other, but the feeling that I had escaped from a cold enclosed place was persistent, as though I had found my way back to the world I should be living in all the time. At the end of safaris you always heard people saying it was time to get back to the real world. I thought that the places they were returning to, most often a conglomerate of dark boxes, a world away from the warm sun and deep blue water, was the constructed place and not the reality. Even in the wind we made, the air was warm all around.

Talking to Teddy, though, I suddenly felt that I hadn't left England at all. Plus, although I was not brave, I couldn't hear too much of this kind of talk without the image of my brown-skinned wife and daughters asking me when I was going to stand up for them and fight back.

'What did you do at school, Teddy,' I said

'Eh?'

'What did you do at school?'

'Why?'

'Because you look like you spent most of your time there eating.'

From high up in the darkness somewhere I thought I might have heard Jody giggle from her hiding place but I couldn't be sure, because all at once Teddy King was roaring with laughter, howling like a shaman, laughing so hard he had to push his hood back off his head and slap himself around the face to make himself stop. When he had recovered Teddy wiped his eyes and spat over the side into the darkness.

'I like him,' he said to Rowdy, whose look was not friendly but suggested he might have to think again about what it was he was looking at, 'he's a cunt, but I like him.'

Then he sighed quietly, as if to say, see, look what happens when you give an inch.

'This is all mine,' he said, and spread his arms as if to include not just the *Shang-Tu*, but the Red Sea and the star-filled, vaulted sky. Then he leaned towards me and spoke softly, for me alone to hear, and this time when he spoke it sounded like he meant every word.

'I could have Bobby drop kick you over the side and nobody would say a word, so don't think you can take the piss. Now sit here,' he said. 'Have a drink and a puff. Tell me why Jody's hiding from me.'

I thought I saw something dark whip across the blue of Teddy's eyes, like the poisonous sea snake that had flashed past me once, off the coast of Baja, twenty metres down in the Sea of Cortez.

Suddenly he looked to where Casey was still sitting and did a double take so that his chins shook and wobbled, acting as though, rather than it being something he had known all the time we were talking, he had just noticed that Casey still hadn't moved.

'I thought I told you to get us a beer.'

Casey looked at him bleakly, and started to move but not fast enough. Teddy exploded at him.

'Move when I fucking tell you!'

Teddy grabbed Casey around the neck and then shoved him until he fell on the deck. Casey quickly scrambled back up and went below. Everyone tried not to look at him. I sat in the empty seat. Rowdy still had that thinking look on him. Casey, for whatever reason, had lost his place at Teddy's right hand,

and Rowdy's look suggested, almost as if he was speaking the words out loud to me – a sudden recognition of what was for both of us an unwelcome idea: that Teddy might be fitting me for a replacement. It seemed clear that the relationship both Casey and Rowdy had with Teddy – the relative positions they held in his world – were fluid and fragile, and this was how Teddy wanted it. He could keep you scared and make you want him to like you, at the same time. That was how I felt about him, at first. And purely for reasons of self-preservation, and because it would make the trip go better, it made sense to accept any offers of friendship Teddy made.

Casey came back with armfuls of beer and a cigarette in his mouth. Teddy stood up slowly and went to him. In his hooded robe he took cans and passed them round to all of us as if the beer was a sacramental offering. He kept two cans for himself. He ripped the ring off one and raised the beer to the sky, grinning at me as he did so.

'Here's to you, Case. Anybody calls you a cunt, don't listen to them. We've been all over the world together, me and him,' he said to the rest of us, 'fucking mates, we are.' Teddy drank his beer in one and threw the empty over the side. Casey stood looking at Teddy. He had no beer, and there was no can left for him, and I wondered if Teddy knew that by taking two he would leave Casey empty handed or if it was just something that had happened.

'Don't look like that,' Teddy said to him, 'I didn't mean to hit you. Give me a hug. Go on, give me a hug, I didn't mean it.'

Casey let Teddy smother him inside the violet robe. Teddy

let him go and said, 'Watch out, mate, you nearly burnt my tit off.'

Teddy looked at Casey as if he was waiting for forgiveness.

'Look, I didn't mean to whack you,' he said. 'I was just having a laugh. You know how it is. Here, have some of this.'

Teddy gave Casey a small glass dispenser full of white powder.

Casey took two hits and handed the little bottle back.

'Cheers, Ted,' he said.

'All right, mate,' Teddy said.

Casey sniffed and huffed the cocaine to the back of his throat, the sound setting off inside me a flash of recognition and desire. Casey lit another cigarette. The dispenser was still in Teddy's hand and he could see me looking at it. He seemed to come closer. He loomed over me. He held out the little bottle to me and shook it so that I could see the powder.

'You want some?' Teddy said.

'I'll have some,' Rowdy said.

Without looking at him Teddy held up his hand and said, 'Hold on, Aussie, just wait a minute. You want a snortie?' he said to me. 'Just a little one?'

Don't get sucked in, I said to myself, and reached out my hand.

≈ ≈ ≈

When the rising light and not Jody's warm skin woke me early the next morning, it was easy, not for the first time in my life, to wish that I had not done the things I had the night before. The inside of my head felt scorched. I remembered that sometime in the night Bobby Ballet had begun showing us stunts. Chewing glass, and throwing himself off the flybridge on to the sun deck. Bobby, horse-faced, expressionless, flying through the air and landing with a bang on the hard deck, close enough to Teddy to make him jump, though the big man pretended not to. Bobby getting up and doing it again, almost like he was challenging Teddy to react. Later, high and half-drunk, I found myself watching a film about the discovery of the lost sunken city of Pavlopetri in the Peloponnesian Sea off southern Greece. As divers hovered over the ruins, using strong halogen lights to illuminate traces of courtyard gardens and main streets that had not been seen for over five thousand years, Teddy King said to me, 'Have another bit.'

Araba had been trying to get me to meet my responsibilities. Some men would have buckled down, but I didn't. The trouble was that for as long as I could remember I'd fought against people telling me what to do. Ever since I'd managed to break free of the room Dug had held me prisoner in. It was difficult to change that even for Araba. I looked at the vial of powder in Teddy's hand. Taking it meant partying, and not having to think about anything except having a good time. I felt entitled. I always did.

'Cheers, Ted,' I said.

I hit the cocaine again, while on screen divers carefully lifted Stone Age ceramics to the surface, ceramics belonging to a sunken city pre-dating Plato's Atlantis story and so maybe this was Atlantis itself. And sometime after that, I remember Teddy and the journalists sniggering over what I found out later was one of Teddy's huge collection of underwater porn films. He watched them every night.

The camera was wobbly. You could hear the breathing of whoever was holding it. In shallow water, a woman in a tight, shiny wetsuit, the zipper pulled down, was diving on a bleached-out and dead reef. Her hair was loose and waving like a torn black flag in the water. The cameraman's air bubbles blew across the screen. The woman did a kind of awkward dance. She looked embarrassed. She pulled the zip of her wetsuit down to the waist, exposing first one big white breast and then the other. The dance seemed to go on for a long time. Teddy's eyes were glittering and one hand was inside his robe. Another diver, naked except for his dive rig, and with a big hard-on, swam to the woman. They started touching each other. I looked away. Teddy took his hand out from under his robe and put it on my shoulder. His hand was sweaty and warm.

'No,' he said, 'wait.'

There was a storm of bubbles on screen. Suddenly the man pulled out the woman's mouthpiece so that she couldn't breathe, and he was holding her off while she kicked and struggled. She was fighting to keep her mouth closed. Her exposed breasts were the same shocking ghost-white colour of the dead coral.

'This is for real,' Teddy said.

'Come on,' Tristan said, whether to Teddy or the woman on the film I don't know.

The cameraman moved closer to the woman. Terror made her eyes enormous. She clawed desperately for the man.

Finally the woman had to open her mouth. She seemed to vomit her last breath. The naked man dropped the woman's mouthpiece. He masturbated as she sank down to the reef. Her eyes stayed open. As she lay still on the reef the camera slowly left the woman and focused on the man's cock.

'I pay bundles for the real stuff,' Teddy said. 'I'm not going to waste my time on fucking actors.'

Nobody said anything. The man came. His spunk pulsed in the water in thick beads and little ribbons, like a number of unknown and colourless invertebrates, last survivors of the dead reef.

Later I climbed up to find Jody in her bed on the flybridge. I hadn't seen her all day, but already I took it as my right that I could get into bed with this girl, whose last name I didn't know, whenever I wanted to. I just pulled the zip down on her sleeping bag expecting to get my hands on her.

She fought me with punches and kicks and whispered fuck offs. I stopped then, and I heard her say, 'Oh Kim, he hasn't got you on that shit already, has he?' I went down to the sun deck and wrapped myself in one of *Shang-Tu*'s red blankets and tried to sleep as the party raged around me.

We were anchored off the low, red Big Brother island. I could see the lighthouse, sandy-coloured in the morning light, corralled by a whitewashed one-floor building, a jetty and a smaller island, Little Brother, a kilometre or so to the south. Black igneous rocks, solidified volcanic lava, showed at Big Brother's shoreline, and above that the island was made from what looked like a porous, crumbling, sandy sediment over-laid by hard rock. There was no vegetation. Nothing grew on the islands. Just below the surface of the water the top of the fringing reef showed. And then all around as far as I could see, blue water, and above me a rose-blue sky.

A handful of dark men, in worn and sweat-marked olive-green uniforms, watched me from Big Brother. I waved and some of the men waved back and called to me to come ashore. They were conscript soldiers, and they manned the lighthouse on Big Brother in three-month shifts. They made T-shirts decorated with a screen print of the islands and sold them to divers.

I went below to the dive deck. It was still early and only the crew were up. Even Garland was nowhere to be seen. *Shang-Tu* was anchored to a permanent mooring and the only sound was the sea. I wondered who had got into the water and tied us on. That was my job. I prayed Garland hadn't tried to wake me and then got in himself. That would explain why he was still asleep. When he woke he would be on the warpath again, and he would ask me why I kept messing up. Things inside me seemed to be breaking up and I didn't know why.

Suhail saw me from inside the saloon where he was laying the breakfast table and opened the sliding doors. We said good morning.

'Coffee?' he said.

'Thanks, I'm going to swim first, then coffee.'

Suhail smiled and pointed at the water and made a fin shape with his hand – fingers straight up while tapping his head with the knuckle of his thumb – and said, 'Gersh,' saying the Arabic for shark with the hard G sound the Bedouins gave the word.

'That's good, mate,' I said, 'sharks are good, that's what we're here for.'

'Sharks good!' Suhail said, and laughed and slapped me on the back. To be honest I was lucky to run into him. In my rush to get in the water I hadn't thought to tell anyone what I was doing. Suhail would give me boat cover until I came back. Stories of people being lost because they hadn't told anybody they were getting in the water were a favourite in conversations among dive professionals. We were never surprised by the eye-watering stupidity of the people we taught and then let loose in the oceans of the world.

Suhail watched me as I grabbed and put on my fins and face mask and he laughed as I jumped off the dive deck with a yell. Water is the only hangover cure I know that works.

I duck-dived and finned down, head first, twenty feet or so then turned on my back. When I stopped to look, I found myself in an eternal colour field of variegated blues. From space, Yuri Gagarin said, the earth has a beautiful blue colour. Long finger rays of low morning sunlight made an almost horizontal penetration of the water above me. A handful of barred flagtails – small, narrow silver fish with a black and white tail – sparkled as they passed through the golden beams of sunlight. Barred flagtails are rare in the Red Sea, and I knew these fish to be outriders from a school that lived just off Big Brother's jetty. A pair of small sergeant-majors – a species of damselfish that is striped and coloured like a bumblebee – floated past me as though it were a summer day at home.

I didn't feel wet. Instead, the experiential change was one from heavy clumsiness on land to a lightness that put my body in alignment with – what exactly? Call it my consciousness, or my soul maybe, because that's what my wife would call it. Just as I know she believed my love for the water was because it was, for me, a numinous space, when, to tell you the truth, it was the impossible beauty of what I saw underwater that made religion seem a bunch of silly stories. Stories that are wholly insufficient as explanations for how the wonders I saw before me came to be.

You know the way your thoughts go anywhere they want? Well, underwater your body can too. You can hang suspended upside down if you feel like it. Free-diving offered me a short burst of this harmony. On scuba the feeling of rightness stayed with me for as long as I could make my air last. We wanted breathing equipment, Cousteau said, not so much to go deeper, but to stay longer, to simply live a while in the new world. And if that were only for an hour, how many of us get to feel that release for even such a short time?

I swam up to the boat and along the hull where *Shang-Tu* was written in block letters. These days there is most often more than one dive boat at anchor over a dive site, and because holidaying divers are sometimes less than good at finding their way back to their own boat, it had become common practice to write the name where divers could see it. Under the hull a single great barracuda – maybe four-and-a-half-feet long, hung sullenly. Bow and stern anchor lines went out from the boat, the stern line straight down and the bow at a forty-five-degree angle. Following the direction of the bow anchor line I could make out the dark hills of the reef.

Hanging vertically in the water column I looked up. I had

read somewhere that the wonder of diving is that we become transformed, a different animal in a different element. Looking through the surface of the sea into the world I had left, I could make out dark movement in the early morning sun; and then it was as though Jody tore a hole in the sky. She came shooting through the opening she had made, uncountable numbers of tiny bubbles streaming from her body, and flew down to me.

Most people imagine that a dive's beauty lies in the movement through the air, that the story is over when the diver crosses the border separating air and water; I would guess because that's the only perspective they see it from. But for me it isn't. Jody was a dark, fishtailed outline backlit by the sun. She was super-streamlined as she dived, and she arched her back to slow her descent, finning herself upright as she reached me. She was wearing a black bikini and black elongated Cressi-Sub free-diver fins, much longer than scuba fins. Her white locks waved in the water. With the sun behind her she was Mediterranean dark, Greek-looking, like a water ghost of the ancient sunken city of Pavlopetri returned. This was the first time I had seen, rather than felt, so much of her body. She was narrow-hipped with small high breasts, and there were freckles splashed across her chest and shoulders and chevrons of raised scars on the insides of both her arms. She was smiling, and her green eyes were magnified behind her mask. She reached for my hand.

I had dreamed about Araba making such a dive into the blue, coming to me to share the place where I really lived. The vision of Araba coming to me through the water was connected to stories in which the brown-skinned girl is, for the white sailor, the longed-for realization of a sustaining dream. The ship finally anchored in the warm blue water of the South Seas after a long voyage of unvarying hard work, brutality and danger. Brown-skinned Polynesian girls swimming out to meet the sailors who were already drunk on the tropical funk and the electrifying sight of green land in a world of water.

Blue sea, warm sun, brown girls. A dream corresponding to my own, imprinted in my mind by the brown-skinned beach girls of my boyhood, and by reading Richard Dana, Melville's *Typee* and *Omoo*, Robert Louis Stevenson. The mutiny on the *Bounty*: Fletcher Christian and his desperate shipmates conspiring against the tyrant William Bligh in Tahiti. Even after I finally got to Hawaii, and saw what the Americans had done to that place, the dream of an island paradise persisted. In my imagination it would be something like the mixed-race rebel state Christian is said to have established on Pitcairn after leaving Tahiti.

Jody pointed at me, screwed up her face, and mimed banging a hammer against her head. She asked me if I was OK by making a circle of her thumb and forefinger. I shrugged, and mouthed 'I'm sorry.' We solemnly shook hands, and then laughed. She made the shark sign, and I shook my head. I had seen no sharks. My heart was thumping. We swam up to breathe.

'Hey,' she said, at the surface.

I could feel the heat of the early morning sun. It was bright on the white sides of the boat, and the surface of the water sparkled with what looked like a million star-shaped silver jacks. With the sun above and behind him, Suhail was a dark outline looking over *Shang-Tu*'s side.

'I'm sorry about last night,' I started to say, but she put her wet salty finger to my lips.

'How's your head?'

'It's fine now.'

'Do you have to get out yet?' she said. 'It's beautiful with just us.'

'I reckon I could get away with another ten minutes without getting into trouble.'

'Any more trouble.'

'Yeah, any more trouble.'

Just then Suhail whistled and when I looked over to him he was pointing beneath the boat.

'Sharks!' he shouted, and waved us back to the boat. I gave him the OK sign to show I'd heard him. Jody was tough; if she was scared she didn't show it. She didn't freak out at the first sound of the word shark.

'Should we get out?' she said.

Our voices were distorted by the masks over our noses, as though we both had head colds. Like a good diver she kept her mask on at the surface rather than push it up on her head where it could easily be knocked off and lost.

'Probably.'

Jody laughed. 'Probably? Is that what you said? We should probably get out?'

'Yeah, well, I've been in the water with sharks before, and they're mostly gentle as Labradors, but these are likely to be oceanic whitetips, and they're fairly well known for getting more aggressive the longer you stay in the water with them. Plus we're on the surface, which isn't good.'

Hass and Cousteau had proved that sharks will not attack a diver unless provoked, and often not even then. Certainly I had rarely heard or read about a diver being attacked underwater. At the surface was a different matter. Sharks attack from below, and so it was humans near or on the surface – snorkellers, surfers, swimmers who were most vulnerable. I'd heard about a boat chartered by Russian divers a couple of months ago. A bunch of them got drunk and started throwing fish chum over the side, then went snorkelling off Little Brother with the blood still in the water. One of them was attacked by a whitetip. The story was, she'd lost a leg. 'Good,' said Garland when I told him, 'serves her right.' He also said, of course, that the sharks you had to worry about weren't the ones in the water. I was pretty sure Jody and I would be all right if we didn't panic, but all the same I was mad at myself for putting Jody in danger.

'OK, so I'm scared now,' she said, 'what do we do?'

We were off the bow, within a few feet of the anchor line. To get out of the water we would have to swim to the stern where the ladders to the dive deck were.

'You can hold your breath a pretty long time, right?' I said.

'When I'm not scared to death, yeah. Why?'

'They're circling under the boat. We've got to swim towards them to get back. I reckon they're around the boat because they've got used to people, and because some of the people that come here feed them. I honestly don't think they're dangerous, but I'd rather not surface swim back. With the fins on it's only going to be splashy and loud and attract them. I reckon we drop down and swim back underwater. That way we can keep an eye on them. And seeing them would be pretty cool, don't you think? OK?'

'OK, I guess.'

I put on my best Cousteau accent. 'If ze shark gets close to you punch him on ze nose.'

Jody laughed. 'You're really not scared, are you?'

'No,' I said. 'I don't know why not, because sometimes I think I'm scared of everything else.'

It was true, I wasn't scared. In the water I was often able to practise a stillness, an effacement that meant I projected nothing – no fear or aggression. It was a recognition, I think, of my own insignificance. When I had dreamed of escape this was what I had dreamed of escaping to. There was something about the idea that not many people I ever went to school with would be able to say they had swum with sharks.

'Look,' I said to Jody, 'here's what I know: shut down everything you think you're supposed to feel. Don't give off any vibes good or bad. Don't project anything on to the shark. Make yourself not matter.'

'OK, OK,' Jody said, laughing again, 'I'll do it, anything to shut you up, Jesus, I didn't know you were such a hippy.'

We took in a few deep breaths and dropped down again. Holding hands we swam towards the stern anchor line. Suhail had let down the two metal ladders off the dive deck, I could see the sunlight catching the metal, and Jody and I swam towards them, looking into the blue for the sharks. We reached the ladders, still looking down. We came to the surface. Suhail was on the dive deck. Holding on to her ladder Jody took off her fins and handed them up to him.

'Shark,' Suhail said, pointing just over my shoulder. I put my head under the water to look. Sun-dappled, tawny and wide, with rounded white-tipped pectoral fins, the shark came cruising towards me. She was accompanied by a handful of striped remora fish, fluttering close to her back and head like royal banners. I let go of the ladder and dropped back down into the water. I turned and faced the shark. Long before there were people there were sharks, moving stately and unseen through the world's oceans, and there will be sharks long after we're gone. Just as they now patrolled the deserted ruined streets of Pavlopetri, Alexandria, and all other drowned cities of the world. The shark moved towards me. I was just a few feet away from her but separated, as Cousteau said, by an abyss of time. As she swam alongside, I reached out my hand across the centuries to touch her snowy fin. Almost imperceptibly she moved, not allowing me to touch her, and she sailed on into further fields of blue beyond my sight.

Finning back to the dive ladder, I saw Jody's face in the water, grinning at me through her mask. I got out and we stood on the dive deck and sprayed each other with cold water from the shower. We were laughing like crazy, our teeth chattering with the cold and the wind. We wrapped ourselves in towels and I held her close to me and rubbed her back hard through the towel to warm her up. There are pictures of us somewhere with these huge grins on our faces, like we'd found sunken treasure or just got married. Suhail snapped a couple with his camera phone, he was always taking photos, and when I looked away from Jody for a minute I saw Johnny, the photographer from *Banker*, standing with his camera up on the sun deck.

'Where's your mate?'

'Tristan? He's writing. Mate, he's always writing.'

I wondered what he was writing. What happened last night? I wouldn't have thought that was the kind of coverage Teddy thought he was paying for.

'How's your head?' I shouted up at Johnny.

He made a sour face. 'I've been worse,' he said, 'but I don't remember when.'

'You want to get in the water, bit of swimming with sharks will sort you out.'

He gave me a look and waved his camera at me.

'I've got it all on here. And you,' he said, 'you're off your head.'

≈ ≈ ≈

Garland stood on the sun deck, close by the whiteboard where I'd drawn a map of Big Brother. Garland had tied his hair against the onshore wind, although loose white strands still whipped across his face. The sun was hammering down and the wind was a hot blast. Sitting under a canvas awning, Teddy and the rest looked like potential mutineers guiltily assembled in the bright glare of morning. Bobby Ballet was as blank faced as he had been when I'd seen him last, flying through the air and crashing to the deck. Teddy still wore his hooded robe – the concentrated vibrancy of its gold and violet colours diminished under the vastness of the morning sky and the scorched light of day. He hid his eyes behind a big pair of creamy, chunky-framed O'Neill sunglasses, but he couldn't disguise the death-pallor of his bloated face. He had still been going strong when I'd gone to raid Jody's sleeping bag, Teddy arm wrestling with both *Banker* journalists at once, and I wondered if he had been to bed at all. I suddenly remembered that the last time I had seen the cream-coloured sunglasses, they had been stuck on Johnny's face. Rowdy, a high colour to him, his vulpine ears red to the tips, looked ready to explode if offered any slight, real or imagined.

'Welcome to El Akhawan,' Garland said, 'the Brothers Islands.'

Rowdy mumbled something that sounded like, 'Bloody bloke thinks we don't know where we are.'

Garland had been lying on his bunk and absent-mindedly thumbing the melody of the meteor song on his mbira when I'd brought him coffee after my swim with Jody. He had looked up at me and I saw that he was tired, the cast in his eye pale, like the sun seen through the clouds.

'You're up late,' I said, 'I've been swimming with sharks already.'

Garland looked at me and the cast in his eye flared brightly.

'Free-diving?'

'Yeah.'

'Tell me you didn't take the girl in with you.'

'Yeah, I did. So what, I know what I'm doing.'

'Mate, have you lost your mind? It's bad enough that you'd get in without your kit where you know there are sharks.

But taking a client in? How stupid do you have to be to do something that dangerous? That's the kind of thing that can finish you if it gets out. You told me yourself they've attacked swimmers here just recently. More than likely it's the same sharks. Did anybody see you?'

I wasn't about to tell him that Johnny had it all on film.

'Was everybody at it again last night?' he said.

'Pretty much. I expect there'll be a few sore heads.'

'Yeah, well, some of us were up in the middle of the night tying the ropes on to the moorings. It was no good asking you to help from what I could see. You were out for the count.'

'Look, Garl,' I said, 'it's not unknown on a dive boat, is it, people partying? We've got to expect it surely? They're on holiday after all.'

'You're not,' he said. He rubbed his face. 'I know you and Araba have problems, but partying with low-lifes like Teddy King isn't the way to deal with them. Let alone sleeping with the girl.'

'There was a time you'd have joined in with the partying.'

'When we were younger maybe, and with the right people and at the right time, but never with somebody like Teddy. The bloke is the wrong side of crazy. He's dangerous. If I'd known somebody like him was running this show, I'd have never signed us on.'

'Didn't you used to tell me that it's a good idea to get onside with the bloke who's paying our wages?'

'That's just an excuse. You're not twenty-five and free any-more. You might want to be a kid still, but you aren't. When are you going to figure out that getting high is not the answer to

124

everything? Apart from anything else you're putting yourself and the people you're with at risk every time you get in the water. I can't have that.'

Garland twanged the mbira and then threw it down on the bed.

'We're in the middle of nowhere with a bunch of people who've got no business being out here,' he said. 'I shouldn't need to ask you to back me up. If you keep on the way you are, I won't be able to carry you. This is my living.'

'It's mine too.'

'Then act like it is.'

'I'm all right.'

'Are you sure?'

'Yes, mate, I feel good, honest.'

'All right then, no more screw-ups. Go and get them together. Let's go diving.'

Garland swung his legs off the bunk and planted his big feet on the floor. He shook out his long hair and sipped at the coffee. 'And draw a map of the island. We're diving the inside reef wall.'

'Rowdy won't like that,' I said, 'Teddy neither. They'll want to get on a wreck.'

'Listen, Kim, we're going to do these dives my way. The first dive will be a shakedown whether they like it or not.'

Standing by the whiteboard Garland was all business.

'You can see we're anchored off the southern end of Big Brother,' he said. 'The lighthouse here was built by the Brits in 1880. The *Aida*, the wreck Kim's marked on the map about two hundred metres north of the jetty, was coming to transfer troops to man the lighthouse when she hit the rocks in 1957 during a storm. She's fused to the reef at a ninety-degree angle – the bow's at about twenty metres, the stern's at around sixty. I know you want to get on it, and we'll dive her for sure, and the other wreck too, the *Numidia*, but only after we've got a few dives in and got used to the conditions.

'For the first dive today we're getting in at the inside reef wall of Big Brother, just south of the *Aida*. Suhail in the Zodiac will take us to the drop-off point up here, just about where Kim has put this fifty-metre mark on the map. We're going to be diving in three groups. We'll change the order around every day so that the same people aren't always getting in first or last. The first group today is Casey, Tony and Susan. Kim's going to get in with you and he'll lead the dive. Everybody OK with that?'

'We've come all this way,' Rowdy said. 'When are we going to dive the bloody wrecks?'

Garland looked at me. I stood up and spoke to everybody.

'When we're all happy in the water,' I said. 'So maybe in a couple of days. We've got some pretty new divers along with us, Rowdy, and we haven't had a chance to do a shakedown. That sound fair to you, Teddy?'

I could see that Rowdy was fuming, and I thought that Teddy might stir things up, but for now he was gazing reverently at Jody. She was sitting in the shade and holding a bottle of water. She had pulled back and tied her hair, and was already in her black wetsuit. She had drawn her feet up under her and she was hugging her knees to her chest. Not many people look good in a wetsuit. Most people, in fact, whether in or out of the water, never look anything other than awkward and uncomfortable in diving gear, and this discomfort we feel is a physical reminder of how much we have to transform ourselves just to explore that tiny fraction of the ocean we are able to visit. It is not our world, however much we'd like to think it is and however much we'd like to own it. Jody was austerely beautiful in her plain black wetsuit and scraped back hair. Her locks fanned out behind her head. Looking at her then I had no doubt that Jody would perfectly integrate herself underwater each time she dived, and leave no trace of her presence once it was time to leave.

Garland said, 'Everybody OK with what Kim said? Rowdy?'

Rowdy reddened but said nothing. Bobby, stone-faced, gave me and Garland the OK sign.

'All right then,' Garland said. 'The second group in is Rowdy, Ted, Bobby and Jody. Bobby and Rowdy will lead the dive.'

Teddy gave Jody a little finger wave and smiled at her, but Jody didn't see him. She had felt me looking at her and she stuck her tongue out at me and crossed her eyes. Teddy stared at us from behind his creamy-coloured shades. To be honest he was so fat, and the sunglasses looked so ridiculous, that he seemed grotesque rather than menacing.

When we were getting high together I tried to get Teddy to talk about Jody but he wouldn't. He was foul-mouthed about women who had been his girlfriends. There was one, he said, who wanted to have surgery to make her breasts bigger. Teddy said that when they were out together afterwards he would say to her, in front of people, 'Show us your tits.' He would make her do it. 'I paid for them,' he would say, 'so get them out.' Evidently Jody was different. Whatever he thought about her seemed to be inviolable, and not to be spoken of.

Casey, standing apart from his boss – standing, in fact, apart from everyone and not so much smoking as conducting smoke – was studying the map I'd drawn and whistling quietly. I'd thought he might be unhappy not to be diving with Teddy, but if he was he didn't show it. I was glad for that. I was going to need his help with Tony and Susan, and I wasn't looking forward to asking him.

'The third group is me and you guys,' Garland said to the journalists.

Johnny didn't look too terrible, considering how bad he said he felt, but Tristan was wrapped up in a blanket, hoodie, hat and shades. He lay still, and I suspect he would have been in his bunk if he could have found the energy to move from where he was. It was difficult to believe that he had been writing that morning, like Johnny had told me.

'We're going to skip this one,' Johnny said.

'How come?' Garland said.

'Just feel a bit rough. Maybe the dinner last night.'

'It sounds more like a lifestyle problem,' Garland said, with no humour in his voice.

Tristan waved feebly.

Teddy laughed and said, 'Lifestyle problem my arse. Fucking raghead shitter of a cook has poisoned him.'

Rowdy and Johnny laughed. Tristan gave a weak smile.

'All right,' said Garland, 'Let's get back to the diving. I guess I'll get in with you,' he said to Teddy.

Teddy smiled.

'Jeez,' Rowdy said, 'that's just what we bloody need. Diving with the cops.'

Garland ignored him.

'You need to know that the currents here are strong and they're changeable,' he said. 'It should be coming this way.'

Garland pointed to the board where I'd shown the current coming from the north-west.

'You can see it's pretty windy this morning, and it's likely the current is fairly stiff. We should be able to have a nice drift along the wall, diving with the flow and keeping the reef on your left-hand side. Everyone's got an SMB, right?'

An SMB – Submersible Marker Buoy – is a brightly coloured inflatable bag attached to a line and reel. They are used to mark a diver's position in the water, so that the surface boat cover can pick you up. A small amount of air introduced to the bag at depth sends the SMB accelerating to the surface, the air inside expanding as the atmospheric pressure decreases with the reduction in depth as the bag rises.

'One last thing,' Garland said. 'You've all heard it before but I'm going to say it anyway. Don't touch the coral. Reefs like the ones you are about to dive on support a quarter of all marine life. They keep healthy an ecosystem that a billion people depend upon for food. All over the world coral reefs are at threat from rising water temperatures, increases in the amount of carbon dioxide going in the water, pollution.'

Teddy yawned loudly.

'Every time you touch the reef, crush the polyps or break a piece off, it takes years for the coral to recover. These are some of the best reefs you'll ever see and I'm going to help them stay that way. Keep your hands to yourself or stay in the boat.'

In the early years of the twentieth century, a man called Roy Miner was curator of zoology at New York's American Museum of Natural History. On an expedition to the island of Andros in the Bahamas in 1923 – the same place Rob Palmer would make his record-breaking dives fifty years later – and using crowbars, hatchets, hammers, and block and tackle, Miner and his team took forty tons of coral from the reef. They transported thirty-one cases in ten boatloads back to New York, where Miner made an artificial reef from the dead coral, painting it and coating it in beeswax to look alive.

Garland and I believed that we were seeing the last days of the reefs. We had both dived too many times on whited-out reefs, heartbreaking fields of bleached and dead coral. Bleaching is due to the expulsion from the coral of zooxanthellae, the protozoa that give corals their colour – and this is caused by the rising water temperatures that are happening everywhere in the world. Plus, the huge amount of CO_2 we produce in the world is exceeding the capacity of the oceans to process it, meaning the water becomes more acidic. This acidity affects the levels of carbonate in the water – which in turn prevents the coral from growing skeletons. They will have to get Miner's artificial reef out of storage to show my grandchildren what corals looked like.

But Garland's threat to keep people in the boat was an empty one. Maybe he could talk to the skipper. Maybe Nawfal could tell Suhail not to take the Zodiac out, or he could make sure the tanks weren't pumped. I didn't think it would happen.

Teddy owned the boat and employed the crew. They were obviously more likely to do what Teddy said whether they liked it or not.

I couldn't figure out if the insurrectionary vibe Teddy and his people were giving off was one that meant, you don't need to tell us this stuff, we know what we're doing, or as I feared and believed more likely, you can say what you like, but when we're down there we'll do whatever we want. You're just here because the rules say you have to be, but you're outnumbered. Teddy winked conspiratorially at me. He pulled out a meshed black collecting bag and waved it at Garland.

'I won't be needing this then, no?' he said.

Garland pretended not to notice, and for the rest of the briefing Teddy, now and again leering at Jody, his hands in his lap, occasionally flopped the long, tubed-up black bag back and forth so that it made a light slapping sound against his thighs. Jody smiled at me and rolled her eyes at Teddy's behaviour. Teddy shot us another unfathomable look.

'All the drop-offs here are steep,' Garland was saying, 'and they all go down thousands of metres. Keep an eye on your depth gauges – especially if you're looking out into the blue for the big stuff. Your max depth is thirty metres. I expect you to keep to those levels and not go deeper. Max dive time: one hour or fifty bar, and a five-minute safety stop at five metres, please. Any questions? OK, the first group – Kim, get your guys kitted up.'

≈ ≈ ≈

Seawater washed over the exposed, three-sided dive deck as *Shang-Tu* rocked lightly at her mooring. Tony and Susan gripped the safety rail. Casey stood on the deck without holding on. He smoked and looked casual. As if he hadn't been partying for most of the night and wasn't carrying a full twelve-litre steel tank on his back. Of course, if Casey wasn't holding onto the rail then I couldn't either, and I stood leaning forward slightly to balance the weight of the tank, my bare feet splayed on the warm wet deck. I held my fins under my arm, mask around my neck. I was hot in my wetsuit, and I could feel sweat running down my back. Above me I could hear Teddy hawking and snorting on the sun deck. I heard him spit hugely.

'Oi, Aussie!' he shouted at Rowdy. 'Where's the fucking decongestants?'

'Lifestyle problems, Ted?' said Rowdy.

'Fuck lifestyle problems,' Teddy said, 'just fucking hand them over.'

Cocaine can cause sinus congestion, and if you had a blocked nose it made it difficult, if not impossible, to equalize the increasing pressure you encounter as you descend underwater. And if you can't equalize, you can't dive. It sounded like Rowdy had anticipated this and brought along decongestant tablets. I wondered if I needed to get hold of some myself. If you took too many of them, as I imagined Rowdy and Teddy did, you became dehydrated, which can be a contributing cause of decompression sickness, or the bends. And we were probably already dehydrated from drinking. I sniffed and spat over the side. My nose didn't seem too bad.

Tony said, 'I've never been in one of those before.'

He was staring anxiously at the little Zodiac inflatable Suhail had brought alongside. Suhail would ferry us to the entry point one group at a time, and then stay out on the water, picking up divers as they surfaced under their marker buoys.

'It's a bit rough, isn't it?' Tony said, looking at the water foamed around the deck.

There was a wind blowing, not too strong, and out on the open water the sunlit waves seemed to me to move in quick but low and gentle terraces.

Suhail was ready for us. 'OK!' he shouted. 'Let's go!'

Tony was pale to begin with, but against his black hair and his new black Mares wetsuit, his face looked bleached out. He was licking his lips, and taking little sips from a bottle of water. With her free hand Susan held a bulky, brand new Sea & Sea DX-IG underwater camera, complete with strobes and a wide-angle lens. I'd never be able to even think about buying a camera like it, so I wasn't certain of the price, but I reckoned she was holding over a thousand pounds' worth of kit. She took turns looking at Tony and at the camera. I held a hand up to Suhail.

'It's only a short ride out there,' I said to Tony, 'and once you get in you'll be fine. You might want to put on your mask when you're in the boat, and keep hold of the handle at the side, you see it? Are you all right?'

'He's fine,' Susan said, the neoprene hood she wore stretching the skin on her face and making her mouth look unnaturally wide, 'aren't you, love?'

'Yes,' Tony said, 'I'm fine.'

'There are just a couple of things. Because the water is warm and the visibility is so good you can be fooled into not taking seriously all the safety stuff Garland went through, but you need to. You heard what Garland said about max depth, and I know that later Casey's going to be putting you through some deep dives for your course, but today we won't be going anywhere near as deep as thirty. Are you guys OK with a max depth of eighteen metres? You'll have done one dive that deep already, for your first course.'

'OK, that's good,' Tony said. 'I wasn't sure if he meant us, so that's good.'

'We'll swim to the reef and down to eighteen, and then on my signal we'll cruise back up to twelve or so for the rest of the dive. Say, forty minutes max or fifty bar.'

Susan awkwardly shifted the camera to her other hand.

'Are you sure you want to take that in on the first dive?' I said. 'You don't want to taskload until you get a feel for the conditions.'

'I want to take pictures,' she said firmly, 'so I need to get used to the camera.'

'Have you got a clip for it for when you need your hands free?'

'Yes,' she said, and showed me where the camera strap clipped onto a D-ring on her buoyancy jacket.

'Maybe you should leave it for now, Sue,' Tony said.

'No, Tony, I'm going to take it.'

'Let me know if you want me to carry it,' Casey said, and blew a couple of smoke rings that drifted and collapsed into themselves.

'Thanks,' Susan said, 'but I'm sure I'll be all right.'

'OK,' I said, 'Casey will buddy up with you, Sue, and I'll go with Tony. Casey and I will be in charge of putting SMBs up. We're not sure of the strength of the surface current so we want to get down quickly. We'll make a negative entry. You know how to do that?'

Tony and Susan looked at each other and shook their heads.

'No problem, it's pretty simple. You need to make sure all your air is dumped from your buoyancy jacket before you go over the side. When you get the signal to go, backroll into the water and go straight down, don't wait at the surface because you might get swept away. Just go down and stop at five metres and make sure we're all together, then we'll head down to the reef. All right? Let's do a buddy check.'

Tony and Susan went through the pre-dive ritual of making sure their air was turned on, and everything else was connected and functioning properly. They showed one another the release clips on their buoyancy jackets and weight belts, in case anything went wrong and they needed help. They identified the location of the secondary air hose the other could use in an out-of-air emergency. When they'd finished, I went through the same routine with, it seemed to me, a clearly uninterested Casey.

'OK,' I said, 'good job. I think it's also a good idea to visualize the dive before you get in. Close your eyes and go through all the stages of the descent.'

'You're full of good advice,' Casey said.

'Mate, that's the job.'

'If you say so,' Casey said. 'I thought you did the job in the water.'

Suhail called to us again.

'Everybody ready?' I said. 'All right, let's go.'

We handed our fins down to Suhail, and Susan passed down her camera. Tony and Susan got in and I followed. In his torn and sun-faded wetsuit Casey stood quietly smoking and watching us. When he'd finished he flicked the butt into the sea, and threw his fins down into the Zodiac. Then Suhail handed him in.

'Isn't that really bad for you,' Susan said, 'smoking just before a dive?'

Casey either didn't hear her or ignored her.

In the water the waves were bigger than they'd looked from the boat. Suhail babied the Zodiac, throttling hard and then cutting back to try and ride up the inside of the bigger waves and not bring the little boat down too hard, or flood her. Still though, the Zodiac came smacking down a couple of times, and Suhail couldn't do anything about the petrol blowback from the engine. We sat sweating and hunched up. We took turns putting our fins on so as not to kick one another.

Suddenly Suhail cut the engine and shouted 'Yalla!'

I gave Tony the OK sign. He signed back, and we backrolled over the side. My last sight of the surface world was a vision of my overlapped fins making a black cross against the morning sky. There was the familiar moment of chaos as I exploded into the water, violently leaving one world and passing through to the other. I flipped over and began to descend to five metres, where I had told the others to wait. Automatically,

I equalized and cinched tight the straps on my buoyancy jacket. The sound of my breathing was loud in my ears. After the white-water storm of my entry I was, for just a second, back in the panoramic blue, and then Casey finned in front of me and kicked my mask off my face.

The water instantly lost its brilliant variety and became a blurred and almost muddy grey, faintly backlit by sunlight. I spun in the water, feeling the increasing pressure against my exposed eyes, hoping but not believing I might somehow be able to see the mask, perhaps as a ray of sunlight more penetrating than the rest illuminated it sufficiently before it spiralled away down into what were now for me entirely invisible depths. I was comfortable enough without a mask underwater – I'd practised being without one or taking it on and off too many times to count – but I couldn't carry on the dive because I wasn't carrying a spare, as I certainly should have been and had taught others to do. For all my talk to Tony and Sue about planning and visualizing the dive I had rushed my preparation, and when it came down to it I had been made to look pretty stupid. And then there was what I had been up to the night before.

I prayed Tony had the sense to surface, as he had been trained to do if he was separated from me. I was free floating in the sea with no mask on, and with a strong current pulsing against me and sending me in who knew which direction and for how far, but the burning embarrassment I felt meant that I could happily have stayed underwater rather than go up and face Garland.

I couldn't read my computer or see the numbers on my

depth gauge. As intended I had gone into the water with no air in my buoyancy jacket, and I could feel the increasing pressure squeeze the compressible spaces in my ears, and I knew I was still descending. I equalized, pinching my nose and blowing down it. Feeling for my inflator, I slowed and then stopped my descent by putting little jets of air into the bladder of the jacket until I was neutrally buoyant. I had been planing headfirst through the water at a forty-five-degree angle.

I straightened up and rolled on my back until I could sense, rather than see, the canopy of lightness that was the sun shining in the water above me. Hovering, I unclipped the reel and submersible marker buoy from the D-ring on the lower-left front of the jacket, and pulled the rolled bag from the surgical tubing bands that held it to the reel. I felt for the clip at the end of the line that attached to a D-ring at the open end of the buoy, then brought that end of the buoy up to my regulator mouthpiece.

The buoy unfurling in front of me was a wide bright colour without delineation. I blew through my mouthpiece into the opening. Holding the open end with one hand, my other hand on the pistol grip handle of the reel, I felt the buoy firm up as it began to fill with air. The line tightened as the buoy strained to rise. I pushed the brake lever down and released the line. The line played out fast as the buoy accelerated up through the water, the air volume inside it expanding as the pressure decreased. When the line stopped playing out I knew that the buoy had broken the surface of the water. I reeled in to tighten the line and hopefully make the buoy stand up and be more visible to anyone looking for me. I went slowly towards the light that brightened as I ascended, taking in line and venting air from the buoyancy jacket to control the pace of my climb. The heavily salted water felt grainy against my naked eyes.

I broke the surface, and my heart jumped when I saw how far west of the islands and out into the open sea the current had already taken me. The waves pushed into me and whipped salt drops hard into my face. There was no sign of Suhail and the Zodiac. If Tony had surfaced as he was supposed to when we separated I couldn't see him. I carried on being taken west. I reeled the last of the line in and clipped the reel onto a D-ring just below my left shoulder.

I reached behind me and pulled out the big collapsible flag from where I'd secured it to the tank with neoprene bands. The three pole sections came together. The flag was a large bright yellow square. I reached behind me again and managed to get the pole back under the bands on the tank so that the flag flew three feet above my head.

I had done everything automatically since losing my mask, but now I was scared. I was being carried further out to sea every second. My best hope was that Tony had come up straightaway and raised the alarm. Suhail should know which way the current was running and so know roughly where to look, but even then I knew from experience how difficult it was to see a diver, or anything else, in the open sea. If Tony hadn't surfaced Suhail would be following the divers on the reef. A lot of things had to go right, it did me no good at all to realize, for me to come out of this OK. My one piece of luck was that it was still early morning. There were hours before it got dark. I shivered, and imagined the thousands of metres of water below me. There was no doubt about it. I was, and maybe had been for a long time, out of my depth.

≈ ≈ ≈

How quickly I was lost. Adrift on the immense wild sea, above me the burning sun. Seventy-two hours before I'd been a husband and father, living with my family in a city of eight million people. Now I was quite alone in the world. The current swept me further and further away from the islands until the lighthouse disappeared. I was surrounded and dazzled by endlessly repeated flashes of sunlight in the moving waves. In all that shoreless water, under the bright glare of the sun, there was nowhere for me to hide from myself. The protective identities I had assumed – father, husband, waterman – peeled away like layers of sunburnt skin, and I was a scared kid again. The sun crunched down on my head. I wanted to take my tight black neoprene hood off, but I knew I'd burn if I did. My head felt squeezed, and I remembered Dug pulling on my long hair and wrapping it tightly around his hand. 'Keep your pretty head still,' he'd said. I'd puked up the first time and he wouldn't let me get clean. Stop thinking about it, I told myself. I can't help it, it's what I think about when I'm scared. I pissed in my wetsuit. I could hear the yellow flag fluttering in the wind. Sweat and salt stung my eyes. Under the surface of the water, dark shapes passed back and forth below my hanging legs.

'Fuck off,' I said out loud, 'fuck off you dirty greaser bastard. I haven't got time for you.'

I felt all the old terror. I hated how familiar it was, and to know how close I was to giving in to it. I made promises to a God I didn't believe in. To be a good father, a better husband. I'll leave the girl alone, I promised. Stop that. Try doing what you're supposed to. Try fighting against it. Stop, breathe, think, act. That's what you've been taught. The lead weight I carried was making me drift faster. My buoyancy jacket was fully inflated but I was still in the water up to my neck. My head was scorched but I was starting to get cold. I reached down and pulled the ripcord on my jacket and dumped the weight. I sat up a little higher. It wasn't much but it felt like something.

I turned on my back and kicked in the direction of the islands. My fins were useless against the current, but I could try to hold my position in the water, and maybe stop drifting. I could keep my discipline. I could stop letting ghosts back into my head. I had fought to be here, so this was not the time to reconsider whether it was not really me, but only some other imagined Kim who belonged in the oceans of the world: so ill-prepared was I if the smallest thing went wrong, so weak were the foundations on which I had built my sense of self. It was a lie, and I knew it was, but I told myself I was out here alone because Casey had deliberately kicked the mask from my face. It would be an almost impossible thing to accomplish on purpose, but I wanted to believe it. It gave me the anger to do something. I began to swim furiously, and by the time I heard the Zodiac coming I was raging, and determined not to show how scared I'd been.

Suhail was touching his head, his arm bent in a kind of half-circle. Are you OK, he was asking me. Yes, I signed back at him, both hands on my head, I am OK.

Suhail cut the engine and with her bow in the air the Zodiac skated across the top of the waves to me. I reached up and felt for the hot rubber mass of the boat. The inflatable gunwales towered above me and I had to stretch up to reach the hand-hold. I kept the reg in my mouth and unclipped the reel with one hand and threw it in the boat. I heard it clunk on the floor. We were drifting in the current and Suhail put the outboard in neutral and the Zodiac idled on the swells. I swallowed petrol fumes. Gripping the handhold I rose and fell in the water. I unfastened the Velcro waist straps and shoulder clips of the buoyancy jacket and took the reg out of my mouth. I let go of the handhold and shrugged out of the kit. Suhail leaned over the side and held onto the pillar valve of my tank. I kind of got underneath the tank and the kit and pushed it up into the boat while Suhail pulled.

Sea water drained from the kit and came down on me. We got the kit in the boat and then I put my hands on the hot rubber sides and pushed myself up and down in the water to get momentum and kind of finned and jumped to get myself up onto the side of the boat. Suhail tried to help me but I wouldn't let him. I sat on the side and took my fins off and threw them into the boat. I spat into the water and breathed heavily. 'Fuck,' I said. I swung my legs into the boat and said to Suhail, 'All right, let's go.'

Suhail swung the boat round and headed into the wind for the *Shang-Tu*. How often had I ridden in the bow of a speeding Zodiac after a dive, secretly thrilled about how cool I must look in my black wetsuit, the sun on my face, another dive logged? These memories of action, cherishable, self-forming. Now, in the Zodiac that against the wind roughly rode the swell of the waves and then punched down on the water with a bang as the waves broke, I let my rage build. I drank warm water from a bottle on the floor of the boat. I kept my burning face turned from Suhail.

I jumped out as soon as we pulled alongside *Shang-Tu*. I rushed to Casey and put my hand to his throat. He didn't even try and get out of my way. I saw my hand there, the fingers corrugated by the water they had absorbed, my wedding ring flashing in the sunlight, the freckled skin on the back of my hand beginning to tan. Recognizably it was my hand and no other that gripped Casey's neck and squeezed tighter. My shame and rage were always there.

'What the fuck was that?' I shouted at him.

Casey reached up and slowly put pressure on my wrist until I relaxed my grip without taking my hand away from his throat. He was looking at me with green, buggy, sad eyes. He wasn't angry. It seemed to take him a big effort to give his attention to me. I wasn't at all important to whatever was really happening in his life. I let go of Casey and stepped back. He held up one hand and reached into the velcroed back pocket of his shorts with the other, and pulled a photograph out of a thin plastic wallet.

It was a picture of a chirpy-looking mixed-race girl who must have been about eight years old. The girl was green eyed and smiling, and at the same time unsuccessfully trying to hide the brace on her teeth. In embryonic form she had her father's bug-eyed look, but she was not unpretty. She was un-mistakably African. Like my daughters her hair had the same frizziness that defeated my attempts to care for it until Araba showed me how. Her skin shone with the same shea butter I had learned to treat my daughters' skin with every day.

'That's Abidemi,' Casey said. 'My daughter. Her name means "born during her father's absence". Her mother went home to Nigeria and left Abidemi for me to look after. I'm bringing her up. You've got kids?'

'Yes.'

'Then you know they cost money. Whatever I do to get it for her is none of your business. Instead of accusing me of stupid shit you want to thank me for not telling Teddy about you and Jody.'

'There's nothing to tell him,' I said.

'Is that right? Well, I know you think Teddy likes you,' Casey said, 'but who do you think he'll believe and what do you think he'll do to you? Let me tell you something: you don't know anything about Teddy King and the best thing you can do is keep it that way. In case you haven't noticed, we're in the middle of nowhere out here. Anything can happen.'

He spoke quietly, but every word was clear, without the ingratiating whine I had presumed was a permanent fixture of the man. This sudden and unwelcome connection with Casey – that he knew about me and Jody and the fact that, like me, he had a mixed-race daughter – made me if anything angrier than if he'd really meant to kick the mask from my face. I didn't know any white fathers of mixed-race children. There were plenty of mixed-race kids in my neighbourhood, but there were no other families where the dad was white. At another time and in another place I would have wanted to talk to him.

To compare stories. Now I didn't want that connection with him, but I couldn't help remembering that when Teddy King was playing the racist routine with me, Casey's silence had seemed to own a particular edge.

'We came up as soon as I realized you weren't there,' Casey said. 'It was an accident, or maybe you just need to look where you're fucking going.'

'All right,' I said, 'All right, fuck it.'

'Yeah, that's just about your level,' Casey said.

Garland and Jody and the others were still on their dive. I looked at my watch. It was only forty minutes since Suhail had taken us out in the Zodiac. I hadn't been very far away after all. Suhail had gone back out to wait for Garland and his group to surface. He'd taken my kit out of the Zodiac and put it on the dive deck.

I grabbed my gear and humped it up to the kit-up area and put it in my rack. I turned off the air and purged my second stages. I unscrewed the regulator's A-clamp from the tank, disconnected my regs and loosened the Velcro straps on my buoyancy jacket to lift the tank out. I took the tape off a new tank, got fresh weights and set my kit up with the tank and put it in the rack, looping my spare mask round the pillar valve. Then the Zodiac's motor came puttering up and I went below to meet them. Rowdy and Teddy were whooping and high-fiving on the dive deck. Garland looked like thunder. He stormed past me without speaking.

Later, Jody told me that at the agreed maximum depth of thirty metres, Rowdy and Teddy King had just carried on cruising down the reef, going deeper and deeper. Bobby Ballet stayed with Jody and Garland. As they sank, Garland was trying to signal them by banging his knife against his tank, but Rowdy and Teddy ignored him. As they were swallowed up in the blue Jody said she saw Teddy flip Garland the finger. Garland was so furious he didn't ask me about my dive. I couldn't forget about it though. I seemed to have sailed on *Shang-Tu* into a territory where my past and present seemed not so much to have come together as collided. I had not managed, as I'd hoped, to escape my past. I still carried it all with me – all the panic and rage and shame – and though I'd spent years thinking other-wise, diving hadn't really allowed me to get away from myself. I felt this at the time – I'm not just saying so looking back. First Jody, and now this near-miss and the way I had acted. Casey's African daughter. Something, maybe even my future, was to be decided. I needed to pay attention. It's the same as being underwater: there are no obvious paths to follow. You have to know where you want to go and how to get there.

≈ ≈ ≈

The days and nights that followed our first ill-starred dives at the Brothers settled into a pattern that soon became familiar. Despite my promises I went straight back to Jody's bed on the night of my rescue. I spent my days diving with her, and I like to think we became friends as well as lovers. In the beginning she had kept her kisses for our nights in her progressively funky smelling sleeping bag, but now she kissed me in the day too, as long as nobody was around – at the breakfast table, as we were kitting up, on the dive deck before jumping into the water. I was sure somebody would catch us.

'Teddy can't find out about us,' I said to her one morning. We were hiding out up by the bow after the early dive, and Jody's legs were wrapped around me and she was kissing me.

'I know,' she said, and kissed me again and made a moaning sound deep in her throat. 'I know.'

Underwater she sometimes took her regulator out and sneakily smooched me when I wasn't expecting it, giggling like crazy afterwards and finning away as cascades of bubbles escaped from her. Other times she'd hover in the water column, a vision suspended in bright blue space and illuminated by great beams of golden sunlight that shone radiantly down on her. She would dance for me in her tight wetsuit and mermaid fins, as impossible numbers of tiny technicolor reef fish showered the water all around us like blossom falling from the sky.

When she wasn't dancing, or scooting in on my blind side to kiss me, Jody presented an undemonstrative, tucked-in and streamlined black profile underwater, with just the ends of her blonde curls peeping out from under her black neoprene hood. We swam close to each other, and I was happy to see that she was always reliably within touching distance, her buoyancy control spot on. Because of Jody's admiration and presence, my confidence in the water returned.

Just the sight of Jody lying in the sun would explain things better than I can ever hope to. Her skin got dark and her hair whitened with the lemon juice she put on it, and she kept her locks, dressed with bone beads, copper cuffs and cowrie shells, tied back under a black bandeau. Her eyebrows and the hair on her forearms were white. In the day she wore cut-offs and a black bikini top, and silver-framed Arnettes in the lenses of which anything she looked at, the islands, the shining water, was doubly reflected. Often I would look at her and see my twin selves, dark forms framed by the sun and sea, looking back at myself and smiling. My world was reduced to this boat, to this girl and the warm and rich water of these small, remote islands far out of sight of home.

Jody refused point blank to get in the water with Rowdy and Teddy King after the first dive. Teddy pleaded with her but she wouldn't do it.

'There's too much testosterone down there,' she said, giving Teddy her best impression of Johnny Utah's tomboy girlfriend in *Point Break*. 'You want to go to fifty metres on a single tank, Teddy, it's your funeral, but count me out.'

Despite the way Teddy and Jody spoke to one another in public, and what I took to be aspects of menace in the desperate looks he gave her, there was an obvious fondness between them, no matter how unlikely. I was taking the sun between dives one day, high up on the flybridge, when I heard Jody's voice coming up from below. Crawling to the side, I looked down and saw Jody and Teddy alone on the sun deck. It wasn't because Teddy had his big arms around her that I was disturbed, but the helpless way he was looking down at her. Without anybody to see him or play up to, the look on Teddy's face was one of pure longing and submission. Jody had her hands flat on his massive chest, and she was scolding him about something I was too far away to hear. Now and then she moved her hands to pick at something that was stuck to his robe.

Garland never spoke directly to me about my nearly being lost, and I thought that was because he had failed to control Teddy and Rowdy on his own first dive. I was surprised that Tony and Susan seemed happy to continue diving with me and Jody, and didn't want to carry on with the course they had paid for with Casey. I guess they didn't want any part of Teddy King's craziness, and no doubt they regretted being on the boat at all. After the first dive I made sure that when we got in we were organized and mellow, and I think Tony and Susan appreciated that. I showed them some things that quickly improved their diving. Keep your arms folded and still, and all your hoses squared away. Nice, calm, steady breathing. Kick from the hips and not the knee. Dive side by side with your buddy, not above or below or behind. Maintain eye contact and communicate with clear uncomplicated signs. Navigate using the environment.

For a few days the four of us got shark fever. We spent whole dives with our backs to the vibrantly alive, mountainous reef, staring instead out into the blue where a shark might appear at any time from a point beyond our vision. When the fever struck you imagined that if you turned to look at the reef for just a second sharks by the hundred would be streaming by behind you. So we would hover, peering out into limitless blue space, straining to cover as much territory as we could but able to see only a fraction of the world we were in. And no matter how good the visibility, your field of sight is dramatically circumscribed underwater compared to on land, and your dive mask cuts out peripheral vision. Even in the Red Sea the water can be cloudy, and the shark can almost be on top of you before you see it, so believe me, it's hard to keep your mind off everything you *can't* see. Just as civilization's territory was once limited to those places within the range of illumination given by campfire light. Beyond the light lay a dark wilderness.

A shark sighting was the prize awarded for patience, and gave you a rush that stayed with you for a long time afterwards, a sharp reminder of the true possibilities of your life. Divers value a good shark spotter, and follow them underwater. I wasn't bad, but Jody was better, as if she were locked onto a shark frequency other people couldn't hear. Compared to me she had no experience in the water, but she had the gift. Most often I'd be staring hard out into the blue and I'd hear her yell through her mouthpiece, or bang her knife against her tank. I'd turn and see her pointing above or below me or to the side, and there would be a shark, a thrilling, relentless, missile-shaped apparition that was always moving away from you, swimming fast without appearing to move at all. As if, like Garland had once said, they had the good sense to keep away from people. Man is the exclusive object of a shark's attention only, I would think, at the moment the man is trying to kill the shark.

I wondered if we had turned the thing we feared – in this case sharks, but it might just as easily be people who were a different colour or who worshipped different gods – into something fearful to justify the slaughter we visited upon them. Time and again in the Yemen, and again in Mexico, we would pass beaches piled high with the bodies of sharks, their fins removed to boil down for soup, the corpses abandoned to rot under the sun.

Rowdy, Teddy King, Casey and Bobby now made what was more or less an ungovernable four, though sometimes Garland still got in with them, I guess in a doomed effort to try and police what they got up to. I knew that Teddy and the others were still diving recklessly and going way too deep. Rowdy was one of those blokes who likes to push the limits of how deep you can go on a single tank of air and still come back, though I reckon it was for the buzz of getting 'narced' as much as the numbers. When you dive on air, the concentration of nitrogen at depth can cause narcosis: a feeling of manic, even hysterical euphoria that some divers love but that can be deadly. Like a lot of blokes who dive, Rowdy loved going deep and getting narced. He charged his dive computer where nobody could see the recorded maximum depth of his dives, and he kept no logbook. When Teddy had called off the shakedown dives on our first afternoon out of port, Garland had handed me a banded stack of certification cards and logbooks. I had opened a beer and spread the cards out on a grey blanket. Without a shakedown dive, this was the only information I had to begin to get a sense of how competent the divers on board were. Logbooks documented your diving history, showing where you had dived, and how often. Details included the maximum depth of each dive. Neither Rowdy nor Teddy King had handed in logbooks.

Bobby Ballet remained a near silent, almost stuporous presence. He always wore dark glasses or a dark-lensed dive mask, but even so I could see that the bruises he had got – from where? from Teddy? – had turned to autumn colours that began to spill out beyond the frames.

Garland never said anything to Teddy about the way he and his friends were carrying on – the drug-taking and the deep dives – but if you were going to look for a reason why, you wouldn't have to look far. Garland was outnumbered, and he clearly no longer trusted me to back him up.

Garland's problem with Teddy was that, apart from everything else, he was exactly the sort of diver Garland hated. Teddy was a sight in the water. He wore no wetsuit, the great rolling mass of himself insulated Teddy from the cold. He was vast, pale, drifting, moon-like in the water, the tank on his back small as a toy. Teddy was not skilful, and he showed no interest in improving. He followed Casey around underwater – you never felt that he knew or cared where he was going. Instead of clipping his hoses and gauges to his buoyancy jacket, he left them hanging, so that when he passed over a reef the loose hoses with their heavy gauges on the end would crash through the coral. Teddy gave the sea no value – he gave it no thought at all unless he was in it – and even then I wonder whether he thought of the water as anything other than the environment of a game made especially for him.

It's speculative to say so, but I do believe that he welcomed the freedom from his own weight that he encountered underwater. But I also think it didn't matter to him whether the place where he free-floated was a reef full of fish or a cloudy and lifeless swimming pool. It was the experience of weightlessness he loved, not the things he saw. He was only ever impressed by sharks and that, I suppose, was because he had to be impressed by anything that could eat him.

Teddy had neither Garland's reverence and concern for the ocean, nor my sense of wonder at the miracles I encountered there. Underwater for Teddy was a place where you could have a laugh – where you could grab hold of a sea turtle and make out the animal was towing you through the water. So, sooner or later, that kind of behaviour was going to make Garland explode.

In the same way that I dived with Tony and Susan, Garland took on Johnny and Tristan's diving education. I say that, but Tristan didn't seem interested. He almost never got into the water, and when he did he would stand trembling on the dive deck afterwards, his mask fogged and half full of water, his tank hanging halfway down his back, while Garland helped him out of his fins, and he would swear that he was never getting in again. 'If I wanted to dress in rubber and put a gag in my mouth,' he said once, 'there are plenty of places back in London I could go.'

Mostly he sat in whatever shade he could find, writing on an A4 pad. Tristan remained defiantly pale, while the rest of us were changed by the sun, and he had the permanent sneer of somebody who was always coming down with or from something. Johnny seemed to enjoy diving though. He never looked at home in the sea, it's true, and Garland could never get him to swim horizontally, but he seemed to get a buzz out of it, and spent hours in the water with Garland, and talking to him afterwards. On the boat Tristan and Johnny kept a low profile, so that it was easy to forget about them, but they were always around. I'd look up and see Tristan under an awning, sneering and writing, or there would be a sudden flash, and Johnny would have taken another photo of Teddy smoking a huge joint, or Garland looking wild against the setting sun.

Garland began to keep to himself, spending more time than usual writing in his dive log. Before each dive he always gave the same briefing. Spelling out to us all the maximum allowable depth and the duration and depth of the safety stop that was required on each dive.

Because he quickly realized how much he got under Garland's skin, Teddy started digging at him every chance he got. Garland's habit of wearing a futah and speaking Arabic, his identifying of fish by their Latin names, the lectures he often gave to Johnny after dives in which, it sometimes seemed even to me, he did talk about the sea and the animals that lived in it as though he were their best if not only custodian – so that Jody whispered to me once that, 'If it looks like a Bodhi and talks like a Bodhi . . .' – all of this was ammunition for Teddy. I remember once at sunset when Garland, looking heroic and just against the burning sky, was talking urgently and along familiar lines about our responsibility to the oceans. Teddy, wrapped in an ectoplasmic cloud of pot smoke, said loud enough for everyone, but particularly Garland, to hear, 'Fucking bollocks.'

I was high enough to giggle, and I still remember the look Garland shot into me when I did. It was a look that said he had been betrayed but didn't understand why, and the force of it whumphed into me and sent me in shame from the sun deck, until I heard the familiar sounds of the party starting back up and knew that it was safe to return, because Garland would have gone.

There were times during those hot partying nights when, feeling the sludge freeze of Teddy's cocaine begin its slow drip at the back of my throat – the frenzy the drug most often made me susceptible to, smoothed out by weed and cold beer and the promise of Jody's caresses to come – I'd connect to the light shining in Teddy's blue eyes that were violet in the electric evening light – a different light to the blaze in Garland's eye – this light saying, 'Aren't we high, though? Aren't we high?' and flying underwater and getting high would seem to me to be parts of the same thing. And I'd think that in a world that seemed to promise and want from me nothing but work, I'd been let in on a great secret.

And I honestly believed it was a secret that Araba and Garland didn't know. That in a world where life is short and death is certain, the only thing worth pursuing was the next high – wherever you get those highs from. At night I'd feel the truth of this as a rush in my heart that was the same feeling as love, or freedom, and whenever the rush subsided there was Teddy King, always hooded, always robed, with the stuff to fire it up again.

Most nights I would have a couple of lines of Teddy's cocaine and five or six beers, and later I would sneak away and have a spliff with Jody. Generally I needed to jump over the side in the morning and get into the water before I felt human. But I was strong, and the fierce sex with Jody every night left me feeling blissed out – buried between her warm brown thighs that smelled of after-sun and ozone and another scent that was hers alone. In the day I was high on underwater flights, precious soul-altering missions to inner space. I felt like I could get away with how I was behaving. And if I didn't think too hard I would think I was happy. I had what I thought I wanted – not just sunshine and water but a pretty brown girl to share them with.

Sometimes I would try and talk with Tony and Susan, who read nothing but celebrity magazines and ghost-written books about footballers and models, and who, so far as I could tell, knew nothing about the world except for what free newspapers told them to know. I would try and make them feel as though they had wasted their lives working hard and buying a house and saving to go on holiday twice a year. Once when Garland was passing and heard me talking that way he turned on me and snarled, 'You want them to be like you? Running away from your wife and kids whenever you feel like it?' So I knew he was really mad at me.

Some nights, though, a fragile if deceptive peace settled over *Shang-Tu*, and things were cool between me and Garland and almost like they used to be. One night, as oceanic whitetip sharks circled the boat, hunting squid by the brightness we made, the tawny backs of the sharks spangled by electric light as they cruised by, the brown arms of Suhail and the crew pointing from the gunwales, Garland showed me Jupiter and Saturn in a sky so thick and bright with the stars of the Milky Way we couldn't make out the separate constellations. I say that, but Garland did manage to find Cassiopeia for me, and

I know he did so because once, years ago and a long way off the Pacific coast of Mexico, we had sailed on a boat of that name into a three-day storm. We had felt the electricity in the air for days, and so had known the storm was coming long before the late afternoon when we had finally seen the horizon ahead of us turn roiling black, and watched lightning crash into the sea in lances of broken golden light.

≈ ≈ ≈

I never liked Casey, and I wonder if deep down it was because I believed him to be a better father than I was. Was it because, as far as I could understand it, he did things he didn't want to do to support Abidemi, and paid for somebody to take care of her when he was away, while I had not only left Araba to look after our kids on her own, but was cheating on her as well?

Maybe so. I know that even though it was unfair, I blamed Casey for everything that was wrong on *Shang-Tu*. I came to hate the sight of him, wearing the same dirty shirt day after day and sucking down his Marlboros. He made my skin crawl. I mean when I wasn't laughing and partying with him, Teddy could scare the life out of me, but it's hard to think badly about somebody you get free drugs from. Of course I worried that Teddy would find out about me and Jody, and I worried about what he would do if he did, but mostly I tried to shunt whatever fears I had about him clean out of my mind. And Jody tried to reassure me that everything was OK, and the way he carried on was just the way Teddy was.

'That's how he controls people. He'll lay on something like

this, pay for everything, and part of the deal is that you have to put up with how he behaves. Nobody's holding a gun to anyone's head. And the way he is with Casey – the thing is, Teddy needs him, and they're as close as brothers. Don't look at me like that, it's true. It doesn't matter what it looks like, or what you think you know. Jeez, Kim, don't you ever fight with the people you love? Teddy doesn't know anything about diving, really, so he relies on Casey to run the dive shop, and more than that, he trusts him underwater. He'd be lost without him down there. And, all right, they're rough with each other, but they all party so hard it's not surprising they feel shitty sometimes and take it out on each other. It's how they are. We can't all be saints like Bodhi.'

Maybe so, but Casey just wasn't likeable. He never washed, for one thing. Maybe he thought the sea would take care of that side of things, or maybe he was just a dirty bastard. Either way he began to hum after a few days. When he was on deck in the heat of the day the sun brought out the sweat-stink from his dirty yellow skin. Because we weren't fighting the cold and darkness of British waters, single-tank dives at the Brothers would often last for an hour or more. It's fairly common for people to piss in their wetsuits on dives that length. Of course when you get out you rinse your wetsuit with fresh water and take a shower, but Casey didn't. And he never changed out of the one pair of shorts he wore. After a dive he would sit up on deck, bug-eyed, smoking and smelling strongly of piss. You really didn't want to be near him. Bobby Ballet was the only one who treated Casey halfway decently.

You couldn't imagine a more unlikely waterman, but to see

Casey in the water was to come close to forgiving him for everything else – his misery, his hostility to me and Garland, and to Suhail and the rest of the crew, his dirtiness and constant smoking, his inability, or so it seemed to me, to defend himself to Teddy King. You wouldn't believe it with the amount of cigarettes he smoked, and the lengthy, hard to listen to, attacks of racking coughing he started every day with, but he used less gas underwater than anyone I've ever seen, including Garland. The less gas you use, of course, the longer you can stay down. Other than this advantage there was nothing to choose between them. Both of them, to use Garland's definition of what made a good diver, could put themselves where they needed to be in the water. The sustainment of neutral buoyancy is an art form few divers can perfect.

Could you hover at five metres for a mandatory safety stop in upswelling water, with no line, and be able, by breath control and the venting of just the right fractional amounts of expanding air from your buoyancy jacket, to keep your depth from fluctuating as the water moved? They both could. They could both hover motionless upside down, fin into sandy caves without kicking up the bottom, and penetrate and navigate the deepest darkest wrecks and never get lost.

In all other respects, though, there was no kinship between them. Against Garland's golden radiance anybody might struggle to shine, but somebody like Casey – who, unless he was in the water suggested by his jaundiced skin and rickety frame nothing so much as decay, anti-life – seemed especially pale and insubstantial next to Garland's luminosity and scale.

Casey dived with his arms folded, making a cradle for his

contents gauges. He wore these ancient stubby black fins, and he had a kind of scooping kick to get him through the water and no other part of him moved. Down around fifteen metres we would often experience a thermocline, the temperature of the water we moved through steeply falling, and that place where the water became suddenly colder trembling like a mirage. Once I saw Casey below me, on the cold, deeper side of this layer of shimmering marine light. A long narrow cornet fish, the colour of pale denim through the haze, sat on Casey's shoulder. Casey was hugging close to the terraced reef that was as brilliant and dense as a city with life, alternately sculling with his fins and then gliding down through the water. Teddy was floundering nearby, moving his hands uselessly and kicking up the visibility. With the sound of my breathing in my ears I watched Casey move over the pulsing reef, touching nothing, in absolute control and looking, looking, at the wild architecture and alien vegetation of the hard and soft corals. Nothing he did seemed forced, and I realized with a start of recognition how much more at home he looked down there than he did on board *Shang-Tu*.

Where somebody like Tony couldn't leave his rig alone, and was constantly tinkering with the configuration, or trying out some new and expensive toy, Casey never – with one exception – bothered with his kit at all. I can't imagine any of his kit ever being serviced. He'd come up from a dive looking for his cigarettes, and he'd stand on the deck and let one of the crew take his kit off him and take it away. Casey never looked at it from one dive to the next.

The exception was that, a couple of days into the trip,

Casey fitted his back-up second stage, called an octopus, with a seven foot-long hose – that's about four foot longer than a standard hose – so that when Teddy King needed air he would breathe from the octopus and swim behind Casey. The long hose was introduced by the Wakulla Karst Plains Project, a Florida-based diving organization which holds most of the world's cave diving depth and distance records. If you needed air and breathed off your buddy's normal-length hose you had to swim side by side, and so you would not be able to pass through the tight entrances and passageways that are a feature of cave diving. Teddy always ran out of air before anybody else, and because he was unwilling to surface he got into the habit of breathing off Casey's long hose for the last fifteen minutes of each dive. The long hose was part of the Hogarth system, a utilitarian, less-is-more approach named after its inventor, Bill Hogarth Main, and used and taught by WKPP divers.

When we weren't forced to dive on single tanks, Garland practised the Hogarth system, in which all the components are integrated. He dived with a steel backplate bolted to dual tanks, and a single set of Dive-Rite wings. The tanks are connected by an isolation manifold, with one regulator attached to each tank, so that you can close down a faulty regulator while still accessing the air in both tanks. All WKPP kit is put together using this principle of redundancy. Compare that to a diver using a single tank of air and single regulator. What happens to that diver when his regulator fails or free flows and he's out of air? He comes looking for yours, or else bolts to the surface, which is no good if you have mandatory decompression stops to make, let alone whether you can even make the surface from, say, forty metres down.

I was kind of a semi-Hogarthian diver. I had the backplate and the manifolded twins, but there were elements of the system that I hadn't integrated. I didn't own, for example, a cave light with a cylindrical battery canister worn right up against my backplate so it created no drag. I couldn't afford one. So very often I dived with a hand-held torch or none at all. In the eyes of the Hogarthian divers this made me a 'stroke', and someone not to dive with. Strokes are out there, the mantra says, and they will kill you. Teddy King, of course, was most definitely a stroke.

I remember on one wall dive on Big Brother, the different groups had got bunched up below a large hawksbill turtle that was feeding from soft corals and backlit by the high sun shining brightly down.

I saw Casey, rock steady in the water, a look of fatalism masking whatever else he might have been thinking about having Teddy so literally on his back. Teddy hugely fat and floating behind him and sucking away on the long hose, as if the hose was what was responsible for blowing him up to this freakish size. I wondered what depth they had come up from. As they went by Teddy winked at me, his open eye malevolent and amplified behind his mask, and he pointed at Casey and gave the wanker sign as they passed below the turtle that, rising in the water to where the sun was strongest, became so brightly illuminated it resembled a fabulous and living jewel.

So, yes, trying to square all these different sides to Casey's character, that's what I find difficult. Maybe it can't be done.

Maybe he was just a nasty piece of work who happened to have a daughter he loved, and who was a genius in the water. If the girl hadn't been mixed-race, or if Casey hadn't had the power to drop me and Jody in it to Teddy at any time, would I have thought about him much at all? I don't know, we were all so close together on that boat. You'd try and forget about somebody, and the next minute everything would go dark and they'd be standing in your sun.

≈ ≈ ≈

All the while Suhail cleaned up after us. He swept up the saloon after dinner – where more often than not Teddy would scoff four or five helpings, and throw the food he hadn't eaten, the skin and bones, at Tristan and Johnny. Mostly Garland ate with Nawfal in the wheelhouse, but earlier in the trip he some-times ate with us. The last time he did I remember him staring at Teddy from the other side of the saloon, as Teddy threw food and talked and talked with his mouth full, bits of rice and fish stuck to the front of his velvet robe. Garland looked like he couldn't believe what he was seeing. He stared and stared at Teddy, but Teddy just carried on behaving like a pig. Of course he knew Garland was looking at him.

Suhail got us in and out of the water. He pumped our tanks, and he ferried us to the dive sites in the little Zodiac and he ferried us back again. If you let him, he'd carry your kit from the Zodiac on to the dive deck of *Shang-Tu*, and of course Teddy let him. And when we were diving Suhail emptied our shit bins and made our beds. He folded clean towels into the shapes of dogs and lizards and left them for us to find. Once he made a dummy of Garland, stuffing a pair of his old boardies and a sweatshirt with brocade cushions, and sticking shades on a loose-stringed, straw-coloured mop. In those rare moments when he wasn't working he would take photographs. And God knows why but he wanted his picture taken with each of us. Months after I got home Suhail sent me an email – a picture of the two of us standing at the rail at sunset with our arms around each other's shoulders, Suhail in his Iron Maiden T-shirt, me in a Lahaina Divers top, head and shoulders bigger than Suhail, my tawny hair cropped right down. I am tan and darker still with the blood-orange sky falling into the sea behind me, so that you can't see the shit-eating grin I habitually wore on that safari. It's lost in the approaching darkness, but I know it's there.

In the windless, desert-hot hours between dives one dog-day mid-afternoon, I was woken by angry shouts coming from the sun deck. I had been sleeping in my hiding place up on the flybridge, my head in Jody's lap, and dreaming of going home to Araba and finding another man in our bed. When I reached them, Suhail was being held back by Nawfal and a bunch of crewmen. Suhail's eyes were big and staring and the veins in his neck stood out so that he looked like a wild horse. He was trying to get to Casey, whose look at least owned the possibility of knowing shame. His bug eyes were filming over and he had his arms crossed in front of him. He smoked defensively, hiding behind the grey clouds he made. Rowdy and Bobby Ballet stood by. Looming nearby on a banquette, smoking a fat joint, and kneading his stomach as though it gave him pleasure, was the massive form of Teddy King.

'No diving,' Nawfal said, 'no more diving.'

'What's happening here?' I said.

'He threw it,' Suhail said, pointing at Casey. 'Him, he threw it. There.' He pointed to the sea.

'Teddy told me to,' Casey said.

'What?'

'He was always sneaking around taking pictures, in't that right, Abdul?' Teddy said from his banquette seat. 'I told you not to take pictures. You see what happens when you don't listen.'

'Suhail!' Suhail screamed at him. 'My name is Suhail! There is no right! No right! It was my camera. Egypt is my country, not yours! One day you will see!'

'Yeah yeah. All right, Abdul,' Teddy said, 'keep your handkerchief on.'

'Teddy,' I said. I was conscious that Garland had appeared next to me.

'What is it, boy?'

'There's no need to speak like this.'

'I've already told you,' he said. 'Maybe you weren't listening. Maybe you were whacked out on the free shit I give you. I don't like wogs. I don't like wogs or Arabs. I don't like wogs, Arabs, poofs, pikeys or micks. I don't like foreigners, no offence, Rowdy, mate. I don't like many cunts who aren't from Canvey, to tell you the truth.'

'Teddy, I just think . . .'

'You're forgetting something, boy.'

'What's that, Teddy?'

'This is my boat. I pay these cunts' wages, and once we get back to Hurghada your little mate is sacked. Waste my fucking money standing around taking pictures, the cunt.' Teddy looked around. 'I'll most probably sack all of them. Plenty more of the camel-fucking bastards where this lot came from. Oi, Nawfal, get him out of my sight, and the rest of them, or nobody gets paid. And make sure them tanks are pumped, I want to go diving.'

Bobby Ballet was slowly shaking his head and staring at Teddy.

'Fucking cunts,' Teddy said. 'What do you reckon, Case, everybody has a good time but forgets who's paying for everything?'

Casey looked at him and shrugged.

'You properly lobbed that camera,' Teddy said.

'You told me to,' Casey said.

'Good lad, Case,' Teddy said. 'At least you fucking remember where your money comes from. Go and get yourself a couple of beers.'

'Give me the shit,' Casey said to him.

Teddy looked surprised for a second and then dug into his robe for the little cocaine dispenser. He handed it over and Casey took a couple of hits.

'Suhail,' Garland said. He'd been so still I'd forgotten he was there.

Suhail looked at him. His eyes were red.

'I've got a camera you can have,' Garland said.

I thought I saw Bobby give Garland an indeterminate look, but with the dark glasses it was hard to tell.

Teddy laughed. 'All right, big man,' he said, 'you give him a camera, but if he takes any more pictures of me with it, I'll throw him to the fucking sharks.'

'Teddy,' Garland said, 'if you touch this boy, or any member of this crew, I'll kill you.'

Suddenly, the sound of everybody's breathing was so loud I couldn't hear the waves against the boat. The last time I had seen that tight, white look on Garland's face, it had ended with his hands around the throat of a man in a bar in Hana, in up-country Maui. The bar was full of tough-looking Hawaiian cowboys and dope farmers, and above the bar was a big painting of Willie Nelson over the words 'Yee hah bra'. The man Garland took against was a huge, black-haired French-Canadian who had come to Hawaii after a season salmon fishing in Alaska. He was wearing a shark's-tooth necklace and Garland had ripped the cheap black cord from the bloke's neck. I heard the shark's-tooth make a 'tik' sound as it fell on the wood floor somewhere. Garland had squeezed the fisher-man round the neck until he started to choke, and then he dropped him and left him out cold on the floor. Now Garland was looming over Teddy in the same way, and Teddy just looked him up and down and laughed.

'You're a dangerous-looking fucker, I grant you,' he said, 'but you're not going to kill anybody and you know it, so get back in your fucking cage.'

All this time Teddy was lying down on the banquette and fingering his fat belly. He smoked the last of his joint and flicked it over the side of the boat. He started to smile sweetly at us and then got caught by a fit of coughing.

'You all right, Ted?' Casey said.

Teddy held his hand up, and then leaned over the side of the banquette and gobbed a great lump of green-brown spit on the deck near Garland's feet.

'Fuck,' Teddy said, 'that's better.'

He looked at the mess on the floor.

'Get out and walk, you bastard,' he said.

Garland looked at me, his face leached of colour but for the fiery cast in his eye. I didn't say anything or even move. I just stood there, and felt my heart fluttering. It seemed to me that Rowdy had moved a step closer.

'What,' I said to Garland, 'what?'

Teddy snorted.

'Kim's not going to do anything,' he said to Garland, 'so don't look at him. You're on your own. You need to shit or get off.'

Garland let out a long exhalation.

'Just leave the kid alone, Teddy,' he said.

'All right, all right,' Teddy said, and smiled and kind of waved at Garland without looking at him. 'Listen, can you move a bit, big man,' he said, 'you're standing in my sun?'

Garland shouldered past me and went below without looking at me again. I got more wrecked than usual that night. I couldn't think of a single reason not to. I just wanted to climb into myself and disappear. Garland was up in the wheelhouse with Nawfal and Suhail. They were sitting on the floor, with glasses of tea on a low rattan table. Red lanterns and pictures of sports cars on the walls. I don't know why I went up there. Suhail sat turning Garland's silver-coloured digital camera over and over in his hands. He said something to Garland I didn't understand, and Garland said to me, 'I'm going to talk to these men now, Kim. Go and see your girl.'

'What have I done now?' I said. 'Why can't I stay?'

'If I have to explain that you need to stand with me when I go up against somebody like Teddy, then you and me are finished. You're supposed to be my buddy. If I can't rely on you out here, then where am I? I needed you to give me a sign that you were ready to back me up today and I didn't see one.'

Nawfal and Suhail were trying not to look at us. Steam rose from the tea glasses on the table.

'I was talking to him, Garl, why did you need to come on so strong?'

'Teddy's not going to listen to anything you say. As far as he's concerned he's bought you off by giving you all that shit you've been sticking up your nose.'

'But why did you have to threaten him? All right, he's a bit rough but it's his boat. He's paying us, and I need to take some money home.'

'Rough? That bloke is pure bloody poison, and if you don't realize how dangerous he is you're going to regret it. He obviously cares about the girl. How long do you think you can keep what you're up to a secret from him? I don't know how you can listen to him talking and carrying on the way he does, but I've had enough of it. This country and this sea belong to these blokes,' he said, looking at Nawfal and Suhail, 'not me or

169

you, and certainly not people like Teddy King. How can I take his money and look these blokes in the eye? How can you? The world would be a better place without him in it.'

When I didn't say anything Garland said, 'Answer me something Kim. You're good, really good, at just one thing: diving. I don't think you've ever realized how good you are. That's why I loved working with you. I could trust you under-water. You ever think how rare that is? Now you'd rather party than work. You'd rather side with low-lifes like Teddy than with your buddy.'

'What do you want to ask me?'

'Have you got what you wanted?'

I didn't have any answer to the question Garland asked. My experience is that nobody really gets what they want. I left Garland talking to Nawfal and Suhail, like he wanted me to. When I looked back at the wheelhouse I could see the shadows of the three men moving on the red-lit walls. Were they plot-ting in there? I couldn't tell you, although Suhail could have been forgiven for thinking of ways to poison Teddy and Casey's air tanks. It would be a pretty easy thing to do – just let some of the carbon monoxide from the boat's engine get into the tanks while he was filling them. Like Garland said, it was Suhail's country and Suhail's water, so who could have blamed him for trying to protect it from people like Teddy King? I sat out on deck trying and failing to get high, and not feeling the warmth in the hot wind that came to me from the islands.

≈ ≈ ≈

Since we had been on the boat Garland and Rowdy had managed to avoid each other. That is, Rowdy had thrown out dagger looks every time Garland passed by, while Garland pretended to ignore him. On what, counting back, was the eleventh morning out of Hurghada, Garland and I, with Suhail piloting the Zodiac, got into the water at first light to untie our anchor lines from their moorings, and Nawfal took the *Shang-Tu* the mile or so to Little Brother, where Garland and I dived again to secure our ropes on permanent moorings at the south-west corner of that island. The next day, just before sunrise, we were to dive Little Brother's southern plateau.

At five the next morning I was up and making coffee for everybody as the dark sky paled in the east. It seemed to speak for the quality of the diving at the islands, that even at that early hour everybody was mustered and looking forward to getting in. There was a sweet breeze. As usual I dived with Jody, Tony and Susan. We kitted up quickly. When we were ready Jody squeezed my hand. Susan smiled at me. I had been wrong about them. The couple were tanned now, and looking confident in the water. They wore the salt patterns on their wetsuits like marks of honour. Susan, especially, had a great profile in the water, holding the big Sea & Sea camera straight out in front of her, her body horizontal and still, kicking her long legs from the hips, like I'd taught her, in slow and measured fin strokes.

In near darkness we jumped off the dive deck and swam slowly down to the reef wall, our torches shooting streams of light through the dark water. I looked at Jody, and she was rimmed by little blue-green stars of bioluminescence. The luminous stars were caused by the fire plant plankton we swam through. The fire plants gave off light as they were disturbed by our passing. I turned my torch off and signalled the others to do the same. We descended together through a sea as starry as the night sky far above us. As we swam down, showers of blue-green light sprayed from our fins like sparks from a welding torch. We left trails of light in the water.

We dropped to thirty metres, to where a stand of giant Gorgonian sea fans flared out from the reef wall at right angles – each of the fans larger than a big man. After the Gorgonians, the reef went sharply away to the right, and the four of us hovered in a gentle current like sentinels at the point of the reef. Soon we were joined by the others. We waited, looking out to where the reef wall fell away and the really deep water began. We held our positions in the moving water with varying degrees of comfort. Garland held the pillar valve of Johnny's tank as the photographer moved awkwardly to keep his place, upright and finning like he was riding a unicycle. Johnny in the water looked, as Jody had said to me once, 'like he was about to pull a bunch of flowers from the sleeve of his wetsuit'. Garland held Johnny's pillar valve to keep him from drifting away. I don't think Johnny even realized. His eyes were huge in his mask. He was moving his hands and tripping out at the glowing plankton. Every movement he made was accompanied by flashing stars. Garland tapped Johnny on the head so that he would look at him. Garland pointed two fingers at his eyes, then pointed out beyond the reef. More stars glowed at Garland's fingertips. *Look out there*, Garland was saying.

In the gloom of the water we were black forms outlined

with shimmering lights, and it was as a radiant constellation in a dark sky that the immense, five-metre-long form of the shark suddenly appeared over the bluff of the reef in front of us. The creature's tail fin, fully as long as its body and shaped like a giant scythe, ribboned out behind and left a great trail of misty blue-green stars in its wake.

Fringed with glimmering lights the shark flew over our heads. Jody reached for my hand and placed it just below her left breast. Our hands sparkled. I could feel Jody's heart banging under her wetsuit. She back-flipped and stars exploded from her. I could hear her whooping. I looked at Garland, who was staring at the illuminated shark. He was all lit-up too, and hanging perfectly still in the water, kind of standing up on his huge fins.

The shark swam over us again, and I saw that Susan was following it with the camera, and then the shark went back over the bluff where there was no bioluminescence. Garland and I followed her with our torches switched on. Looking down into the gloom we saw pale fragments of the shark moving between our criss-crossing columns of light, and then she was gone into the deep indigo water. We waited, but no more sharks came. Slowly we swam back up the reef. The morning's lightness was in the water now. On our safety stop we were in the blue again, blue all around, with the canopy of sunlit brightness above us, and below us a wild darkness beyond our reach. Coming up we broke the surface of the water like returning spacemen made golden by the rising sun. Our whoops and hollers were loud in the quietness of the morning. I saw Teddy slap the water with his hand. That was the only time I ever saw him properly stoked by something he saw in the water.

'Did you fucking see that, Case?' he said and laughed. 'That was the shit, mate. The absolute fucking shit. That was better than tripping, fuck.'

That night when the stars came out again we got high and talked about what we'd seen. Even Garland was there for a little bit, and drank a couple of beers. He told us that the bioluminescence was caused by marine algae, called dino-flagellates, that produce light when they're disturbed or hunted by other plankton.

'They're called fire plants, aren't they, Garl?' I said.

'That's right. The light is caused by the fire plant turning chemical energy into light energy. Aristotle wrote about it – he talked about the sea shining at night.'

'Aristotle!' Teddy said. 'What a shitter!'

'What kind of shark was that?' Tony asked.

'A thresher. Did you see the caudal fin, the tail? When they're hunting they use the fin like a whip to stun the fish.'

'That's what I do with my knob,' Teddy said. 'Ain't that right, Jody?'

We drank beer and looked at Susan's pictures of the illuminated shark again and again. We took it in turn to tell diving stories. Not the near-death kind, but the stories about dives where we had seen tremendous things. Schooling hammerheads in the Sea of Cortez. Whale sharks off the coast of Mombasa. Teddy voted for cage diving with a Great White off Dyer Island in South Africa.

'You done that dive, big man?' he said to Garland, friendly

as you like, as though Garland's promise to kill him had never happened. 'I thought my arsehole was going to drop out.'

Garland shook his head. Teddy nudged Rowdy and looked smug. I knew that more than once in South Africa Garland had been in the open water with whites, not hiding in a cage.

'This morning,' I said, 'that was the best, I reckon. The best I've done anyway and I've been to a few places. If you've got enough money to get to the right sites you can always see mantas or whale sharks. Fair enough you need some luck, but you can see them. I'll bet you money none of us will ever see anything like we saw this morning again.'

I turned to Garland. 'What do you reckon, Garl? An illuminated shark – you ever see anything like that before? That was something from outer space, man.'

'That was pretty special,' Garland said softly. 'It was superb, man, it really was. You see something like that, you don't have to wonder any more what you're alive for.'

After the dawn start most people went to bed early. In the end it was just me and Jody and Rowdy, and I was hoping Rowdy would leave us alone but he showed no signs of going.

Jody was stretched out on the banquette with her head close to my leg. I tried not to stare at her, and I kept my hands to myself. Every so often she moved her head a little, making the shells and beads in her hair click, and setting off little flashes of desire in me.

'That whole dive was like a dream,' Jody said, looking sad. 'It's hard to believe it now it's over.'

'Jesus,' said Rowdy, 'it was just a bloody shark.'

'Oh, Rowdy,' Jody said, 'what happened to you? That was a

glow-in-the-dark shark, man. When was the last time you saw one of them?'

Rowdy didn't answer her. He looked at me and said, 'You're looking pretty pleased with yourself. I bet old Garland isn't too happy with you though, is he? Getting on the piss all the time and sniffing up the powder.'

'Don't start, Rowdy,' Jody said, her breath hot against my leg, 'not after today. Today was special.'

'Rowdy doesn't think much of me, Jody,' I said. 'It's all right.'

'It's not all right,' she said. 'Why don't you tell us why you're so angry all the time, Rowdy?'

Rowdy lit a cigarette and his eyes flashed in the glare of his lighter.

'You remember when we first met?' Rowdy said to me.

'Oh man, not now,' Jody said. 'I didn't mean now. I don't want to hear this. Shit, Rowdy, now you're going to ruin everything.'

'Ssh, Jo. In Al-Quseir?'

'Yeah, down there. You were trying to be somebody you weren't. Remember?'

'I remember, Rowdy. I hope maybe I've grown up a bit since then.'

'I don't know, mate. I think you're still pretending to be something you're not.'

'If you say so.'

'I bloody do say so. Making out you're another Garland Rain. Mate, you're not hard enough to be like Garland. Let me tell you a story about him. The time you first rocked up in

Al-Quseir was around the time my sister Tyler left. She was like you. She loved old Garland. She was only eighteen then. We were travelling together when we ran into Garland down in Indo. I thought he was a cool bloke, right enough, but Tyler bloody loved him. I mean, all she wanted to do was to be free and travel. She didn't need a bloke or want one, but Garland put the moves on her and pretty soon they were shacked up. I was pleased at first, that's how stupid I was. My sister and my mate. I couldn't see any wrong in the man. Just like you.'

I realized I was holding my breath. I let out air.

'What happened?'

'He bloody knocked my little sister up. When she was about six months gone he sent her back to Oz to have the baby. We were up in Dahab then. Garland said he'd follow her in a couple of weeks but instead we moved south to Al-Quseir. That was about the time you came. Then Garland says, "We're packing up and going to the Yemen." So I say, "What about Tyler?" Garland says, "What about her, bru?" He flat-out turned his back on her. What do you think of that? That's something you didn't bloody know, eh?'

'I don't know, that doesn't sound like Garland. There's got to be more to it than that.'

'Has there? Why? Because he's Mister Perfect fucking diver? What would you bloody know about it, mate? You think I don't know what I'm talking about? You calling my sister a liar? You saying she didn't have a baby, a little girl, my bloody niece? You think I made that up?'

'That's not what I meant. You don't have kids. Things get complicated.'

'I know exactly what you meant, and you can stick your Garland Rain up your arse.'

Rowdy stood up and pushed past me. He smacked the back of my head with his open hand.

Later I stood up on the flybridge in the warm wind and watched squid swim in the boat lights. Jody came and put her arm around me. I could see Suhail and two of the younger crewmen play-wrestling. If I half-closed my eyes *Shang-Tu* suddenly seemed full of children.

'Don't take it so bad.'

'Take what?'

'Bodhi turning out differently to how you think of him.'

I pushed her arm away.

'Don't call him Bodhi.'

'Why not?' Jody said. 'Can't I tease him? Is that not allowed?

'You don't know him.'

'Do you?'

I thought so. I'd let him down, but at one time I had loved him like a brother. My door was always open to him, and he knew it. He loved my girls, and was Suzy's godfather. He never forgot her birthday. He never complained when Suzy made him sit still for hours while she plaited his hair. Had he shown sadness whenever Suzy or Jay hugged him? I couldn't remember.

At first, I was less concerned that, according to Rowdy, he had abandoned his daughter, than I was that he hadn't told me she existed. Because if he hadn't told me about his daughter, what did that say about how he felt about me? I could not doubt that Rowdy was telling the truth, and so of course what he told me made me think differently about the man who, for as long as this child – who would, by now, be around nine or ten – had been alive, I'd thought of as my best friend.

And then I wondered if Garland's anger at my affair with Jody did not just mean that he simply disapproved, but rather was a sign of a more personal and deeper regret at what he must have seen as the inevitable destruction of my family. If that was true, it meant that the separation from his daughter was inevitably a far more complex issue than the one-sided story told by Rowdy. I do remember telling Garland, when I first moved in with Araba, that although I wanted to be a father I was terrified now it was happening. I talked to Garland about not knowing what to do. About wanting, above all, not to cause harm. Garland said the only thing that mattered was that you showed your children love, and that they lived under your roof. That seemed a strange thing to say if what Rowdy had told me was true.

I thought about Casey's daughter Abidemi: born in her father's absence – and I wondered what that name must have done to Garland. 'He's got a kid, eh?' was all he had said when I had told him. His smooth face became momentarily contorted into a look of awful and, at the time, perplexing sadness before he shut it down. Of course I could read what Rowdy told me as another story about Garland committing himself to the water, and giving up the possibility of having a family. It was not lost on me that this might be my story too. Was this fierce independence worth it? Was Garland happy? What about Casey? He was looking after Abidemi, but working for Teddy to support her certainly didn't make him happy.

That night Jody said to me, 'What are we going to do when the trip's over?'

'What do you mean?'

'What happens with you and me?'

'I have to go home first and sort things out. I told you that.'

'And then you'll be with me?'

'Uh-huh.'

She was quiet then and I could tell she didn't believe me.

'I'm staying here,' she said. 'You talk about it all the time, only having one life and all that, and you're right. I love diving and I'm good at it. I'm going to stay here and do a divemaster course in Hurghada and look for work on the boats. You talk about leaving your wife and moving out here. Well, I'm just saying, I'm going to be here.'

As Jody and I grew closer, her resemblance to my boyhood sweetheart Dawn seemed to recede a little. Maybe Jody seemed to look less like her as she became her own person in my heart and mind. And the less I saw of Dawn in Jody, the less she was able to remind me of my past. That night though, after Rowdy had told me about his sister Tyler's fatherless child, I dreamed about Dawn and her father again. The dream was always the same, of course: I'm helpless and abandoned, tied down in the stink of my own piss and fear in a pitch-black room, until Dug opens the door and stands, naked, dirty, his tattooed body pulsing with excited malevolence, in a drenching opiate light that I knew was the promise of my own oblivion. Not for the first time I woke up shouting Araba's name.

Jody held me and asked me what was wrong, the little

electric filaments of her hair glowing faintly in the starlight like fire plants. I looked at her young and lovely face, and knew what I had to do. When I had first made promises to her, and our bodies had still been stuck together with our sweat, I had been able to dream about a life together for me and Jody. Now I couldn't, and I needed to find a way to tell her. I had to go home and try and make things right with my wife, somehow. I'd tried to sleep again, then, but all the time in the back of my head, like a song you can't get rid of, sounded her name. Araba, Araba, Araba.

≈ ≈ ≈

Three days before we were due to sail back to Hurghada, my partnership with Garland seemingly exhausted, and the consequences of my actions closing in on me like a gathering storm, Jody and I stood on the sun deck drying off after the day's first dive, and watched as a patch of sunlit water fifty yards off our port bow began to bubble and fizz like a hot spring. The sun was still climbing, and shone across rather than straight down on the water. For as far as I could see sunshine reflected off the sea, so that I was dazzled by an infinite number of light flashes as the shallow terraces of waves rose and fell, and it was difficult to be sure that the section of water I was looking at was disturbed in the way I thought it was.

I have thought about what happened next – the next few minutes, the next day and a half – so often, and so hard, that the events come back to me in what I can only describe as a series of especially lustrous but unreliable images. Pictures that are saturated and radiant with sunshine colours, but whose bright clarity does not stop me from remembering odd details, the significance of which I continually question. Like the way the light was on the water that morning. Did it really dazzle me?

There is Jody at the rail, trying to make sense of what she is looking at, while what I see now most clearly is the long shallow swell of her calves as she stood on tiptoes and pointed, the tinkling of the bells on her ankles, her wet black bikini sucked onto her sun-blushed skin that was breaking out in goosebumps, the disturbance of the sea reflected in the lenses of her sunglasses. But which one of us first noticed the moving water? I stood by Jody at the gunwale, with a coarse and bright white towel held to my face, my wet shorts cold and stuck to my legs.

'What *is* that, Kim?' Jody said. 'Fish?'

I remember being almost blinded by sunlight. I put on my sunglasses. The furious disruption to the surface of the otherwise calm water made it seem, like Jody had said, as if numbers of bait fish were being hunted from below by something – bonitos, maybe, or barracudas – and were being pushed upwards until they had nowhere to go. The water became more and more churned up, but there were no little flashes of silver as hunted fish tried to escape out of the water. Below the surface foam I could see a dark shape quickly growing bigger. Nearby an orange SMB popped up in the water.

'Suhail!' I said.

Suhail was on the dive deck, the Zodiac tied alongside. He looked up.

I pointed at the boiling water. 'Get ready!' I shouted. He gave me the OK sign and jumped into the inflatable.

'Get the oxygen ready,' I said to Jody.

'Shit,' she said, 'what is it?'

'Just get it, all right? Now.'

'OK.'

I hurried down the ladder and went out onto the exposed dive deck. I grabbed my fins and mask from the rack. Suhail put his arm out to steady me and I jumped into the Zodiac. Suhail pulled the ripcord and spun the boat in a tight circle and headed out to where the water had become a great up-rush of white foam. The heat of the sun was hidden by the wind we made and I was cold again and shivering when Teddy King surfaced, much too fast, so that he rose high, up to his waist with water pouring from him. I was close enough to see that Teddy's cornflower blue eyes were huge behind his mask. As fast as he'd appeared he began to sink back down.

Suhail slowed and stopped the boat and the heat was there again. I gave Suhail my sunglasses. I put my fins on. The black footholds were warmed and softened by the sun and I could smell the rubber. I spat in my mask and rinsed it in the sea and put it on and back-rolled over the side of the Zodiac. I dived down. The sun lit up the water immediately beneath the surface and the water shimmered in the light and then, as I looked down, became dark where the sun didn't reach. In all the blue space in between, and heading down towards the darkness, Teddy King was alone.

He was breathing – he exhaled a shower of bubbles that rose to meet and tremble against my skin on their way to the surface – but for whatever reason he was not putting air in his buoyancy jacket to slow and suspend his descent, so he was sinking fast. His secondary hose was trailing, the hose's appearance inevitably that of a severed lifeline, so that Teddy looked like a spaceman cut adrift.

Tiny silver fish seemed to be circling his waist and nudging at him, until I realized they were air bubbles trapped in the folds of his stomach. I watched Teddy falling and all the doubts about who I was disappeared. I knew what I could and couldn't do. I knew how long I could hold my breath. There was still time to get to him. My fins were free-diving fins and I moved fast in the water. Teddy had some air, though I didn't know how much. But once I got to him I knew I could breathe. I kicked and swam towards him, the pressure to take a breath beginning to build. I ignored it. I tried to make eye contact with Teddy, but I couldn't tell if he recognized me or even knew where he was. His blue eyes were wide open to any interpretation I might give them, as if they reflected the infinite water he found himself in.

When I reached him, the world was reduced to me and Teddy and the path I had to invent for both of us to get back to the surface. I grabbed the octopus hose and put it in my mouth and breathed. I looked at his contents gauge. His air was showing in the red. He had less than twenty bar: ten per cent of what he'd started with, and thirty bar less than the amount that, by convention, he should have returned to the surface with. Twenty bar was plenty, though. I got behind Teddy and felt for his weight belt. The buckle and release were buried under his heavy pleats of fat, and I had to dig in until I found it. More air bubbles escaped as I moved his fat around. I released the catch and the weight belt fell from Teddy, spiralling down until it was out of my sight. I held onto him and put air into his buoyancy jacket and our depth stabilized at nine metres. I had to stretch to get my arms round him. I made a kind of chair by bending my knees. I made sure Teddy kept his regulator in his mouth by holding it in place with the flat of my right hand; I held his jacket inflator high in my left. I finned upwards. I couldn't tell if Teddy was helping. His legs were moving, but whether intentionally or not I couldn't say. I put more air in the jacket, and as we began to rise and the air began to expand I controlled our ascent by venting small amounts of the air I had added.

As we neared the surface, light flooded the water so that Teddy, already weightless, became striped by sun rays as I looked at him. As we rose to where the light was strongest, and my vision of Teddy became more and more challenged, I could almost believe in the unreality of our ascent. When we finally broke the surface, Teddy was reconstituted to solid mass. I managed to get him on his back, inflate his buoyancy jacket and begin to tow him by the pillar of his tank towards the Zodiac. Suhail brought the boat to meet me. He came alongside, but when he saw that it was Teddy he didn't move away from the tiller. I pushed Teddy between me and the Zodiac. I undid the clips on his jacket and Velcro waistband, dumped the air, and pulled the open jacket with the tank attached down and away from him. I took his left hand and pulled him so that he was square onto the boat, and told him to grab the hand-grip.

'Get hold of it, Ted,' I shouted at him. Suhail hadn't moved. 'Help me!' I shouted at him. Finally, Suhail reached over the side of the Zodiac and grabbed Teddy by his shoulders. I got underneath Teddy and pushed upwards.

'You've got to help, Ted,' I shouted at him. Teddy reached over the Zodiac's side with his right arm and tried to pull himself in. The weight of the three of us threatened to tip the boat.

'Kick, Ted,' I said, and he managed a few fin-kicks, and I pushed at the same time and Suhail pulled and we got him into the boat, where he lay with water streaming from him. Under the limitless sky, the only sound was the three of us breathing hard, and the waves lightly slapping the hot rubber sides of the Zodiac. Teddy lay with his head towards the bow.

'All right, Suhail,' I said. 'Yalla, let's go.'

Suhail stood in the stern looking down at Teddy. His usually open face was closed down. He didn't move.

'Suhail,' I said, 'come on, man.'

'Shit,' he said, and spat over the side, but he pulled the ripcord and the engine started and he began to take us back towards *Shang-Tu*.

'Can you hear me, Teddy? What happened?'

'I'm bent,' Teddy said. 'I'm fucking bent. I come up too fast, fuck, fuck, fuck. What's going to happen to me?'

'Where does it hurt?'

'My left arm, my shoulder, all round there, fuck, I lost Casey.'

'You mean Casey's still down there?'

'I don't know, I lost him. He'll be all right though, won't he? He's on the wreck. He'll come up when he can't find me.'

I heard a whistle. Under the SMB I had seen surface just

186

before Teddy, Rowdy and Bobby Ballet were up and calling to Suhail to pick them up.

I cupped my hands and shouted, 'Teddy's bent, I've got to get him back to the boat. Just stay put for five minutes.'

Bobby gave me the OK sign.

'Have you seen Casey?' I shouted.

Bobby shook his head.

I've tried to explain to Araba about decompression sickness, the bends, but I gave up. Except with God, Araba gets cross about anything she doesn't understand. When we dive, excess gas is dissolved in our blood and tissues, because of the higher partial pressure of the gases in our lungs. When we dive on air, these gases are oxygen and nitrogen. The oxygen gets used up, but the extra nitrogen doesn't. So long as we come up from a dive slowly, this extra nitrogen will leave our body in a safe way. If we come up too fast bubbles of nitrogen can form in the tissues or the blood, and these bubbles can cause symptoms from joint pain and numbness to the kind of hit that can leave you blind and paralysed. But it's not just if you come up too fast. Repetitive diving, deep diving, obesity, drinking, being hungover, taking drugs – all of these things will make you more vulnerable to the bends. If Araba was looking over my shoulder reading this she would say, 'Hah, you better be careful, then.' What she wouldn't admit is that every time I go under the water she's terrified I won't come back.

Jody was waiting on the dive deck. She helped me get Teddy aboard and into the cool saloon. We lay Teddy on the couch and put blankets over him, and Jody turned the oxygen cylinder on and helped Teddy put the mask on. The first thing you should do with a bent diver is give him a high concentration of oxygen to breathe, which reduces the size of the bubbles.

'Sit with him, Jo, will you?' I said. 'Talk to him. Keep asking him if the pain is the same, or worse, or better.'

I took Suhail with me up to the flybridge to tell Nawfal what was happening, and then Suhail went back out to pick up Bobby and Rowdy. Tony and Susan stopped me as I went back below.

'What's happening?' Susan said. 'Is something wrong?'

'It's all right,' I said. 'Teddy's got a slight bend but he's taking oxygen, and Casey's not come up yet. He'll be all right, though, I'm sure.'

'Can we do anything?' Tony said.

'You can keep a lookout up here,' I said. 'Shout if you see Casey come up.'

I went in to check on Teddy. Then Rowdy and Bobby came into the saloon in their wetsuits, dripping water on the floor.

'How'sit, Teddy, mate?' Rowdy said.

Teddy waved at him, and pointed to the oxygen mask.

'He's got a bend,' I said. 'In his left arm and shoulder – it's not spreading though, right, Jo?'

'That's what he says,' Jody said.

Teddy took the mask off. He said to Rowdy, 'Have you seen Casey?'

'No mate, I thought he was with you.'

'I lost him,' Teddy rasped. 'Fuck. I was running out of air, and I looked around for him, you know, to tell him and get on his long hose. And he looked at me and just kept going down.

I must of panicked because I bolted for the surface. Forgot everything he taught me.'

Jody shushed him, and made him put the mask back on.

'Rowdy,' I said, and walked away from Teddy and Jody and stood by the open door. Rowdy and Bobby followed.

'What's this about Casey?' Rowdy said.

'Casey's missing,' I said.

'You mean he's not come up yet?' Rowdy said.

'Yeah, but Teddy said he lost him.'

'He'll come up,' Rowdy said.

'I think so too, but for now Suhail's out there looking for him, and everybody on board is up on deck keeping lookout. Did you see him down there?'

'No, me and Bobby were diving together. Where's Garland?'

'I don't know. He must still be diving with Tristan and Johnny.'

'One of you two should have been in with Teddy.'

'Jesus, Rowdy, since when did any of you want us in the water with you?'

We'd been diving the *Aida* – the troop supply ship wrecked on the rocks of Big Brother in heavy storms in 1957 and now concreted to the reef and hanging vertically, its bow at twenty-five metres, the stern past sixty – and I wouldn't be surprised if Rowdy and Bobby had dived to the bottom of the wreck.

Bobby said, 'He didn't have his computer or SMB.'

'Casey? Why not?'

Rowdy said, 'He forgot them and that bloody Arab wouldn't turn around so he could get them.'

'Who, Suhail?' I said.

Rowdy nodded.

Bobby looked at him. You could still see where his eye was bruised but the colours were faded. 'No, mate,' he said, 'that's not quite right. Suhail said he'd come back and Casey told him not to bother.'

'You reckon?' Rowdy said.

'Yes mate, that's what happened.'

I wasn't interested just then in why Bobby and Rowdy were arguing. I was more concerned to know that Casey had got into the water without key pieces of equipment. The deeper you dive, the less time you have before entering decompression time. In deco time, the diver makes mandatory stops as he ascends, to safely expel the excess nitrogen in the blood. If you get into deco time, and come up without making the stops, you can get bent. We all carried computers that calculated how deep we were and how long we could stay. You should really work out the profile of your dive before you get in the water, but the truth was most divers depended on their computers. If Casey was diving without one he could get into deco time without knowing it. And without a marker buoy, Casey could have surfaced and it would be almost impossible, in all that space, and with the sunlight acting like a glaze on the water, to see him.

'What do we do now?' Bobby said.

'We wait until Garland's group comes up. The skipper's called for a helicopter to get Teddy off, but you know it's going to take hours to get here. They didn't want to send one – wanted us to make for Hurghada, and only agreed when Nawfal told them we had a diver missing too. If Casey's not come up by the time Garland does, then I reckon we'll unmoor from here and start searching down current. You two could go up top and help Tony and Susan keep a lookout.'

'All right,' Bobby said, 'come on, Rowdy.'

I went back to Jody. She was looking at the contents gauge of the oxygen bottle.

'How much of this should I give him?'

'Give him all of it.'

Garland, like Rowdy and Bobby still in his wetsuit, came into the saloon. Johnny tried to follow him in. He was holding a camera.

'Not now, mate,' I said.

'What's going on?' Johnny said.

'We'll talk to you later,' I said. 'In the meantime we've got a diver missing. Get up top and see what you can do to help.'

Johnny went away.

'Who's missing?' Garland said.

'Casey.'

'What have you done so far?' Garland said.

I told him.

'All right,' he said, 'that's all good, but what were you doing jumping in after Teddy without putting a tank on?'

'I got him up, didn't I?'

'You could have both died.'

'I got him up,' I said. 'You weren't there. I didn't have time to kit up. He'd have been gone before I got to him.'

He looked at his watch. 'So, it's coming up to two hours since Casey got in the water?'

'About that,' I said. 'It's not good, is it?'

'No,' he said, 'no, it's not. This has been coming since day one. I just can't believe it's the only good diver that's missing. '

He squeezed water out of his hair. 'All right,' he said, 'we'll do what we can.'

After talking with Garland, Nawfal took *Shang-Tu* down-current, and we began searching for Casey in a pattern of increasing circles. Garland and I stood up on the flybridge. The crew and the divers stood silently and still, looking out at the ocean from the rail of the sun deck. Sunlight flashed cease-lessly in the waves, so that everywhere you looked there seemed to be something moving on the water, but nothing that was moving was Casey.

'We're going to have to get in and look for him,' Garland said to me.

'You want me to tell Nawfal to take us back?'

'I'll do it,' he said, 'you go and check on Teddy.'

Wrapped in red towels, Teddy was lying down, and he had his head in Jody's lap. When he saw me come into the saloon he took the oxygen mask off his face.

'Hey,' he said.

'Don't talk, Teddy,' Jody said. 'Keep the mask on.'

Teddy ignored her and stared at me. His blue eyes seemed alive with these strange black flashes. He gripped my hand. I couldn't tell if he was trying to shake my hand, to thank me for saving him, or if he was just holding me there.

'Have you found him yet?'

'Me and Garland are going in to look for him now.'

Teddy nodded, as if to say he understood how small the chances were of finding Casey in all that water.

'It's my fault,' Teddy said, 'getting on his back all the time. I was just mucking about.'

'We don't know what happened, Ted.'

'You got to find him,' Teddy said, 'to know what happened.'

'Ted,' I said, 'the mask, you need it.'

Teddy nodded, and slowly put the mask back on.

≈ ≈ ≈

Garland and I rigged up twin-sets – two independent twelve-litre cylinders – using twinning bands and crimping blocks to keep the tanks in place. Garland would have liked to shorten any deco time we would get into on the dive by having an oxygen-rich mix of fifty per cent Nitrox to breathe on any stops, but *Shang-Tu* carried no gases other than air, and the single cylinder of oxygen that Teddy King was breathing down.

In the Zodiac, Garland said, 'Listen, I don't suppose I'm telling you anything you don't already know, but there's not much chance of us finding him down there. Any more than looking for him at the surface when he's got no way to signal us. Unless he's in the wreck he's gone down to the bottom. But it's the thing to do, to get in and look for him. He was one of us, whatever he was like as a bloke. You'd want somebody to do the same for you.'

'Shit,' I said, 'I can't believe it.'

'Come on,' Garland said. 'We just have to do what we can

now. You look like you've had the stuffing knocked out of you. Are you up for this?'

'Yes.'

'All right. I'm going to look over as much of the wreck as I can without putting either of us at risk. I'll go to forty metres or thereabouts and have a look around. I've already done a thirty-metre dive this morning, so I'm going to get into deco time pretty quickly. I don't really want more than ten minutes' deco, and I won't have long down there before I get into that. What was your profile this morning?'

I looked at my computer.

'My max depth was thirty metres just about. And I was breathing air when I brought Teddy up.'

'Stay above me,' Garland said. 'There's no sense us both going deep. Have a look around the bows but keep an eye on me. I'll give you this sign when I'm five minutes from deco time. When I'm in deco I'll come up to you and let you know how long the stop is going to be. You shouldn't get into deco but if you do let me know. Then we'll head up and you put the blob up and we'll make our stops. Is that all clear?'

'You haven't said what we'll do if we do find him.'

'Are you spooked?'

'I don't think so. Are we going to lift him?'

'If he's down there we'll bring him up. If we mark him and leave him there won't be much of him left after a day or two. If he's still got air in his tank I'll inflate his jacket to the point where I can move him, and then I'll bring him up the same way you would a rescue drill. If he's got no air, I'll use my own feed.'

'Dump his weight?'

'He didn't carry much did he? But yes, dump his weight.'

'What about the stops?'

'When we get to the stop send the SMB up, and once that's up we'll send Casey up and do our stops. I'll tie my SMB onto him.'

'Suhail won't be able to get him into the Zodiac on his own.'

'No, he'll pull him alongside and wait for us. All right? Anything else? I really don't think we're going to find him down there.'

'That's it, I think. Garl,' I said, 'what do you reckon happened?'

Garland held his clear mask in his hands and looked into it. We were skirting the island.

'I don't know, Kim. Without a body we'll never know. You know how most divers die – they either make mistakes or they have something like a heart attack. Maybe the way he lived his life caught up with him. And you know what, I wouldn't be surprised if Teddy had something to do with it.'

'You really think that?'

'I don't know, but he's a menace underwater. I hate to think how many times Casey had to save his skin. You want to know what happened down there?' he said, and nodded his head at four soldiers who watched us from the island. 'I've got about as much idea as those blokes.'

The four dark figures stood motionless on the rocks and watched. They would watch us until we went into the water and then they would track our position from our bubbles that rose to the surface. They would watch for any sign that we had found the body, and they would wait for us to come up. They were not so used to divers going missing, but they had seen it before, and unless one of them had seen Casey come up, they could do nothing to help us.

'You don't think he killed himself?' I said.

'If he was the kind of bloke to kill himself that's how he'd do it, I reckon,' Garland said, 'but I don't think he was like that.'

'Why do you think that?'

Garland looked at me again. 'He had a kid, didn't he?' he said. 'You know what, I'm not even going to guess what was in his mind. I'm going to do my job, that's all, and then I'm going to get out of here. If I'm lucky, I won't have to think about these people ever again. What are you going to do?'

'What do you mean?'

'What do you think? Are you going home, or are you staying with the girl?'

I gave Garland a true answer almost out of habit, even though I believed he no longer had the right to ask me that kind of question.

'I'm going home,' I said.

'Have you told Jody?'

'Not yet.'

Garland nodded his head. 'That'll be more drama, then,' he said.

Suhail slowed the Zodiac.

'All right,' Garland said, 'we're here. Let's do a check and get in. Remember: keep to the plan. I don't want this turning into a train wreck like everything else.'

We checked our kit and back-rolled over the side. We'd agreed on a negative entry and went straight down. Except when I paused to squeeze and blow down my nose to equalize the pressure in my ears, I kept my arms folded, my contents gauge in the crook of my left arm. I hadn't dived with Garland for a while, but when I looked for him five metres down, he was where I knew he would be. On my right side, arms folded and level with my shoulder and within touching distance. Garland looked across at me. His hair flared out from under his hood and waved in the water. Without taking his right hand from his left elbow he gave me a casual OK sign. I gave him the sign back, in the same way.

I suddenly got that feeling you get after you've lied to somebody you love, and you come out of your own selfishness and understand what you've done, and more than anything you want to go back to the time before you lied, and you know that you can't. You've crossed into a different territory and can't go back. It's like remembering something good about being a kid and then realizing you can never be a kid again.

I flew through a blue cloud of Suez fusiliers, outriders from the reef below. I loved fusiliers the most of all the fish I saw underwater. If you asked Jay or Suzy to draw a fish they would draw a fusilier without knowing it. Start with the pencil at top-left and in one line go rightwards down and up and over left and down again, finishing bottom-left, so that you have an oval shape with two lines sticking out for the tail. You know the fish sign Christians wear? That's what a fusilier looks like.

Specks and filaments floated everywhere in the water. I could hear little clicks and whistles, the strange noises you heard underwater and most often paid no attention to. As we went deeper I tightened my weight belt, the webbing on my buoyancy jacket, and the straps on my watch and computer as the pressure squeezed my wetsuit.

We came to the reef and then I could see the blooming flower corals and tube sponges. Clouds of purple King Solomon fish drifted in the water, and yellow-orange fairy basslets flashed in and out of hiding places. There were more sonic pops and ticks from who knows where, like stones being clicked together. I looked away from the reef wall and then at Garland as we descended. We flashed each other the OK sign again. Twenty metres down, the broken spars of the wreck of the *Aida*, coroneted by unicorn fish, appeared out of the blue.

≈ ≈ ≈

The metal frames of the *Aida*'s smashed-in bows were blanketed with soft pastel corals. The ship's wooden decking was long gone. The corals covered her railings and broken spars, and decorated a ladder that had been bent out of shape and now curved to nowhere in the blue. Thousands of axe-head shaped sweeper fish crowded the gangways in golden clouds.

Below me, forty metres down, Garland Rain swept his torch across the wreckage. At the forward hold he pointed at himself and then at the hold and held his hand palm out to me. He pointed at me and then pointed at his eyes and gave me the OK sign. His signs meant: I'm going inside the wreck, wait there, watch me. OK, I signed back. Garland swam into the hold and disappeared. I hovered motionless in the water and waited, framed by the broken ladder, and sheltered by the wreckage from the currents that pulsed by the reef.

We were searching for a dead man, and so it seemed wrong
to think so, but the Aida was a pretty wreck. As light disappears
the deeper you dive, so do colours, as the water absorbs the
wavelengths of light that colour is made up of. Red and orange
and yellow disappear first, and by the time you get as deep as
Garland was everything seems to be blue and green. But the
corals that covered the Aida like wild roses flared into their
true brilliance when Garland shone his torch on them, as
though Garland were temporarily restoring parts of a painting
whose colour had been obscured by dirt and time. Honey-
combed moray eels gaped from holes in the wreck. There were
so many fish in the water you almost didn't see them, the way
when it's raining hard you don't see the individual raindrops.
Above me swam a large shoal of horned unicorn fish, dark and
backlit by the distant sun.

After a minute or so Garland reappeared from the hold.
He shook his head at me. Slowly, Garland began to climb the
wreck. Three more times he signalled to me that he was going
to disappear inside, and each time I waited for him and
tracked him by his bubble stream. The final time he emerged
from a hole in the wreck and shook his head at me, he looked
at his computer and showed me a vertical thumb underneath a
flat palm and then five digits raised. That meant Garland had
five more minutes before he got into deco time. I okayed him
again. Below Garland, the forward mast pointed straight out
from the reef. Beyond the mast, and down into the blue, there
were plenty of places on the wreck – the bridge and cabins, the
engine room and after-deck – where Casey's body could be,
and that were too deep for us to get to. Always slowly rising,

Garland swam the width of the wreck and back again, and I could read his frustration as his torchlight sawed back and forth.

Garland looked at me and tapped his hood with his closed fist, and then pointed up. Knock it on the head, he was saying, let's get out of here. At fifteen metres we saw three reef sharks, and later, hanging on the SMB line in sunlit water, as Garland made his free-floating deco stops, I remembered him saying that a dead body in the water does not last long. 'The flesh is eaten in a period of days,' wrote Cousteau, 'not only by fish and crustaceans, but by such unsuspected creatures as the starfish . . . The bones will then be efficiently consumed, mainly by worms and bacteria.'

I thought of Casey somewhere far down below me. I imagined him caught in the branches of a giant sea fan, or lost in the deep holds of the wreck of the *Aida*. Most likely he was, as Garland said, all the way down on the seabed, and I couldn't help but see his body falling through water that turned from sunfilled blue to indigo to black, descending past cruising pelagics, squid, innumerable shoals of fish feeding on the smaller creatures, crustaceans and molluscs, who in turn fed on plankton and protozoa. Casey would be food for all of them, until he became part of the marine snow of decomposing remains, dead plankton and faecal waste that ceaselessly falls from the surface to the seafloor. I saw what remained of Casey lying on the seabed in the cold and dark water, attracting a great congregation of alien, bioluminescent deep-water creatures, his body rent and illuminated by the animals that consumed him, until there was nothing left and the creatures dispersed back into the dark, and the place where he had fallen became black again.

Garland and I had done our best to follow Casey to his grave, but we could not recover his body, or even mark with a stone the place where he fell. Death is so close underwater. When we are lost at sea, out of sight of the surface world, it is as though we have never been. My constructed image of Casey on the sea floor – his breastbone broken, light made by the creatures who were eating him radiating out from his ribcage – is one I have not been able to forget, and even though I've never met her, I often wonder what dreams Abidemi has of her father's death.

≈ ≈ ≈

Rowdy said, 'What are you blokes going to bloody do now?'

Garland and I were on the dive deck and Rowdy was look-ing down at us, holding a beer. The tendons in his neck pulsed, and he was red-eyed, as if his permanent anger was beginning to consume him from the inside.

Jody and Bobby helped us with the heavy kit. Jody gave me a towel and squeezed my hand.

'Are you all right?' she said.

Garland looked up at Rowdy. 'You want me to be honest? I'd say he'll never be found. I'm sorry. I know he was your friend, but there's no point stopping here once the helicopter comes for Teddy. We'll have to head back to Hurghada. They'll want to talk to all of us.'

'Look, it was a bloody accident wasn't it?' Rowdy said. 'A heart attack or something. Why do we have to answer questions? They should be asking why Suhail let Casey in the water without his computer and SMB? Or why you blokes weren't with them? We should be asking them why the bloody chopper's taking so long – it's only an hour and a half flight!'

He emptied his beer and crushed the can. He started rolling a joint. When he finished he lit it and opened another beer. Clouds of smoke poured out of his nose.

'Don't be cheap, Rowdy,' Garland said, 'it's not Suhail's fault, and Casey never wanted me or Kim to get in the water with him. You know the score. You know about the helicopter. I explained it when we started out. We're a long way from port and when you call the helicopter up to come out there're always big arguments between the army and the dive companies about who pays for it. They didn't want to send one at all, except Casey's missing. So it was always going to take a while to get here, you know what I'm saying? That's why we tell you not to dive deeper than thirty metres. This is not the place to push your luck. They're going to need to know we told you all that, and they'll want to look at your computers to check your depths.'

'Yeah, I know what you're saying, Garland. The bloke's not been gone five minutes and already you're saying, "I told you so." You're a cold self-righteous bastard, and you can stick your bloody questions. Nobody's going to be looking at my computer.'

'Jesus, Rowdy,' Jody shouted up at him, 'they're not even dry yet. What have you done to help!'

She handed me a beer.

'Here,' she said, 'get this inside you. You and Garland have done all you can.'

I wondered about that, but she had given Garland a can too, and after I watched him pop the beer and drink deep, I did too.

'How's Teddy?' I said.

'I think he's all right. Sometimes he says it hurts worse than before. He wants to know when the helicopter's going to get here. I think he's nervous about what's going to happen. He's broken up about Casey.'

Jody and I went back to check Teddy in the saloon.

'You should sit up, Teddy,' I said.

'You didn't figure it out?' he said.

'What?'

'Casey. You didn't find him so you don't know what happened.'

'No,' I said, 'I'm sorry, but the chances are we'll never know.'

'All right,' Teddy said. 'Well, I'm going to miss him, I am.'

'What's going to happen to Abidemi?'

'Who?'

'Casey's daughter, Abidemi, somebody's going to have to tell her.'

'I'll look after her,' Teddy said, 'that's a promise.'

I could hear the helicopter coming.

'That's you,' I said.

'Come on, Teddy,' Jody said.

With Jody by his side, Teddy, wearing his robe once more, with a red towel around his neck and carrying the oxygen cylinder under his arm, walked in a slow, heavy procession from the saloon, past the kitting-up area, and out on to the dive deck. Rowdy and the others and the crew all stood and watched him. Nobody said anything. Garland was waiting in the Zodiac. Teddy finally let go of Jody and looked at me. He pulled the oxygen mask down. 'See you,' he said.

I stood with Jody and together we watched Garland gently help Teddy down into the rubber boat. Garland and Teddy made for Big Brother, where the helicopter was waiting. The brightness of Teddy's violet robe diminished against the sun-spangled water, as Garland piloted the little boat closer to the island. I guess Garland went with Teddy because Suhail wouldn't take him. The Zodiac got smaller and smaller, until all I could swear to was Garland's bright head, shining like the water all around. Then I couldn't see him at all. After a while the helicopter rose straight up from the island. The shattering, violent noise of the rotor blades got louder as the helicopter flew over *Shang-Tu* towards Hurghada, and then lessened as it flew out of sight, until the only sound I could hear was the familiar one of the little Zodiac, and I stopped looking at the sky for signs of Teddy King and stood on the dive deck and watched Garland Rain returning.

Later, Rowdy got a party going. Drinking to Casey, Rowdy said, though when he was alive Rowdy had shown him no love or kindness that I could see. Maybe released from Teddy's surveillance and control they could show how they really felt, or maybe, like Garland said, they didn't need an excuse to get wrecked. Rowdy seemed genuinely upset though, while Bobby was the same as usual, so calm I just thought he was stoned.

I didn't join in with them. I took some blankets and found a corner of the boat away from everyone – even Jody. I didn't see her. Strange now to think about Jody on that night – the strong life force beating in her on a day of death. I watched the big Arabian moon and thought about the same moon over my family's house. I wondered what was the proper way to feel about the death of somebody you didn't like when they were alive? Think about the people who would feel the loss of him. Who would they be? The girl, Abidemi, of course, for all her life, and the girl's mother, who must have loved him once.

I understood that I had heard pride in Casey's voice the one time he had spoken to me about his daughter, a huge differ-ence from the beaten way he usually spoke. That was my best memory of him, when we had nearly fought one another. That, and seeing him in the water, where he was a master. I fell asleep thinking of Casey, with the sound of loud drunk voices in my head.

In the morning I picked my way through the debris of the party. Rowdy was crashed in the saloon, the fiery redness of his colouring muted in sleep and the dimness of the room. On the sun deck, in the pale morning light, the air soft as though after a storm, Garland was performing sun salutations. I watched him and then, as I had once used to do, I stood and faced the sun and joined in. Garland gave me no sign of recognition, no welcome, but even so, I followed and repeated his movements in the early brightness, the exercise slowly releasing the deep aches in my body and mind, and I felt the warmth on my skin.

≈ ≈ ≈

The captain of the tourist police questioned us from behind a desk covered by stained and faded brown-paper files, in a stuffy, windowless room in an anonymous one-floor building close by the harbour, while we sat on soft, faded-brown chairs that had exhaled dust when we sat on them, and watched the smoke from the captain's cigarettes twist slowly and push against the yellow walls of the room like coastal fog.

We had left the islands early that morning. All day we motored into a headwind that whipped the waves into skeins of white foam, and made *Shang-Tu* buck in the water. We sighted land just before the sun disappeared from the sky, and the clear delineation of the different elements of the coast-line we sailed along – the mountains and flat-topped cliffs, the desert, the sky and sea – began to be lost in the fading light, appearing first as fluid washes of deepening roses and oranges that bled into one another, until, after the sun fell but before the stars came out, the sea and the sky turned indigo, and the desert and the mountains became dun-coloured and barely visible, when the lights of the town appeared.

There wasn't a lot of talking on the way back. The headwind kept most people below. Garland spent the journey up on the flybridge with Nawfal and Suhail. Taking turns piloting *Shang-Tu* towards Hurghada, the three of them looked like they had taken possession of Teddy's boat, now that he was gone. Rowdy came out a couple of times to smoke a joint, the sweet smell of hashish now and then catching on the wind and reaching the sun deck, where Jody and I lay together. Jody sat wrapped in my arms. Her head was tucked under my chin, and she rested her hands on my forearms. We both wore high-factor sun cream against the burning wind. You could almost hear the things we didn't say. After a time the silence felt like something neither of us wanted to break. I don't know, nothing I could say was going to make Jody happy, and she knew that, and I guess too that she didn't want to hear me lie. So we sat silently together, watching the brightness of the coastline diminish until it finally disappeared, as silver-backed dolphins and flying fish leapt out of the water in advance of our charging bow.

Tristan came up to the sun deck as the light first began to fade, wearing his pristine, pale-blue Adidas tracksuit. He sat nearby on a banquette and smoked a cigarette. Jody and I didn't move. Tristan flicked his cigarette over the side and said to me, 'Can I talk to you about what happened?'

'Nope,' I said. 'Talk to Garland.'

'He's not talking either,' Tristan said.

'There you go then,' I said.

'I've got to write something.'

'Mate, write what you want.'

At Hurghada Nawfal slowed the engine, picking his way through live-aboards reflected at anchor in the shallow water, and docked in a slip among a row of tiered white dive boats shining under the harbour lights. It was turnaround day, when the live-aboards put ashore one set of divers, and the boats were cleaned and resupplied before taking on another. The harbour was busy with crewmen loading sacks of rice and potatoes, pushing stackers jammed with plastic-wrapped slabs of beer and cola, and carrying boxes of fresh fruit and vegetables.

Wild dogs scavenged after the men who carried food. Two sandy dogs who looked enough alike to be litter-mates, with bullish heads and thin bodies whose ribs showed like those of a shipwreck, fought viciously and loudly over a couple of tomatoes. A bored-looking harbour policeman hit them with his stick and the dogs ran into shadow, their fur stained by what might have been blood, or the pulp of the fruit they had crushed in their fight for it.

Teddy sent a minibus with blacked out windows waiting to take us to a hotel in the Sekala district of downtown Hurghada, where we would spend the night before flying home the next day. I wondered how he had been able to organize the bus from his bed in the Naval Centre's hyperbaric chamber. As the crew started to unload bags, two men with sunglasses pushed up in their slicked-back hair, smoking and wearing shiny European suits in the heat of the Egyptian evening, stepped on to the dive deck of *Shang-Tu* with half a dozen armed and uniformed men. Nawfal and Garland were expecting them, and looking grim-faced they went forward to meet them.

Jody said to me, 'Shit, what's this?'

Rowdy, quickly throwing his kit into his dive bag, glanced at the men in suits and muttered something to Bobby.

'Tourist police,' I said to Jody, 'it's all right. Nothing for you to worry about.'

'What are they doing here?' she said.

'It's routine,' I said with a calmness I didn't feel. 'We lost a diver, and Teddy had to be airlifted off the boat. That's bad for business. The police will be under pressure from the diving and tourist industry, and from the government, to find out what went on out there.'

'So, what happens now?'

'These guys will want to talk to the skipper, and to me and Garland.'

'Are you all right, Kim?'

'Casey died on my watch, Jo,' I said. 'That'll be on my record for ever.'

'It wasn't your fault,' Jody said, 'there was nothing you could have done about it.'

'We both know that's not true,' I said. 'If I'd done my job properly from the start this wouldn't have happened.'

'Are you saying if you hadn't slept with me Casey would still be alive?'

'That's not what I meant, Jo.'

'Yeah? Well fuck you, because that's what it sounded like. That's the first time anyone's dumped me and said it was because somebody died.'

Jody turned her back on me, and jumped down to the marina's boardwalk.

'Jody!' I shouted. 'Wait!'

She flipped me the finger and ran to the bus and went inside, disappearing behind the blacked-out windows.

Crewmen from the other dive boats shouted questions at *Shang-Tu*'s crew as they carried dive bags and suitcases to the minibus. A couple of boats down from us, a deeply tanned white man wearing boardies and a long-sleeved white T-shirt, sat in a foldout picnic chair on the afterdeck. He was drinking beer from a can as a crewman polished the marker lights that illuminated him.

'Garland!' he shouted. 'What's going on, mate? It's like bloody *Midnight Express* over there.'

Garland acted like he hadn't heard him. The policemen continued talking to Nawfal. Garland said loudly for all of us to hear, 'The bus is here to take you to a hotel. You can get cleaned up and have something to eat. It's all paid for. The police may or may not want to come and take statements from you at the hotel.'

'Hey, Garland,' Rowdy said, 'has Teddy paid for the hotel?'

'Yes.'

'Would it kill you to bloody say so?'

Backlit by the bright lights of the harbour and the town, Garland suddenly looked worn out. 'Kim,' he said, 'these guys want to talk to us now.'

'OK. Here?' I said.

'No, we go with them.'

Before I stepped off the boat Bobby Ballet handed me a folded sheet of paper.

'Everybody's signed it,' he said, 'even Rowdy.'

'What's this, Bobby?'

'It was an accident, what happened. There's no way it was your fault. There's no need to drag people through the mud.'

I had been long enough at sea to notice the change when I stepped on land. The men in suits took Garland and me in one car, and Nawfal and Suhail in another, for the short drive from the docks to the harbour offices. A couple of uniformed tourist policemen stayed on board to talk to the rest of the crew.

In the car I looked through what Bobby had given me, then I handed the paper to Garland. 'Read this,' I said.

Bobby had got everybody to sign a statement saying that Garland and I had followed proper safety procedures through-out the safari. Divers were given proper briefings before each dive, in which safety plans, dive times, maximum depths and safety stops for each dive were detailed. All divers were told to carry SMBs, the statement said, and it was Casey's decision to go into the water without one. The statement ended by saying that in the opinion of everybody on board Casey's death had been a tragic accident.

'That's pretty decent of them, don't you think, Garland?'

He folded the paper and tapped it against his teeth.

'Rowdy and Bobby are covering themselves, that's all this is. I've got a log here where I recorded the safety instructions I gave before each dive. Each entry is signed by the people I dived with. Rowdy might want to go after me about Casey – he might reckon he can do me some damage. I told him about the dive log. I even got Johnny to film a couple of briefings. If Rowdy decides to kick up, I'll show the police all this and ask them to have a look at Rowdy and Bobby's computers – ask them why they were diving fifty metres plus on every dive, and who they were diving with. Rowdy and Bobby don't want black marks against their names. Teddy will be running more trips to the islands, and now that Rowdy and Bobby have dived here I reckon they'll be his full-time guides.'

'You've got it all figured out.'

'Yeah, well, this trip had the makings of a mess from day

211

one. I was just looking out for us. I don't want it to be any worse for us than it already is.'

'I didn't help much.'

'No, mate, you didn't.'

I hadn't expected absolution, not even after I had got Teddy safely out of the water. Absolution was not Garland's way and I knew it. I waited for him to say something else, but he stayed quiet until the car stopped. Once more Garland's restraint meant that I was left with the unwanted but familiar feeling that I was in debt to him, and would remain so until I figured out whatever lesson it was he wanted me to learn.

We got out of the car and Garland said, 'What happened on the boat stays there, all right? Be careful what you say to these people.'

'You don't need to tell me how to talk to the police, Garland,' I said.

I wondered if the man sitting behind the desk, wearing the dark blue shirt and crumpled uniform trousers, with grey in his hair and nicotine staining his moustache, had deliberately loaded his desk with hundreds of paper files to give the impression that he was, indeed, a man weighed down by bureaucracy.

'I am Captain Mahfouz,' the man said. 'May I see some identification, please?'

We showed him our passports and diver certification cards. He handed the suited man our documentation and said something to him.

Captain Mahfouz lit another cigarette and said, 'Would you like some tea, some juice?'

Garland shook his head. I had put on a long-sleeved T-shirt to hide my tattoos, and it was hot in the room. I could have used some water, but I shook my head like Garland. The captain said something else to the man and he went away.

'He has gone to copy your paperwork, although I am sure he would rather be driving a fast car and chasing the bad guys. You'll have them back very soon.'

Garland reached across to give Captain Mahfouz the signed statement. 'You might want to copy this too,' he said.

The captain read the statement. 'Good, this is very good, very supportive. I will have him make copies when he comes back. Now,' he put out his cigarette and lit another, 'I must ask these questions. First, as observers: did you notice any bad feelings among the divers, among these four men in particular?'

'They seemed to be close friends,' Garland said. 'The man who's missing – ' he paused, looked at me, and began again. 'The man who died worked for Mr King, as did the other two men. It was my understanding that the trip was a thank you from Mr King to the people who worked for him.'

The captain looked at me and said, 'Do you agree with your colleague?'

'If you're asking me whether there is any reason for this not to be what it looks like,' I said, 'then no, there isn't. I don't know what happened down there, but I'm sure it was an accident.'

'Of course. Please, I have to be satisfied there was no foul play. Were either of you in the water when the accident happened?'

'Yes,' said Garland, 'I was, but not with the party who had the accident. My colleague was out of the water. He was the one who rescued Mr King.'

'Why were these four – Mr King and these other men – diving without a guide?'

'Mr King's companions were all very experienced divers,' Garland said, 'and they had consistently expressed a wish to dive without a guide. The dead man was an instructor with over two thousand dives. After the first couple of dives it was clear to us that this group could be trusted to dive alone. We were able to give our time and attention to the less accomplished divers.'

'But the diving at these sites is very challenging.'

'As the document makes clear, we gave very detailed briefings before each dive,' Garland said, 'and we were all pretty much in the water at the same time.'

'Yes, indeed. What did Mr King tell you about his experience of the dive?'

'He said that he needed air,' I said. 'That he had gone to Casey to breathe from his octopus, and that Casey had acted like he hadn't seen him and had, in fact, descended away from Mr King.'

'And what did you think when Mr King told you this? That his friend was already unconscious for whatever reason?'

'It seems the most likely explanation.'

There was a knock at the door, and a uniformed policeman came into the room, gave the captain a brown folder, and left. Captain Mahfouz opened the folder and read the contents.

Garland and I sat waiting. The captain closed the file and added it to the piles on his desk.

'Do you attach any significance to the fact that the dead man went into the water without his computer or marker buoy?' he said.

'Well,' Garland said, 'perhaps it was over-confidence.'

'Do you think the crewman in the Zodiac is to blame for letting him in the water without these items?'

'No,' said Garland, 'he was in an impossible position.'

'This young man and the dead man had an argument some days before the fatal dive?'

'Yes, but I must tell you the boy is entirely blameless.'

'Because he could not have stopped the dead man from getting in the water?'

'That's right,' Garland said.

'He did not have the authority, of course.' Captain Mahfouz lit another cigarette and looked at us. 'But,' he went on, 'you did, had either of you been leading the group on the dive. We will never know if this was significant. We will talk to Mr King, of course, when he is quite recovered, but I must say that this man's death appears to be nothing more than a terrible accident. A confluence of misfortunes. Even the most experienced divers, gentlemen, need guidance and leadership – especially when they are diving the more remote sites. I'm sorry to say that the plain fact of the matter, Mr Rain, is that too many people come to my country thinking they know what they are doing in the water, when the truth is they are really just playing.'

In the car that took us to the hotel, Garland withdrew into

what I recognized from my fights with Araba as a loud silence. When the lights of other cars momentarily illuminated Garland's face, he looked both ashamed and angry. For Garland to have his professionalism doubted, even in the most indirect way, was to feel himself attacked to the heart. And to have to answer questions that forced him to consider whether he had contributed to another diver's death would really burn. As it did me.

It didn't matter that Captain Mahfouz would eventually decide that Casey's death had been an accident, or that the packed-out charter planes would continue to fly in to Sharm and Hurghada every day. Garland and I had been hired as dive guides, and, once you stripped away everything else, the job came down to getting everybody safely back home. Hopefully you showed them a great time, but the one real responsibility you had was that everybody lived. And we had failed.

We were supposed to control the boat and control the diving. Dive guides decided where to dive, how deep and for how long. It was our responsibility to make sure people dived safely and obeyed the rules. Plan the dive and dive the plan. That meant if a diver repeatedly went deeper than the maximum depth allowed you kept him on the boat. You didn't let divers in the water without standard kit. You didn't let people in the water if they'd been up all night. You told people they could party or dive, but they couldn't do both. It didn't matter if you liked the people you were working for. You didn't play favourites. You got in the water with everybody, good divers and bad, nice people and shits. You shared out the dives between them over the course of the trip. You were professional. You didn't disrespect one diver in front of another. You didn't get high publicly. You didn't say 'fuck it' and leave people to get on with it. You didn't sleep with the clients.

I don't know whether it was because I had been at sea for three weeks, or because the smoke that filled the policeman's room seemed to permeate my skin, or just because the interview with Captain Mahfouz had left me feeling dirty inside in a way I thought I might never get rid of, but I stayed in the shower until the water ran cold. I shut my eyes and put my head against the black tiles as the spray pounded on my back. When I at least felt clean on the outside, I got dry and put on after-sun, and wearing flip-flops and clean Lee jeans and a Lahaina Divers T-shirt, I went to get drunk. I suppose I went to find Jody. I had made promises to her I was never going to keep. I'd had practice at closing down my mind to my own shame and regret, and I didn't want to see her, but I went anyway.

≈ ≈ ≈

She was sitting in the hotel bar, unwashed and wearing dirty shorts, her hair looking heavy and glutinous with the salt in it. The bar was called The Sherlock Holmes, and an animatronic, life-size figure of the tall, hawk-faced detective in a dusty black suit greeted me at the entrance. He was holding a magnifying glass in one hand, and a rusty pistol in the other. As I passed Holmes to enter the bar, he raised the glass to his eye, accompanied by lots of clanking and whirring noises, and lights flashing on and off. A metallic voice came from the figure. 'The game's afoot, Watson,' it said.

Inside the gloomy bar, that was decorated like some American's idea of an English pub, large framed pictures of Margaret Thatcher, Frank Bruno and Freddie Mercury hung next to hunting prints on the carmine-coloured walls. Jody was wearing a deerstalker on top of her locks, and sucking on a plastic pipe that blew soap bubbles. She was drinking pints of Carlsberg with Rowdy and Bobby Ballet, and her eyes were red. The three of them, sunburned, in boardies and flip-flops, were strung out along the bar with their feet up on one another's stools so nobody else could get close. They were throwing peanuts at each other and ordering round after round of cold beer. There were two barmen behind the bar. One wore a deerstalker while the other was bareheaded.

Rowdy turned to look at me. 'What do you bloody want?'

'I'm getting a beer, Rowdy.'

'Yeah, well get it somewhere else, yer bloody mongrel, this is a party for Jody. She's staying in this shit-hole for some reason. But you knew that, right? She's staying and you're bloody leaving.'

The young Egyptian in the deerstalker stared at Rowdy. The two barmen were standing with their arms folded, as far away from us as they could.

Bobby Ballet looked at me and gave a small shrug.

'Garland was here,' he said. He looked at Jody. 'He was talking.'

'About what?'

'He said you were going home,' Jody said. 'Were you going to let me know, or did you ask him to tell me because you didn't have the guts to do it yourself?'

'Rain's another bloody mongrel,' Rowdy said. 'You blokes think you can root who you like. Behave like bloody rock stars.'

'I'm here now,' I said to Jody. 'You want to get something to eat, have a talk?'

'Fuck. Off.' Jody said. 'What do you really want? One more ride before you go home to your wife? Just fuck off, all right?'

She got off her stool and picked up her pint glass. I thought she was going to throw it at me, but instead she walked away into the dark interior of the bar, trailing a stream of soap bubbles, the stupid hat wobbling on top of her locks. I watched her go and then I sat at her place. I started absently picking up the peanuts that were scattered all over the bar.

'What else did Garland say?' I asked Bobby.

'He just said you were going home, and he wasn't.'

'Is that right?'

'That's what he said.'

'Fucking arsehole!' Jody shouted from the dark.

'Did Garland say where he was going?' I said.

'Nope.'

'You mean you don't bloody know?' Rowdy said. 'Reckon he's not your bloody mate any more then. Not if you're the last to bloody know.'

'Have the cops been to see you?' I said to Bobby.

'Yeah,' he said, 'about an hour ago.'

'They say it was an accident?'

'No shit, Sherlock,' Rowdy said. 'If you did your bloody job properly maybe Casey would still be alive.'

'You told me yourself it was an accident. And that's what the cops said, right?'

'Yeah, well,' Rowdy said.

'Get off my fucking back then, Rowdy.'

'What are you going to bloody do about it,' said Rowdy, standing up.

'Hey,' Bobby said, 'just sit down, mate, will you?' He shucked his chin at the barmen, who were nervously looking at Rowdy, his face reddening, standing with his fists clenched.

'I've had enough cops for one night,' Bobby said. 'Haven't you?'

Rowdy slowly sat down. I looked at the barman and pointed at the empty glasses. I signalled for three more beers.

'Have you been to see Teddy?' I asked Bobby.

Bobby shook his head.

'You going to?'

'Mind your own bloody business,' Rowdy said. 'What do you care anyway?'

'It was me that got him out of the water, mate.'

'You did one thing right in the whole bloody trip, is that what you're saying?' Rowdy said.

The barman put the beers down. Bobby drank a mouthful. Rowdy pushed his away.

'You want to drink with this bludger, Bobby, you go ahead,' Rowdy said. 'I'll be fucked if I'm going to. I'm off.'

'This is bullshit,' I said, 'I'll go.' I drank off my beer and stood up to leave.

'That's right,' Jody shouted at me from the darkness, 'run away! Run home to your wife! When Teddy finds out what you did, he's going to kill you!'

Rowdy blew a stream of bubbles from his plastic pipe.

'That bloody elementary enough for you, mate?' he said.

I went up to Garland's room and knocked on his door, but he didn't answer. I stood alone in the overexposed light of the hotel's corridor. 'Fuck,' I said. 'Fuck!' I said again, louder this time. 'Garland!'

A door opened a little way along the corridor, and Susan came out. She shut the door softly and walked towards me. Her short black hair was wet and she was wearing flared black sweat pants and a black vest. She was barefoot and close up she smelled of after-sun cream.

'What's happened?' she said. 'Is anything wrong?'

'No,' I said, 'everything's fine. Sorry if I woke you.'

'I wasn't sleeping,' she said. 'Tony's dead to the world. I don't know how he can sleep, he's more freaked out than I am, but as soon as he hit the bed he was out.'

'He'll be OK, you both will. Once you've been home a day or so, you'll see. Nothing that happened had anything to do with you, you just got mixed up in the craziness. You knew Casey better than me, but there's no right way to feel about what happened. Go on some more dive trips, and you'll be able to forget this one.'

'I don't think I'll ever be able to forget this trip,' she said, 'and neither will you.'

'No,' I said, 'I suppose not.'

'Don't beat yourself up too much,' she said. 'You're a good teacher, and you saved that awful man.'

'The training kicked in, I guess.'

'Don't sell yourself short. It was a brave thing to do,' she said. She was looking hard at me. 'OK, Kim,' she said, 'I'm going to try and get some sleep now. You should too.'

'All right,' I said. 'Thanks, Susan. Hey, did you know I've got a daughter called Suzy?'

'No,' she said. 'I bet she can't wait to see you.' She leaned in and kissed me on the cheek. 'Goodnight, Kim,' she said, 'and thanks.'

'For what?'

'For finding us the illuminated shark,' she said. 'I won't forget that, not ever.'

Susan went back to her room. I took the lift to the lobby, and got a taxi back downtown. I don't remember much about the rest of my last night by the Red Sea. I know I went to the harbour first, and wandered around the marina looking at the dive boats. Because it was turnaround day the boats had new divers on board. They sat out on deck drinking cold beer. At some point late in the night they would take off. Some of them would be going as far as the islands, as we had done three weeks before. I walked back and forth on the boardwalk, first one way and then the other, and wished I was going with them. I didn't want to leave the water, but I couldn't find anywhere to get a beer in the harbour, so I went into town. I bar hopped for a while, talking to sunburned divers who were all drunker than I was at first, until I caught up. I remember Tropical Murphy's and Moby Dick's, but there were lots of other places. I hooked up with a bunch of young, well-off Egyptians who took me to a bar with no name, where I was the only westerner. I half remember a messy, failed attempt to buy cocaine that got me thrown out of there.

The last thing I remember is standing outside Garland's door again, drunk this time. I say it was Garland's room but I suppose it might not have been. I banged on the door and shouted, but nobody answered. Susan didn't come out of her room again. Somebody called hotel security, and when I saw the guard in his too-big, dark suit, walking along the endless corridor towards me, I put my hands up and went away from there. In my room I turned off the air-conditioning, and took the single mattress out onto the balcony and lay down. Winter was coming in England, and I wanted to remember the heat.

SHORE LEAVE

I was still drunk when I got on the plane, and on the way home I took as much beer as they would let me have. I piled the dead cans in the empty seat where Garland should have been. I threw the beer into me as quick as I could, but it didn't stop the feeling that, although Garland wasn't there, everything else was going to follow me home.

Araba and I lived in one of three small, cheaply renovated ground-floor houses that were part of an L-shaped five-floor block of flats on Railton Road, in the middle of what had once been Brixton's Front Line. Back then, in the late seventies, the building had fallen derelict. The squatters that moved in were the usual mix of idealists, chancers, druggies and transients. The majority of the first squatters had been white, but the building was left untouched during what Araba had taught me to call the Uprising in 1981, while the whites-only pub next door had been burned to the ground.

Over time, some of the long-term residents began to organize themselves. They formed a housing co-op, fought for and won a leasehold from Lambeth Council, chased out the hard-drug dealers and cleaned out the two flats that were long established shooting galleries, and started painting, planting, and rebuilding. Araba was one of them. She had arrived in Brixton as a seventeen-year-old black punk girl from the West Country, and had been brought to the building by her first boyfriend, a junkie musician. Lee's dad. He was long gone – ran away in a hand-painted bus as soon as he knew Araba was pregnant. I spent most of my time there after Araba and I got together, but I hadn't moved in with her until Suzy was born.

I didn't think I'd get along with living there at first. The living spaces were built very close to one another. Everybody knew when Araba and I had been fighting. I did get friendly with a huge, big-handed, slab-faced bloke called Co-op Mick who looked like a docker and dressed like a hippy. Mick was strong on his Buddhism – his chanting was often the first thing I heard in the morning. Sometimes me and Mick would get up on the roof to have a beer and a smoke and watch the sunset. Mick would try and sell me the power of chanting, and I would watch the planes coming out of Heathrow fly across the fiery sky in an endless parabola that made my heart ache.

I walked into the yard carrying my kitbag. There was a banana tree and a large bed of sorry-looking flowers – hollyhocks and delphiniums – and a small medicinal herb garden – wormwood plants, things like that. The beds were littered with rubbish. There was a late-night bar next door that had taken the place of the burned-out white pub. People who stood outside the bar to smoke dropped cigarette ends and joints, crack vials, cans and bottles. Used condoms and chicken bones. They pissed in the yard, even shat in it sometimes. At the last co-op meeting before I went away, I had said I would take responsibility for looking after it.

I could hear kids playing in the garden and along the walkways. Before dark there was never a time when you didn't hear children somewhere in the building. There were maybe fifteen or twenty kids and they went about in a huge mixed-raced gang, the babies and the little kids trailing soft toys and blankets, following the bigger kids like Suzy and Jay, all of them worshipping the teenagers like Lee. The kids had worn out the grass in the garden so that it was bare dirt in dry weather and mud all other times.

My electronic pass-key to the security gate didn't work. I didn't understand why. I walked out of the front courtyard and around the side of the building. I looked through the railings and saw my children playing in low splashes of sunlight that made dappled patterns in the dirt. Suzy was writing on the side of the fort with coloured chalk. Her hair was in china buns. Her arms and face were patterned with rainbows, the seat of her jeans dusty with dirt. Jay was playing a fast game of 'it' with the other kids. Lee was sitting at the top of the fort listening to her iPod. I couldn't see Araba, but my front door was open.

'Lee,' I shouted, 'Lee!'

Lee took out one earpiece and looked around.

'Lee,' I shouted again, 'what's going on? I can't get in.'

Lee ran into the house. Jay and Suzy came to the fence. Their small fingers gripped the squares of wire.

'Daddy-Waddy!' Suzy shouted.

'Dadda!' Jay called.

'What's going on, kids? Somebody let me in.'

Araba came out of the house.

'Come round to the front,' she called.

Araba's hair was tied up, and her face was set like a wooden mask against me. She was carrying a small cardboard box. On the ground by her feet, and dusted with yard dirt and flower seeds, was a black puppy dog.

'Hello, honey,' I said, 'what happened? I'm locked out. Why did you change the keys?'

I could hear Suzy screaming, 'Let me go, Lee, let me go! I want to see Dad!'

Araba was looking at me. I was dressed in a T-shirt, jeans and flip-flops, sunglasses pushed up.

'You've always lived in your own world, Kimmy,' she said, 'and you're the only one in it. There's no room for anyone else. Not me, not the kids, except maybe Suzy. Sometimes I think Suzy's the only person you care about.'

'What's that supposed to mean? Let me in. Why's Suzy screaming?'

'I can't let you in,' she said, 'I wouldn't even if you weren't drunk.'

She shook her head.

'You haven't seen your family for three weeks, and you have to get drunk to see us? What's that supposed to tell me?'

Suzy and Jay were crying.

'Lee, let the kids go!' I called.

'No, Lee!' Araba shouted.

I gripped the black bars.

'What's going on?'

'Have you brought money back for us?' she said. 'Have you got a full-time job? Are you working tomorrow?'

'I've just got off the plane, mate, give us a chance. I'll see about work tomorrow.'

'You're not my mate,' she said. 'I don't know why I couldn't get you to listen. I tried really hard.'

She pushed the cardboard box through the bars.

'Here,' she said.

I took the box but didn't open it.

'It's a phone,' Araba said, 'so we can speak to each other and you can talk to the kids and arrange to see them. You can see them anytime. It's pay as you go, the phone. There's twenty pounds on it.'

'Oh shit, Araba,' I said, 'I don't want this. Let me in, sweetheart, please. Don't cry. I'll do whatever you want, I promise.'

'It's too late.'

'Don't do this.'

'Look at the mess in the yard. You were supposed to clear that up. I have to live with everybody in there, my friends, feeling sorry for me because I'm with a man who won't take the simplest responsibilities.'

'I'll do it now. Let me in and I'll do it now.'

'It's too late, Kim,' she said, 'there might be somebody else.'

'What? Who? Fuck, somebody else, who?'

Araba bent down to pick up the puppy.

I wanted to break things. I wanted to beg. I wanted to touch her. The dog nuzzled her and licked the side of Araba's face.

'You don't like dogs,' I said.

'Sandy got her for the girls.'

'Is it Sandy?' I said.

'No, it's not Sandy,' she said.

'Who then?'

'Oh, Kim,' she said, 'I'm not going to tell you that.'

The kids were screaming. I couldn't see them. Araba kept looking over her shoulder.

'Use the phone,' she said. 'I've got to go. I'm glad you're safe.'

She put the black dog on the ground and it ran away and she followed it.

I heard Lee shout, 'Kim!' She came to the gate.

'Where are you going?' she said.

'I don't know,' I said. 'I'll be back to see you and your sisters soon.'

'I'll hate you for ever if you don't come back. So will Jay and Suzy.'

'I'll be back soon.'

Lee reached her hand through the metal bars of the security gate.

'Promise?' she said.

'Promise,' I said.

My step-daughter glared at me through the bars. Lee wore a black sweater, jeans, black Vans, and her blue hair was tied in two ragged bunches. At fifteen she was taller than her mother. There were holes torn in the sleeves of Lee's sweater that she had her thumbs looped through. She had crumbling black varnish on her nails, and silver rings on her fingers and thumbs, and in her nose and ears. Through the bars I passed

Lee two fluffy oceanic whitetip sharks for her sisters, and a black Red Sea Divers hoodie. I could hear Araba trying to shush Suzy and Jay as my daughters sat screaming in the dirt of the building's communal garden.

'Your promises are shit,' she said, and tried to laugh.

'I know,' I said, 'but I promise.'

'Wipe your face,' Lee said, 'you can't go out there crying.'

I sat in the dirt of the yard, among the dying flowers and medicinal plants I had promised and failed to look after. In a place like that, where people were trying to live communally, and more than one woman was taking refuge in the building from a man in the outside world who beat her, my failure to live peacefully with Araba seemed in my imagination to move in repeated sonic waves through all the badly laid floors and chipped walls.

I went back out on the street carrying my bag full of dive kit that was suddenly useless to me. How could I have ever believed that the things in that heavy bag were all that made me who I was? It was cold after the heat of north Africa. I could feel the black winter coming. I was still in that space where the faraway reefs and islands were what I knew best.

I walked to the pub. Road dust and tufty seeds and smoke danced in the last of the sunlight. I drank for two or three hours, and then I punched a number into the phone Araba had given me – one of the few numbers I knew by heart.

'Sandy,' I said, when he picked up, 'I'm in trouble.'

It was late before Sandy's Volvo pulled up to the pub. By that time of night the street people – the crack whores, vividly bruised white girls whose pimps waited out of sight up the street, the junkies, the homeless mad whose minds pin-wheeled with unknown psychotropic visions – were out begging money and cigarettes from the late drinkers who stood smoking outside the pub. I shouted at and chased off a young prostitute who wore red pedal pushers bright as the marks on her face. She was only a couple of years older than Lee. I was still shouting at her when Sandy got out of the car.

Sandy was dressed all in black, his long, straw-coloured hair was untied and loose. A man asked Sandy for money. A dirty white bloke, whose uncut and uncombed red hair and beard had become locksed. He was barefoot and wrapped in filthy blankets. Sandy gave him money. I was drunk, and my own feet were dirty, and I was shouting at a girl young enough to be my daughter, who had already lived a lifetime of being abused.

'Come on, mate,' Sandy said.

'Come on, mate,' repeated the man in blankets.

'Sandy,' I said, 'why'd you buy my kids a dog, for fuck's sake?'

'The dog needed a home,' he said, 'and Araba needs some love.'

Sandy drove for a little way and pulled up alongside the girl in red shoes I'd chased away. He reached out and gave the girl something, and drove on.

That night I dreamed that I was a supernaturally fast runner. I could run to a tropical reef, and run back to Araba in England in no time, but no matter how fast I ran, when I came back home there were hundreds of men I didn't know, all standing with gifts at my wife's door.

≈ ≈ ≈

When Sandy was younger, and had with little notice been sent to Berlin or Cyprus or Northern Ireland, he'd had to leave his young wife and sons and not tell them where he was going or when he'd be back. I knew that Sandy believed that these forced separations – and the secrets he was made to keep – were the reason he was alone now.

'Only the strongest woman can continue in a marriage where the husband is continually going away to places he can't tell her about,' Sandy said, 'and be expected to wait for him for an unknown amount of time knowing he might not come back at all. My wife was strong, and she was patient and she trusted me, but even so the relationship became impossible for her. Because when I did come home I couldn't tell her about what I'd been doing.'

It was a Saturday morning in November. I'd been staying at Sandy's for six weeks. We were drinking coffee as the wind-driven rain crashed loudly against the windows. Sandy was wearing an oversized grey sweatshirt and clean, very old tan cords. He was barefoot and his wet hair was in a topknot. I was just getting up when he'd returned from his daily run round Brockwell Park. While Sandy showered, I put away my camp bed and made coffee, got in the shower when Sandy got out. This was the routine on Saturday mornings. Weekdays, I was out the door and on my way to work just as Sandy was getting up.

There were photographs of Sandy's blonde ex-wife and children on the walls, and a picture of Sandy in diving kit. There was a print of a dark woman wearing a bright skirt, and standing against a blue sea and a dun-coloured landscape above the words 'You are on Aboriginal land', but there were no photos anywhere of Sandy in uniform.

'Did she want you to leave the army?' I said.

'Yes, of course, and I should have,' Sandy said, 'I see that now. But I loved it. I'm sure you feel that way about diving. Now I think a lot of it was self-indulgence on my part. Playing the Great Game and all that rot. That book. Kipling. Your namesake. I read it too young, huge impression. If you're going to live for yourself that's one thing, but it's unfair to drag a woman, and especially children, into that kind of life. We can go over it and over it, but it's what we do now that counts.'

'I should go, really,' I said. 'I don't want to be late.'

Sandy looked out of the window.

'Right, of course, yes, you must go. I should think you're glad not to be working in this today,' he said.

'Mate, it's not like rain is unusual in this country. That's one of the reasons I keep wanting to get out.'

'If you think this is bad,' Sandy said, still looking out of the window, 'you should try a winter in Belfast.'

'I thought you were undercover,' I said.

We both laughed.

'That's the first time I've seen you smile in weeks,' Sandy said.

'It's Big Paul,' I said, 'after a day working with him I'm too knackered to smile.'

'Nonsense,' Sandy said, 'make a man of you.'

The lido was closed for the winter and I was back labouring. I worked with an old Irish labourer called Big Paul, who was well over sixty-five, and still thick in the chest and arms. Paul worked shirtless in all weathers. He told me he was working because his wife died and he didn't want to sit at home on his own. The bosses kept him on because even at his age he did the work of two men.

Paul sang as he worked. I would knock-up and bring him concrete for some bricks.

'"I went through the desert on a horse with no name, she said . . ."' Paul would sing. 'Not too wet, Kim, that's grand, throw it on there. Good man, get me a couple more spadefuls. "It felt good to be out of the rain, she said . . ."'

The house we were working on was next door to one owned by a great-grandson of Charles Darwin. This man, who was about Paul's age but very deaf, wore the same auburn-coloured worsted suit and cordovan loafers every day. Darwin had a Filipina housekeeper who never came out of the house and an ancient springer spaniel who was as deaf as his owner. Like his great-grandfather, this Darwin had once sailed to the Galapagos Islands.

'When I was a young fellow, like you,' he told me, 'life was a great adventure.'

When I told Darwin about the illuminated shark, he said, 'Oh, yes, I can quite believe it. It sounds absolutely marvellous.'

Every morning, just about the time I got to work, Darwin, smelling slightly stale, his face spotted with small pieces of bloody tissue, would walk very slowly with his deaf dog along the quiet mews street to the newsagents to buy his paper. His full head of white hair was always beautifully Brylcreemed in place, so perhaps Darwin trusted the Filipina woman to brush his hair but not to shave him. Each morning the dog would slowly lift his leg on our skip. The dog's piss smelt very strongly of fish. This used to drive Paul mad, and he would go out and shout at Darwin who couldn't hear much of what Paul said, and what he could hear I don't imagine he understood. I would stand at the open window of the unfinished house and watch the huge shirtless Irishman try and make himself understood to the natural historian's great-grandson.

Paul was always exasperated after trying to talk with Darwin.

'You can talk to him until the cows go blue in the face,' he would say to me, 'but he can't stop that effing mutt widdling up against our skip. Can he not get it to do its business some-where out of our road? He's got soft hands, that's his problem. Never done a day's work in his life.'

Paul started work as a twelve-year-old immigrant. He con-demned anybody with soft hands as useless. My hands were slowly getting hard again. I wondered if I would be like Paul at sixty-five, a shirtless labourer arguing in the street with a deaf old man about an incontinent dog.

About a month after I got back from the Red Sea, Tristan's long article about the safari, with Johnny's photographs, was published in *Banker*. I read it in my dinner hour, sitting on a bench by the Church of the Immaculate Conception in Mount Street Gardens, where robins hopped in the laurel and camel-lia bushes and the city sky always seemed to threaten rain. I could never look at a church without thinking about Araba. I would watch people pass from the bright alive light of the day and cross the threshold into the dark church. I looked at them and tried to understand what Araba got out of it.

Maybe she felt the same way when I went below the surface of the water and passed, she believed, from light into darkness. Like Araba after a service, many of the people leaving Immaculate Conception had the kinds of looks on their faces I had seen on people coming up to the sun after a morning wall dive. There are lots of places where you can find the compensation of a belief in life after death. But I was on the side of the people who found heaven on earth, even if I hadn't, unlike Garland, come to feel more strongly about the huge islands of plastic rubbish in the Pacific and Atlantic oceans than about bombs in the high street. Garland said we behaved like people on a long and difficult voyage, who poison our own water supply, punch holes in the only boat we have, and fill it with our own waste. 'You get the picture,' Garland said. 'Maybe the people in charge know something we don't, maybe they've got another boat lined up, but I don't reckon so, do you?'

Tristan's story of wild partying under Arabian stars, diving with an illuminated shark, and the drama of Casey being lost at sea, fuelled the fantasies of the young, frustrated office workers reading *Banker* as they headed home on the commuter train for a ready-meal and a wank. It must have seemed to more than a few of them that Teddy King was living the dream. There were lots of posed photographs of Teddy. There was one of him holding a fish up to his mouth, with the caption: 'Pass the lighter, it's gone out again.' Tristan said nothing about my rescue of Teddy, or about his bend.

I didn't realize at first how badly Garland and I came out of it, and it wasn't until the article was picked up by the scuba magazines a week or so later that things really started to get hot for us. In the diving press Garland was condemned for an apparent disengagement from clients whose behaviour was getting increasingly out of hand as the three-week safari went on. He was written up as somebody who would be looking meaningfully out to sea, or performing sun salutations up on the flybridge, his snowy hair blowing in the wind – in the article there had been a couple of Johnny's photos along those lines – while the clients we were being paid to safely guide, on dives in deep, capricious water eight hours from the nearest land, were getting high and staying high, and kitting-up for a dive the next morning still, if truth be told, pretty fucked up.

They put the boot into me for joining in with the partying and for taking Tony and Susan to thirty metres, where we saw the illuminated shark, when they were only qualified to go to eighteen. Put together, the stories about deep dives and parties, and the sly references to pot and cocaine, meant that Garland and I were done for in the sunshine and guiding business. They slaughtered us and all but came out and said Casey's death was our fault.

I beat myself up for staying in England, until Saturday mornings when my daughters would come barrelling out of their mother's house and into my arms, and I would be just about all right for another week of muck and rain.

'Be a shark, Daddy!' Jay would shout, swimming towards me as rain drummed on the vaulted roof, and black clouds massed and pulsed against the pool's huge arched window.

Suzy dived down to the dirty bottom again and again. Looking for treasure – hair grips, scuzzy scrunchies, cheap hooped earrings. Suzy kept them all in secret hiding places at the side until it was time to pick out the best pieces to show me. She never wanted to get out of the water.

'I want to stay in the water with you for ever,' she'd say.

'Make sure you wash all the chlorine off,' I'd tell her when I finally got her under the shower, 'or you'll get itchy.'

Jay, in mask and snorkel and little black fins, would tread water while I dived down and swam below her kicking legs. I'd rush up through the water and grab Jay as she tried to escape, and as we rose out of the water together, I'd feel her heart thump against skin that had paled in the winter months.

'Shark!' Jay would scream, 'Shark!' She'd wriggle out of my arms and swim away, her arms by her side, finning from the hips the way I'd taught her.

In a cafe near the pool one December Saturday, Jay said, 'Dadda, why don't you live with us any more?'

'Jay!' Suzy said, her lion hair all fluffed out by the dryer she had stood laughing under in the changing room. 'Shut up!'

'It's all right, Suze,' I said. 'Mate, I bodged it up with Mum.'

'Why do you call Jay "mate"?' Suzy said.

'It's just the way I talk.'

'It's funny.'

'Are you ever coming home?' Jay said.

'I don't know, Jay.'

'Dadda, sometimes I dream that I'm lost. I can't find you and I can't find our house,' Jay says.

'That's scary, Popper,' I said, 'but you know it's just a dream.'

'I know that, Dad, but when I wake up and you're not there it's sad.'

'Jay, shut up!'

'Suzy, it's OK. Come on, kids, eat up. If you don't eat your chips you won't get any ice cream.'

'Dad!'

≈ ≈ ≈

One night, a couple of months after I'd come back from the Red Sea, Sandy had my winter diving kit spread out all over the floor. My drysuit and Thinsulate undersuit, the thick hood and gloves, my regulator hoses and manifolded twin ten-litre tanks that were fitted with a steel backplate and harness, and my Dive-Rite buoyancy wing.

Sandy was kneeling down, attaching my regulator hoses to my tanks. He had a big spares box open in front of him, full of O-rings, spare fin and mask straps, a huge set of allen keys, a tube of silicon grease and lengths of surgical tubing. He closed the isolator valve on the manifold. He opened the righthand tank and breathed through the mouthpiece of the reg he'd fitted to it. He turned off the air without purging the reg, repeated the process with the other tank, reopened the isolator. He clipped the hoses to the stainless steel D-rings I'd fitted at the harness. When he was finished, he stood up. His own twins were set up, and his dive bag was packed.

'All right, Sand,' I said, 'I'll bite. Where are we going?'

'Where else?' he said. 'Stoney Cove.'

Stoney Cove, a freshwater quarry in the Midlands, was the UK's national diving centre. Because Stoney was landlocked, and not subject to tides and currents, offshore or onshore winds, you could dive there all year round. During the season and deep into the winter, hundreds of divers who could not reach the sea, and working instructors who needed to know that their training dives would not get blown out by the weather, would come to Stoney every day. In the very early morning, with mist rising off the undisturbed water, the quarry could look pretty.

By mid-morning the place would be mobbed. The water would be thick with drysuited instructors leading groups of students freezing in their wetsuits. The novices kicked up Stoney's shale bottom in dusty clouds as they struggled with their buoyancy, and ruined whatever visibility there might be. The dive shop vans parked by the waterside would have pissed-in dive suits hanging up to dry over the open doors.

'Stoney? What, you want to swim with a few dodgy old pike? What else have they got in there, an old helicopter? A broken-down van?'

'And much more besides,' Sandy said. 'Come on, it'll be fun. You remember when you used to have fun?'

'It'll be pitch black and freezing in there, is what it'll be.'

'So what, where's your sense of adventure? Have you stopped diving altogether?' He patted my yellow tanks – yellow because that was the colour of the tanks Cousteau's people had dived with on the TV shows I had watched as a kid.

'You sure you don't want me to sell these so you can piss the money up against the wall?' he said.

'All right, Sandy, all right,' I said, raising my hands in surrender. 'When do you want to go?'

'Tomorrow, before you change your mind. First thing.'

Driving north, the winter morning slowly revealed a mean landscape. The permanent roaring jam on the southbound side of the motorway, exhaust miasma, terraces of look-alike houses giving way to fields dominated by garish rape seed. I saw corralled horses running along the fences of a high, pinched field. The traffic noise had the permanence of tidal water, and I wondered if the horses heard it this way, as something natural, or if the never-ending noise had driven them crazy, and that's why they were careering around the too-small field. Whenever I craned my head to look skywards it always seemed as if skeins of baleful Canada geese were passing below the grey clouds.

'In the late fifties,' Sandy said, 'after they stopped quarrying and let the place flood, people were jumping over the fence to get in and dive at Stoney. There was nothing in there but you couldn't keep them out of the water. They glued their own wetsuits together and converted old gas cylinders to breathing tanks. Wouldn't have the sport if it wasn't for people like that. Remarkable.'

I didn't say anything. My beanie hat was pulled low over my ears.

'You don't seem very excited to be going diving,' Sandy said.

'I'm just outwardly calm, Sand,' I said, and yawned. 'Despite appearances, I'm bursting with excitement.'

Sandy chuckled.

'You're not just going to take it, are you?' he said after a while.

'Take what?'

'You know – all that rot about you and Garland.'

'I don't know. Maybe I deserved it.'

'What about Garland?'

'What about him?'

'Look, Kim, bloody well wake up, will you? Garland doesn't deserve all that horseshit written about him and neither do you, and you know Garland wouldn't dream of saying anything himself. You've got over a thousand dives. Are you going to let some snot-nosed bugger who's been in the water half a dozen times at best, and with somebody like you holding his hand, say you're not a diver? You mustn't just drift along letting things happen to you. Tell people what really happened and back Garland up. It's a chance to do the right thing.'

Even in December Stoney was busy. All around us people were unloading kit from their cars and vans.

'Jesus,' I said, 'it's a cult.'

I put on my thick undersuit, stepped into the built-in boots of my drysuit, and pulled the heavy suit up to my waist. Sandy did the same, and then reached into his kitbag and pulled out a container of baby powder. The drysuit had latex seals at the neck and wrists to stop water coming in. Sandy dusted the seals with talcum. It made it easier to get the suit on and reduced the risk of stretching or tearing a seal, which would make the suit leak. Sandy handed me the talcum and I did the same. I gently put my hands through the seals and then my head, and then Sandy pulled the big zip across my shoulders, closing the suit. I reached for the tag at the end of the zip and he handed it to me and I gave it a tug. That way, if I got a leak, I'd know it wasn't because Sandy hadn't closed the zip properly.

I stood up and Sandy helped me on with my twin-set. I pulled on my thick neoprene hood. I had a pair of five-millimetre neoprene gloves. I put on the right one, and strapped on my watch and computer. When I was ready I helped Sandy on with his kit. I pulled on my left glove, and carried my fins under my left arm.

Weighed down with the twin tens, I walked slowly with Sandy to the jetty. Just a little way off it there was a large red buoy on the surface of the water that marked a line going down thirty-six metres to a hydrobox – an upturned metal cube once used to train underwater welders.

It was claustrophobic being overloaded with so much kit. In the tropics I had often dived in just a mask and fins, and a pair of cut-offs, breathing off a short hose I'd put on a tank I carried under my arm.

'Ready?' Sandy said.

'Yep.'

'Just bounce at the bottom, and three minutes at five on the way back?' he said.

'All right,' I said, 'let's go.'

The surface water was brownish. As we began to descend, what light there had been from the low winter sun quickly vanished and we turned on our torches as we carried on down. At thirty metres there was no ambient light. The cold bit into my spine and made my head ache, and even with the thick gloves on I couldn't feel my hands. Suddenly our torches illuminated the five-metre-tall box. At the top there was a round hole with a projecting rim sticking out to make an entrance. I went inside first, with Sandy following. I don't know how it was possible but it was even darker in the box. The box sat on four legs, so that there was a couple of feet of exit space at the bottom. We swam down and out, and then I signalled to Sandy to start making a slow ascent.

As we slowly climbed the quarry's granite walls there was no point pretending that this kind of diving was the same as the diving I had become used to. Because it was cold and dark the feeling was not of a world opening up, but of it closing down. There was the technical challenge, of course, of managing all the equipment you needed. But this kind of diving, it seemed to me, was all about exploration, and not the sensory experience of being weightless and free. Diving was the means by which you got to a place and back again. The destination, which most often in the UK was a deep wreck, was the whole point. You explored but you didn't fly. Could I be one of these blokes? Laden down with kit and diving in the UK all year round – maybe one week a year in the tropics? Diving, ever since I'd been a boy and held prisoner, was an escape from darkness. I knew without being told that, sooner or later, diving all the time in cold, dark water would bring on the old, deadly terror of confinement.

And yet, when I returned to the world in a bright December morning, and broke the surface of the water, my head was clear for the first time in months. The winter sun flashed in the granite. High above me in the cloudless sky, a black-faced peregrine falcon, its broad wings outstretched, its tail feathers splayed like a war bonnet, floated on the air.

I punched Sandy on the shoulder and pointed up.

'What?'

'Fawcon,' I said.

'Fuck on?' he said.

'I can't thpeak,' I said, 'ith too cold,' and, laughing, we swam on our backs to the waterside.

We helped each other out of our kit and stood shivering in our Thinsulates. Divers were getting in and out of the water all the time. You could hear them laughing and yelling. A voice travelled across the water: 'See that pike? As long as my leg, that was.'

'Your third leg maybe,' his buddy shouted back, 'after you've been in there.'

'Christ,' I said, 'they think this is fun.'

'Quite right too,' Sandy said. His thin, hawk-shaped face was white with cold.

'Fuck this,' I said, 'let's get out of here.'

Sandy had the heater on full blast all the way back to London. I said, 'I don't know what the hell I'm doing in this country. Never have. Why don't I just take off for good?'

'You know why,' Sandy said. 'Araba and the kids. You've done a good job with the girls. With Jay.'

'You reckon?'

'Kid hangs on your every word.'

'So what do I do?'

'Take responsibility. Do whatever you can to make things better.'

Sandy asked me a couple of times, but I didn't go back to Stoney. I thought about what Sandy had said. My hands were hard; I was working every day. I gave Araba money at the end of the week. I hadn't left the kids. But it had otherwise been a pattern in my life not to take responsibility for the things I'd done or caused to happen. If I said that I'd meant no harm – that all I wanted was the good time my special history made me think I was entitled to – that was no excuse at all. When I finally got around to writing to *Scuba Sport*, the biggest of the diving magazines, I didn't try to defend myself.

I said that I had behaved badly, and that this meant that my friend and partner, Garland Rain, had been left alone to guide a safari that, by anybody's standards except maybe Teddy King's, had descended into chaos long before Casey took his fatal dive. I explained that Garland had given extensive briefings before each dive. If people chose to ignore him what could Garland do? He couldn't be in the water with everyone at the same time.

I admitted that there was drug-taking on the trip, but I said that Teddy King encouraged this behaviour. I gave examples of the way Teddy abused the crew. I told the story of Suhail and the camera. I quoted the words Teddy used to describe Nawfal, Suhail, and the rest. I wrote how Teddy had prevented us from conducting shakedown dives. If anything, I said, Casey's death was the result of behaviour that Teddy King encouraged and participated in. Teddy himself had suffered a bad bend: why hadn't that been reported in *Banker*? If there'd been drug-taking on *Shang-Tu*, who'd brought the drugs on board? Whose boat was it? Was Teddy the kind of person from whom divers should be chartering boats? I stuck it to Teddy as hard as

I could, and I promised myself that I would meet the consequences of what I'd written, whatever they were.

≈ ≈ ≈

Jody had emailed me regularly when I first got home, once a
week, sometimes more, but I hadn't answered, and eventually
she stopped. Then, in mid-January, just as I had forgotten what
sunshine looked like, she wrote to me again.

She was leaving Egypt, she said. She was staying in Africa,
but moving further south. She'd taken her dive instructor
exams and got a job in Tanzania that started in a month. Was
I still here? How could I stand the cold? She was going to be
passing through London and would come to see me wherever
I wanted.

I thought all the proper things – how I was supposed to be
working to win Araba back, how Jody was only five years older
than Lee, how I was an old man next to her. But then I remembered her playing above a technicolor reef, or somersaulting in
the blue in glow-star showers of bioluminescence. I remembered the warmth of her body under the sun, her long young
brown legs wrapped around me, her fluffy lambswool locks
tickling my face as she kissed me, and I was excited and looked
forward to seeing her again. Tell me you would feel any differently about a smart and lovely young girl you had once made
love to at sea, on a boat out of sight of land in the warm
Arabian night, under a blood-red sky, popping with shooting
stars?

I met her in Brixton. At the Tube station a neat, grey-haired old woman wrapped in kente cloth, and sitting on a stack of large, plastic, multi-coloured bread baskets, sold bright, felt-tip pictures of animals and fish that were framed in tinfoil. She played paper and comb while waiting for people to buy her pictures, and shook her money box like a percussion instrument. Araba always talked to her.

When she saw my wife the old woman's dark face would blossom into a bright smile that showed you what she might have looked like when she was a girl, in the blue mountains of Jamaica maybe, and with a mother and father who loved and cared for her. The old woman might have smiled because Araba always gave her money, but I didn't think so. She would hold Araba's hands and the two women would talk for as long as I had the patience to wait.

'She relies on nobody but herself,' Araba told me, 'that's what I admire about her. She has no family. She lives on the street and keeps herself clean. She doesn't beg. All the money she gets comes from selling her pictures.'

Incense sellers burned strong-smelling sticks of frankincense that put me back in North Africa – Egyptians believed the smell of frankincense represented the life force, and it was a familiar scent in that country. Now when I think of Jody it's burning frankincense I remember. A Christian street preacher told me to change my ways or I was going to hell. A young black man asked a man old enough to be his father for money.

'You should be ashamed fi beg,' the older man said, 'a big bwoy like you.'

I allowed myself to remember how Jody had tasted, and the honeyed texture of her skin, but when she came up the station steps, I saw that her face was set against me, the way Araba's had been when I first came back from the Red Sea. The faces of these two women who had once shown happiness and pleasure when they saw me had become fierce masks. I didn't know what it was that Jody had come to tell me, but when I saw her I knew it was nothing good.

Jody's hair had grown longer and was properly sun-whitened, fat and bulky and wrapped under a head scarf so that only the long tails of her locks showed, but she also seemed changed in other ways that were both invisible and also somehow fundamental. She was a wearing an outsized cagoule and a pair of loose Carhartt jeans, and open-toed Birkenstock sandals. Her face and feet and hands were very tanned. It was raining, and her sandals and brown feet were soaked by the time we got to the pub.

The only person I knew in the Effra was an old Jamaican man called Step-Light. He'd worked as a merchant seaman for over thirty years. He had sailed all the oceans and great rivers of the world, and still walked like a seaman. In part because of the seafaring life he'd lived, I'm sure, Step-Light was divorced and lived alone, and he spent all his time in the pub reading science fiction novels. There were few places in the world he had not been, he told me, and he had strong memories of all the journeys he had made. The only way he could travel now was in his mind, so he remembered, and he read. But he didn't want to read about countries that were still bright in his memory, and that's why he loved science fiction. He got to travel to fabulous worlds he had never been to before. Step-Light had no money but talked as though he were a king. His clothes were so insubstantial they seemed to be a parody of clothes – thin cuffless shirts you could see through, ancient suit trousers that shone with wear. In all weathers he wore paper-thin boat shoes. He was always looking for somebody to buy him a drink. When he was drunk he yelled at you in a high, piercing voice, at the same time leaning in close and hitting you on the arm. He had an empty pint glass in front of him. Paperbacks with pictures of rockets and red moons on the cover spilled out of his pockets.

'Is this the place you told me about?' Jody said. 'I can't see what's so special about it. It's a dump. What do you come in here for?'

'He's in here all the time!' Step-Light shouted. 'My bald-head friend. He's in here more than me, and I'm here every day!'

I bought beer for me and Step-Light, and a juice for Jody.

'Don't you want something stronger?' I said to her. 'A beer?'

'No,' she said, 'I can't stay.'

'Thanks, son,' Step-Light said. He took a big drink of his lager and smacked his lips.

'If you can't stay, why did you want to see me?' I said.

'Wait,' she said. 'I've been thinking about how to say this. I didn't want to tell you at all but I guess you deserve to know.'

'Well, whatever the mystery is, I'm getting another drink.'

'Hey,' Jody said, 'don't talk to me like that. You don't get to be angry with me, not after what you've done.'

I put my hands up in surrender and went to the bar. I necked a rum at the bar and brought another beer back to the table.

'I had this stupid idea that you would come for me,' Jody said. 'I knew you were married, but you made me promises. I don't even know why I'm telling you this. I mean, do you even remember the promises you made to me?'

'Yes, Jesus. Of course. Yes.'

'Really? Then why didn't you write? You can't just drop people like they never existed. Do you sleep with somebody on every trip you work?'

'No.'

'I don't believe you.'

'I don't, it's true. I'm sorry.'

'Are you? I'm sure you're sorry sitting here now, but how often did you think about me after you got home?'

'A lot, to tell you the truth. I was in bits about you. I'd never cheated on Araba, and I guess—'

'You guess what? If you tell me you felt guilty I'll throw this drink in your face.'

'No, I don't feel guilty about sleeping with you, Jo. I loved sleeping with you. I feel guilty about hurting you. I know it's no good saying so now, but I care about you more than you think.'

'Is that right? Well, fuck you. Next time you and your wife have a rough patch I won't be available.'

She moved her empty juice glass around on the table. I wanted to put my hand on hers to stop it moving.

'We split up,' I said.

'Shit, really? Because of me?'

'Because of me, Jo.'

'And you're not diving? Jeez Louise, Kim, you'll go mad if you don't dive.'

'Yeah, well, that's my lookout.'

'Do you see your daughters?'

'Every week.'

'What's that like, not living with your kids?'

'My friend Sandy used to listen to me complaining about my life with Araba. He's been divorced for years. His kids are grown up and he hardly sees them. We were out for a day's diving somewhere and I was going on and on, and Sandy listened and finally he said, "You know all those things people tell you – be careful what you wish for, you don't know what you've got until it's gone, all that stuff? Well you might not believe me but they're all true."' I didn't say anything else for a bit, and then I said, 'Sandy was right, I think. Why are you here, Jo?'

'You mean you can't guess?'

'Are you pregnant?'

'Finally,' Jody said, 'he gets it.'

'Oh, Jo,' I said, 'oh, Jo, I'm sorry.'

'I'm not,' Jody said. 'I was, but I'm not now. I've got a job in a dive centre,' Jody said. 'I'll be behind a desk at first. They won't let me dive until after the baby's born. But after that we're going to travel all over, just like you said we would.'

'What do you want me to do? Come out to Tanzania with you?'

'Are you out of your mind? Jesus, Kim, what world are you living in? Are you saying you'll leave the kids you have here and live with me? Even if I thought you meant it, it would be a nightmare. I know you don't love me. It's true isn't it? You don't love me.'

Step-Light screamed at me from where he was standing at the other side of the bar.

'How's the kids, son? Them all right?'

'See?' Jody said. 'You can't answer me. You don't love me and your head would be wrecked and you'd be no good for us. It's too late. You've got no say in anything I do. Not now. Not when the baby's born.'

'You're telling me I can't see my own kid? You can't do that.'

'I can do what I want,' she said. 'This is what happens in the real world, Kim. You fucked me and dumped me and left me pregnant. That makes this baby mine, not yours. I don't want anything from you, and you don't get to see it unless I say so.'

'What, you don't want money?'

'No. Not even if I thought you'd ever come up with any.'

When I didn't say anything, Jody said, 'You never know when your life's going to change. I thought you were cute, and I wanted some fun. I was just a PA on holiday. Now look at me, I'm a twenty-year-old knocked-up dive guide going to live in Tanzania. A year ago I couldn't have told you where that was.'

She was looking down. There were still drops of rain on her headscarf.

'Are you hearing any of this?' She punched me on the arm. 'Are. You. Listening?'

'Yes,' I said. 'Yes.'

She looked at me, her eyes blazing. 'There's something else,' she said.

'What?'

'Teddy.'

'Teddy King? What about him?'

'You never understood how strongly he felt about me.'

I didn't care about Teddy King. I had saved his life and he had put me out of work, was how I looked at it.

'What about Teddy?'

I watched Jody struggle to find the right words to describe her friend and protector.

'Why did you do it?' she said.

'What do you mean? It just happened. Look, you hit on me first, remember?'

'I don't mean that. Why did you send that story to *Scuba Sport*?'

'I didn't write anything that wasn't true,' I said.

'Teddy went mad. Until that came out the boat was booked solid. Then you tell your side of the story, and suddenly people are ringing up from all over, cancelling. Parents are calling, stopping payment for trips their kids have booked, wives saying to husbands: you're not going on the drug boat, the party boat. Teddy needed the bookings to pay for the boat. He put all his money into it, everything, and he's lost the lot. He's talking about sinking *Shang-Tu*.'

'How do you know all this?'

'He's come out to see me a couple of times. He's not good.'

'Yeah? Well, tough shit.'

'Do you really not get it? There's only two things Teddy cares about. Me and his money. When Teddy was still in the hospital I went to see him. I told him I was staying out in Egypt and not coming back to work for him – that really hurt him. When he got out he sent me emails every day, love letters,

begging me to come back to England. He promised me anything, said he couldn't live without me. Then he came to see
me. What could I do? I couldn't tell him not to come. He'd
come and see me and he'd be off his head, and he'd cry and
beg me to come home with him. The last time he came out
was only a couple of weeks ago. It was awful. I had to tell him
it was you who got me pregnant. He went mental, Kim. He
says he's going to kill you and I believe he'll try. I need to get
him out of my life for good. He doesn't know I'm going to
Tanzania.'

'Come on, Jo. He's not going to kill me. I saved the bloke's
life,' I said.

'You didn't see him, and you don't know what he's like.
The emails he sends me now are sick. He talks about you all the
time: "I'm going to get the scrotey. I'm going to fucking kill
him. He can't do this to me."'

'All right, you say he's going to kill me. What am I supposed
to do about it?'

'I don't know, Kim. Go somewhere a long way away. That's
what I'm doing.'

'I can't do that, Jo.'

'I know. Just say you'll be careful.'

'All right, I promise,' I said. 'But Jo, please let me know
about the baby. You don't have to talk to me. Send an email.'

'Don't make promises to me. You've done that before,
remember. What you need to think about,' Jody said, 'is
Teddy.'

'The baby, Jo.'

She stood up.

'I used to queue all morning in the same internet cafe every day just to see if I had an email from you. And you never sent one. Not even just to ask me how I was doing.'

'You're having a baby, darling!' Step-Light screamed. He had a bunch of children who'd grown up while he was away at sea. I don't know if he saw any of them now.

'You didn't come to tell me you're pregnant,' I said. It wasn't a question. 'You came to tell me about Teddy.'

'If it wasn't for Teddy, you wouldn't have known anything,' she said.

≈ ≈ ≈

In the winter all building sites are the same. Cold and hard and dirty. The wind and the rain blows in through unfinished walls and empty windows. The noise goes through you. Dark when you get there and dark when you leave. My hands grew harder and were always cold. Everything is hard and cold. When I think about that winter I think about cold rain illuminated in the weak beam of my bike lights as I cycled to and from work in the dark. I'm not saying I invented work, and maybe biking home in the winter wind after eight hours spreading concrete is an accurate indication of your significance in the world, but what you want is the warm hands of a woman to hold you when you come in from the cold.

Every morning I went to work angry and the day would drag so that it seemed to me that time was going backwards, and I would stay angry and look for reasons not to go back to Sandy's. Maybe I'd hear some joiner I barely knew asking around to see if anybody wanted to go for a beer after work, and at half-four or five I would hit the nearest pub with a gang of working blokes, all of them ten years younger than me and single, thousands of miles away from homes in Oz, New Zealand, South Africa. I'd still be there when most of them had packed it in for the night, chewing my gums with the last of a buzz from a line of bad cocaine one of the guys had left out for me in the pub toilet.

'How ya battlin', mate? There you go, get it in to yer. Jeez you're fucking hardcore. Have you seen this guy? He's been all over the world mate, diving. Why are you bloody doing this for?'

Jody's baby was a secret that burned in me and it was hard to say nothing. Keeping the secret was hell, and knowing that I was not going to be able to see my son or daughter killed me. I remembered how Jay and Suzy had loved to sleep on my chest when they were tiny. I remembered the rightness of their weight on me. As if they made whole something I never knew was incomplete. The way they locked onto you. You were there and they were safe.

I tried not to think about it, but it was no use. Jody's baby was a consequence of my actions, as were my broken marriage, and what I knew, deep in my heart, to be the authentic threat of Teddy King. I didn't need Jody's word for it. I just had to remember Teddy on the boat, his violet-robed and hooded malevolence, to know the truth. I was going to have to face up to him, and everything else, sooner or later.

Araba came to see me one morning when I was at work. I got called down from the roof. She was waiting for me in the street outside the dark, unfinished house I was working on. I had found it impossible to look my wife in the face in the months since we had split, but her image was always in my heart. The feeling was like the one you have when you remember looking back at a place you have loved from a boat moving away, knowing that you won't go there again. Her hair was wrapped in a plain, tight dark scarf that smoothed out her face and took years off her, so that Araba looked like she had when I first met her. She wore a long, dark-wool overcoat and high, round-toed black-leather boots. Against these dark clothes her upturned face was luminous, the look she wore, one I didn't recognize at first, until I realized she was happy to see me.

'Hey,' she said. When she talked I could see the breath coming from her mouth.

'Is anything wrong?' I said. 'Are you and the kids all right?'

'Yes, we're all fine.' She smiled. It had been a long time since my wife had smiled at me. 'I like the get-up. Very macho.'

I was carrying my hard hat and wearing a safety harness over my dirty jeans and sweatshirt. My heavy boots were worn and stained with concrete and salt.

'Can we talk?'

'I don't know,' I said, 'we've not been very good at it so far.'

'Ha ha,' Araba said. 'Can you take a break?'

I could hear Paul yodelling a Merle Haggard song in the unfinished house.

'"But you see not the danger, she said,"' he sang, '"cos your silly with booze, she said."'

'Paul!' I shouted into the house.

'Yes, son!'

'I'm taking half an hour!'

Paul's big snowy head and red face appeared from out of an empty window frame. He looked at Araba. He saw me shifting my hard hat from hand to hand.

'That's dead on,' he said, 'a hundred per cent. Take as long as you like.'

His head vanished back inside the house.

I took an old newspaper from a pile of rubbish in the house, and we walked to Mount Street gardens in the rain. I put the newspaper on a bench near the church and we sat down.

'Do you want to go somewhere else?'

'What do you mean?' I said.

'The rain.'

'Oh, no, I don't care about the rain.'

'Liar.'

'I don't.'

'Are you coming to see the girls on Saturday?' Araba said.

'Sure.'

'What about Lee? You haven't seen her in a couple of weeks.'

'I know, I need to call her.'

'She wants to see you.'

'Is she all right?'

'She's fine. She misses you. I miss you too.'

'Do you ever think about the fact that we never did any courting?' I said. 'There were always kids. I think I was locked into the first promise I made to you – that I'd be a Dad to Lee and Jay. And then Suzy came along. We never really got to know one another.'

'Lee showed me that magazine with your letter in. That was

a good thing you did. It sounded like you were trying to say sorry to Garland. What happened on that last trip, we never talked about it. I know there was a girl.'

'How do you know?'

'I could just tell. I don't want to hear about her. I don't think I can stand any more surprises. Tell me about the rest of it. The man that died.'

I told her as much as I could. I told her about Casey and how he and Garland were opposite in every way except in the water, where they had an equal brilliance and might have been brothers. I told her about some of the things I'd seen. What I didn't do was tell her anything about Teddy King. I told her about my vision of Casey being eaten until there was nothing left. I said I couldn't get the image out of my head.

'What does it mean to you?' Araba asked. 'It'll probably be stuck there until you figure it out.'

'I know what it means – partly anyway. It means I'll never be able to find consolation in the things you believe in.'

'Like what?'

'Like heaven. We're here and then we're not. Thinking anything else is a kind of fear, I think. We're like butterflies that live twenty-four hours. It's just a question of scale.'

'I'm not asking you to believe in what I believe in.'

'You used to tell me you thought there was something missing in my life because I didn't believe in God.'

'I can say that and think it's true, but it doesn't mean you have to believe. And it doesn't mean I don't love you, which is what I think you think I mean. You said you partly understood what Casey's death meant – the dream you have about it. What's the part you don't understand?'

'We're here for no time,' I said, 'so what matters is how to live right. I haven't figured out how to do that.'

'That's where what I believe is useful,' Araba said. 'Come home, I'll help you.'

These were the words I had wanted to hear and didn't believe I ever would. I wish she'd said them before I knew about Jody. I knew I didn't love Jody, no matter how much I wanted to. Why didn't I? I thought she looked at the world the same way I did. She got what there was to get. She was at home in the sun and the water, and she was carrying my blood child. With Jody I might have had the life I'd dreamed of. But the plain truth is, my heart was taken by Araba. I loved a woman who could look at the sun or the water and simply not see the same things I did. This, and the fact that two of our three children were not my blood, didn't seem to matter. So what was stopping me saying yes, and taking her warm hand? I didn't trust myself to resist the call of the sea, when it came for me again as I knew it would. The pattern of our life together had been that I had run when things got hard and I had the water to run to. I loved Araba enough not to want to do that to her again. What I didn't know was if I loved her enough to stay for good. Plus, I've got to say, I wasn't sure that what she believed *was* useful. I think people need to get in touch with their own impermanence and stop relying on stories intended to compensate for, or flat-out deny, that absolute truth, however difficult that may be.

'I don't wear this harness every day, you know,' I said.

Araba smiled, even though I knew she had not heard me say yes.

'Not even if I asked nicely?' she said.

'Well, maybe.'

'Will you call Lee, and go and see her?'

'Yes.'

'When?'

'Today. After work,' I said, 'promise.'

Araba walked back with me to the house. When we said goodbye she kissed me on the cheek – her touch on me soft and warm, like the Red Sea. Later one of the Aussie carpenters said to me: she's lovely, can I borrow her?

'No mate,' I said, 'you can't.'

≈ ≈ ≈

When I was sixteen, and held against my will in a dark and stinking room, cable-tied by my bloody wrists to a cot bed that still held the vanilla scent of my girlfriend Dawn's dyed hair, it was as though any guiding star that I might have put a claim to had fallen from the sky, and the world turned black and stayed that way for many years.

Most of all, I can't forget the frozen terror of being unable to act. Just days before, it seemed, I'd been a boy playing on a golden shoreline, running whenever I wanted to into surf that dazzled endlessly under high southern sunlight. What happened, I thought, as I lay helpless and sweating in the terrifyingly sudden and personal, and, for all I knew, permanent darkness, what happened? There was nothing I could do except lie in my own dirt waiting for Dug to come back into the room. I owned only the smells and the taste of him. The pictures of what he had done to me already, and what he was coming to do to me again, ran in an endless screaming loop in my head. For years afterwards I believed that what had happened had been my fault. And so I dived to get clean, and to repeat the act of escape. To go back to that remembered and imagined boyhood where I lived in a magic kingdom of sun and water, free from harm, but also free from all responsibility. What I should never have forgotten is that the border separating what passes as a safe life from one of chaos and terror can be suddenly and easily crossed. Worse still: it's often not your choice as to which side of the border you're on. But if you aren't always responsible for the appearance of terror in your life and the lives of the people you love, sometimes you are.

Lee was sitting at a table outside Etta's Kitchen, a tiny Caribbean restaurant inside Brixton market. She was wearing a black beret over her blue hair, and a black leather bomber jacket with a fake fur collar turned up high. It was raining outside, and raindrops still shone like tears in the felt of the beret and in the soft black collar. When she saw me she jumped up from the table and came running to me. She wrapped her arms around me and buried her face in my chest. I could feel her shaking. I stroked her back and kissed the top of her beret. I'd known Lee since she was eight, a smart, funny, curly-haired kid who wasn't scared to tell me off, and who picked at the black polish on her fingernails, habits she had kept. I must have seen Lee crying when she was little, when she had bad dreams, or when she wasn't allowed another biscuit, but

I honestly couldn't remember. Lee's tears crashed through the sea-wall I'd put up around me, behind which I'd tried to hide from taking responsibility for the things I'd done. This is your daughter, I told myself, because unforgivably I still needed telling, this is your daughter crying. While I still held her in my arms, Lee butted me and started to punch me.

'Shit, Kim,' she said, looking up at me with her face all wet, 'what have you done?'

'Hey, Lee, it's all right. It's all right, baby. Come and sit down. Tell me what happened.'

There was a plate of calamari on Lee's table. She hadn't eaten any. She picked off a flake of batter and put it on the side of her plate, where there was a little pile of it.

'He must have been following me. I was walking home on my own. It was late. I was listening to music so I didn't hear anybody behind me. I made it easy for him. Shit. He put his hand over my mouth to stop me screaming and his hand was wet.'

'Who, Lee,' I said, 'who was following you?'

'This fat, fat man. Then I was in a car and he was driving. He drove with one hand, and was stroking and pinching me. I told him to stop and he punched me.'

Lee was crying hard, but there was defiance in her voice too. As though Lee had already decided that she would not allow these pictures to live in her head for ever.

'He punched me between my legs, hard so that it really really hurt, and then he grabbed me around the neck. He was crushing me and I was choking and I couldn't breathe. He hadn't said anything, and it was awful that he wouldn't speak.

I thought I was going to die and I'd never know why. Just like I was a bug that gets squashed for no reason. Oh, Kim, I was so scared!'

Lee unzipped her bomber jacket and turned down the collar.

'See?' she said.

'Oh, Lee,' I said, 'I'm sorry. I'm so sorry, baby.'

The rupturing impact of Teddy King's fat thumb and fingers showed in obscene and huge plum-coloured bruises either side of Lee's neck. I remembered the terrified drowning girl in Teddy's porn film. I remembered his stupefied look of desire whenever he saw Jody in her tight black wetsuit. Jody scared and pregnant, and hiding in Tanzania. The ring of bright bruises around Lee's neck was the final realization that while I thought I had taken him seriously, I had not taken him nearly seriously enough.

I held Lee close until she stopped crying. I breathed in the African Shea butter on her skin that was the smell of home, and that I had allowed to become unfamiliar to me.

'He let go, but he didn't stop touching me,' Lee said. 'We drove around some more. He still hadn't said anything. He seemed to forget about me almost, like he was stoned or something. He just drove, and his hand stopped moving on me, and just, just rested on me.'

Lee let out a deep breath to stop herself from crying again.

'And I was thinking, maybe if we stopped at a light I could maybe get out, you know? But then my phone rang. I knew it was Mum checking to see where I was. It made both of us jump, and it woke him up. He didn't need to tell me not to answer it. We were by the park and he stopped the car and reached across to open the door. He put his face right up close to mine and I could smell skunk on him. "Tell that scrote you call your dad," he said, "that your slag of a mum is next. Tell him I'll do much worse to her, and before I come to fuck him up for good I'll make him watch a film of me and his nigger wife." Then he pushed me out and said, "You're a nice-looking little bitch, for a half-caste."'

Lee couldn't stop herself from crying again.

'Ssshh,' I said. 'Ssshh, Lee, I'm sorry, but it's going to be all right.'

'How can you say that?' she cried. 'How do you know? What's going to happen to Mum?'

'Nothing's going to happen. Have you told her? Have you shown her the bruises?'

'No,' Lee said. 'Should I tell her? What should I do, Kim?'

'Don't say anything. Keep the bruises covered up. It'll be all right, Lee. I know what to do. Really, I know what to do. You won't see this man again.'

We sat not talking for a little while. A young woman brought Lee's bill and I paid it.

'Mum told me what happened to you,' Lee said, 'when you were my age.'

When I was Lee's age I got sucked into a world of boys and gangs where blood settled every argument. In those days I may even have believed there was glamour in violence. Maybe it's different if you have money, but all the boys I knew in our town were connected in a constellation in which your brightness was measured by how tough you were. Fighting was how we established our worth in the absence of anything else. I never felt I was tough enough, and was always trying to prove myself – not just to my brother Scott, who was the toughest boy in town – but to the man who even before I was born had decided I was not worth sticking around for. This was a near-fatal mis-judgement that, nearly twenty years later, I'd never been able to stop blaming myself for, even though I knew it was not my fault. It was just that I was a kid, and there was nobody there to look out for me. Ultimately, it led me to the alley behind Dug's garage, with a flaming molotov cocktail in each hand, only to be caught, beaten unconscious, and dragged by my red hair into his filthy house.

Dug waited until I woke up before he started raping me. Later he hacked off my long hair. I remember that each time he came into the bedroom where he held me prisoner, I could see into the front room. The only light there was came from a table lamp shaped like a biker riding a chopped Harley to nowhere. While Dug did what he did to me, I used to try and concentrate on the lamp, but it didn't do me any good. It's a terrible thing to say, but the worst thing was waiting for him. It got so bad in the dark, I almost wanted him to come. Just to get it over with. When I started thinking like that, instead of thinking how to stop him, I really began to hate myself.

When Scott and his friends broke into the garage to set me free, Dug rushed at the boys naked and raging, slashing at them with a broken cutlass, his chest tattooed with a massive skull and crossbones. His long black hair was tightly plaited, and the stale air around him was hot and sulphurous with the burning kitchen matches he'd stuck between his greasy braids.

Blood covered the walls and spread over the floor. Scott and the skinheads kicked Dug halfway to death, and then drove him out of town and dumped him in a place called Paradise Woods. Dawn was there, and after it was over she helped me on with a pair of jeans, and stroked my cropped and bloody head. I never saw her again after that.

I had tried hard to leave violence behind after that summer, but it seemed to me I had no choice now but to confront Teddy head-on. This was a bitter realization, but no more bitter than knowing I had failed to protect Lee. What I had to do would not be about misguidedly trying to prove my own value, but to keep safe those people I loved, and who loved and valued me, and without whom I would have long ago been lost.

'Nothing like that is going to happen to you,' I said to Lee.

'How do you know it won't?' she said.

'Because I'm not going to let it.' I said.

≈ ≈ ≈

A week later, outside the Effra, I watched a slim, mixed-race boy in white shorts and sparkling white knee-high socks, with a silver afro-comb standing up in his hair like a feather, play keepy-up outside a three-floor Victorian house. Garland was coming and I was waiting for him. A smaller child in pale pyjamas was hanging out from the open upstairs window with his head and arms hanging straight down like a dead bandit folded over the saddle of the sheriff's horse. The only light on in the house haloed the boy in the window. On the wall of the house somebody had painted, in the African unity colours of black, red and green, a mural of animals – giraffes, lions, elephants – going two-by-two into the Ark. A rastaman holding a staff, his hair wrapped tightly in a turban, was calling the animals in. It was night, and I stood at a distance from the house, but I could see that the colours of the mural were faded. The rastaman's once-luminous white turban was washed out to the colour of a distant winter moon.

'Let me out, Sky,' the little kid called down.

'Daddy told me not to,' his brother said.

'Oh, Sky,' the little kid cried, leaning even further out the window and stretching out his hands, 'let me fwee, Sky. Let me fwee.'

The three of us watched a thin black man in a torn shirt, and a broad brindle pitbull crossbreed showing pinky gums, with its tongue hanging out like it was too big for its mouth, walk past the pub. The dog pulled the man. The man held fast to the dog by a studded leather lead clipped onto a leather harness. The harness went across the dog's shoulders and around his chest. To shorten the lead the man had wrapped it round his hand. When they passed the boy, Sky, on the other side of the road, the dog turned his head to look at him. The dog's grin became wider, and he pulled even harder on the lead. Putting on a stone face, Sky flicked the ball up high, let it fall, caught it, and watched the dog pass before continuing the game of keepy-up.

The little kid in the window said, 'Ooh.'

'You know why the man so thin?' Sky said quietly to his brother as the man and the dog moved on ahead.

The thin man wore a huge, wobbling tam-o'-shanter held

in place on his head by an elastic belt with a snake clasp. The dog pulled the man so hard he had to hang back on the lead, and when the dog passed behind a car and became invisible it looked like the weight of the man's dreadlocks wrapped inside the vast tam was what was making him lean so.

'The man so thin,' Sky called up to his brother, 'cause the dog eat all the food.'

I'd come straight to the pub after work. I'd ridden south across the shining river, coloured beaten gold in the falling light. They'd found asbestos in the building I was working in. I've been given a white protective suit and mask and told to get rid of the poisonous material. While I worked, I'd been thinking about Teddy King.

Shang-Tu had been named after Kubla Khan's Mongolian summer palace, and like Khan's monument to himself it was where Teddy kept close by those things he loved and that mattered to him. Cocaine, pornography, skunkweed and lager. Men to bully and abuse. A girl to have violent fantasies over. Now, like Khan's fantastic estate, Teddy's floating palace was nothing more than a sacked ruin, a wreck somewhere at the bottom of the Red Sea. Teddy couldn't afford to keep it running, Jody had said. It was an insufficient consolation to me that *Shang-Tu* would be colonized and slowly become a living reef.

I thought about Araba, Teddy King, Jody and my different children. I called Sandy. He was watching the house. Araba and the girls were safe inside. A couple of days after I'd told him about Lee, Sandy had said, 'I've done some digging into this fellow King. A thoroughly nasty character, but then you know that. Specifically, a long history of drug dealing. Money laundering through legitimate concerns. Use of intimidation and violence carried over into business. I spoke to one chap he had beaten so badly he was hospitalized for a month. Chap said he thought he got off lightly. Said he thought King capable of far worse.'

'You don't need to tell me, Sand,' I'd said, 'not now.'

'You know there are people I could call to take care of this,' Sandy had said, his hawk face sad and serious. 'From the old days.'

'Thanks, Sand,' I'd said, 'but this is my problem.'

'Well, anything I can do.'

Garland texted me to say he was five minutes away. It was winter, dark and cold now the light had gone, but when he appeared at the crossroads by the pub, Garland had his shades pushed up into his hair, like it was always summer in his mind.

He was wide and tawny as always, his hair still sun bleached and shoulder length. He was wearing a worn, dust-coloured combat jacket, old jeans and a battered pair of work boots. He seemed to me to have aged more than was warranted. I put it down to hard work, the same way that, when I looked in the mirror, the accumulated years of labouring and partying had chased away the young man I had once been. I was pushing thirty-five, so Garland must have been forty. He hugged me, wrapping me in the ozonic funk he carried with him everywhere. Love dented his grey eyes.

'How'sit, bru?' he said. 'Long time.'

He'd been living on the sea-bed in a small pressurized

diving bell, working maintenance on the pipelines in the Baku oil fields in the south-west of the Caspian Sea, off the coast of Azerbaijan. He was coming to the end of a three-month contract.

'It's not a sea at all,' Garland had told me when I'd called him up a few weeks back. 'Did you know that? The Caspian Sea, it's a salt lake, the largest body of inland water in the world.'

'How's the work, Garl?' I'd asked. 'Is it tough like everybody says?'

'It's tough enough, Kim,' he'd said.

In the past I might have laughed at the way his voice had gone all high with the gas mix he was having to breathe down there. I knew that if I'd mentioned it, Garland, once again, would have confirmed that what he saw as my shallowness betrayed a fatal lack of understanding about how things really are in the place he never had any trouble in calling the real world. I wanted him to know that I was serious.

'I saw the magazine,' Garland had said. 'It meant a lot to me, that you'd do that. And I'm sorry that Lee had to get hurt before you opened your eyes. You know Teddy killed Casey. You've got that straight now?'

'What? How do you know?'

'I didn't know, but I suspected him from the off. So I went to Rowdy.'

'Rowdy? I thought he hated you. You got his sister pregnant and then dumped her.'

'That's what he told you?'

'Yeah.'

275

'And you believed him? You didn't think to ask me about it?'

'You never told me about it,' I'd said. 'I thought we were close, and I had to hear about your daughter from somebody else. What was I supposed to think? Why didn't you tell me?'

'I don't know. When it happened we'd only just met, and later, well, by then I guess I'd got too used to being your hero.'

'Really?'

'It meant a lot to me that you looked up to me. I figured that if I told you about the baby you'd think less of me. I really admired the way you looked after your kids. That's why I was so pissed off when it looked like you were going to muck things up with Araba. From where I was standing it looked like you had everything. You were the only one who couldn't see it.'

I'd held the phone tightly. I couldn't say anything for a while. I could imagine Garland far below the surface of the Caspian Sea, with all that cold water bearing down on him.

'What happened with Rowdy?' I'd said at last.

'I knew he must know something about it, but I also knew he'd never talk to me. But if he *had* seen something, I thought I could get to him if I talked to Tyler first.'

'Rowdy's sister?'

'Rowdy got what happened all wrong. When Tyler got pregnant she wanted to go home. I wanted us to bring the baby up on the road. For Tyler though, back then, what we were doing was just a holiday before she settled down. And she wanted to get away from her brother. Tyler thought Rowdy was always trying to run her life. So when she got pregnant she saw a chance to make her own decisions. Tyler's red-haired, but otherwise she's completely different from Rowdy. Tyler's level-headed, calm, peaceful. I loved her, and it was what she wanted, and that was it. It nearly killed me but I had to do what I said. I still love her.'

I thought of Jody and her unborn baby in Tanzania. How the feelings of guilt and powerlessness descended on me when I least expected them. Together with the sure knowledge that these women we had failed were better than us.

'After the Brothers I went out to Oz to see Tyler and my daughter,' Garland said. 'I was cut up. We'd fallen out, and Casey was on my mind all the time. I told Tyler about what had happened. Nobody had ever died when I'd been guiding. I couldn't stop thinking about it. I know he had all the bad habits, and I guess he could have gone at any minute, but I never believed it was an accident. He was too good in the water. And, like it or not, he was one of us. I had to find out, for my sake as much as anything else. I told Tyler that I thought her brother knew something about Casey's death and that I needed him to talk to me. I asked her to tell him the truth about what had happened between us, and see if he'd get in touch, but he didn't. I should have known he wouldn't.'

'What did you do?'

'What I should have done first. I talked to Bobby.'

'Bobby Ballet?'

'I knew Bobby had a big reason to have it in for Teddy – the money Teddy had taken from him – but I believed what he told me. Bobby said Teddy got hammered one night and confessed. Teddy told him he'd taken Casey's long hose as usual, when they were coming up from the wreck. Except Teddy thought it would be fun to let out Casey's air. So instead of breathing off the hose, he presses the purge button and Casey loses his air in about twenty seconds. God knows what Teddy was thinking. I suppose he thought they were near enough to the surface for Casey to swim for it, and Teddy would get a big laugh out of it, but something went wrong. Maybe Casey didn't realize what was happening until it was too late. I don't know, but once Casey started sinking Teddy panicked. You know Teddy was no kind of diver. He couldn't get close enough to give Casey any of his air or he was too scared to go after him. So he bolted for the surface. Then he pulled that stunt about having a bend.

'I still saved his life,' I said. 'It wasn't a stunt, it couldn't have been.'

'And I'm telling you that when he pretended to be bent, that was an act.'

'Mate, I was there,' I said. 'You weren't. How do you know that was a con? Because it didn't look like it to me.'

'I got in touch with the hyperbaric centre in Hurghada. Teddy got out of there with a clean bill of health. No evidence of a bend. Nothing wrong with the bloke.'

I saw Teddy falling through the water, still colossal but becoming smaller as he sank beyond sunlight's reach. His final breaths, rising in bubbles that seemed to contain the departing light of his life, brushing gently against my face as I swam down to him. It was possible he was faking it. Maybe I'd been too quick to want to redeem myself, and so saw only what I wanted to see. Certainly it was possible he'd been out of control on his ascent – it was more common than you'd think for unskilled divers to come up much too fast but get away with it.

And Teddy was quick-witted and cunning enough to know that by inventing a bend, he wouldn't have to immediately answer for Casey's disappearance.

'Bobby says Teddy's gone stone mad. His business has tanked. He's blaming you for everything.'

'That's what I hear,' I said. 'I didn't believe it at first but I do now. I've got to do something, Garl. You didn't see what he did to Lee.'

'That's what I figured, Kim,' he said, 'but I'll be honest, I'm going to have be looking you in the eye when we talk about this.'

≈ ≈ ≈

Garland had Bobby Ballet with him. Bobby wore his red wool Cousteau beanie, a navy pea jacket, jeans and Blunstone boots. His silver chain glittered on the surface of the black crewneck jumper he wore, and he was rubbing the shining medal of St Jude between his fingers. His long horse face was pale, but otherwise his expression was unreadable, as I remembered it had been when I had seen him last.

'Hello, Bobby,' I said.

'Kim,' Bobby said.

The pub was quiet. Step-Light sat at the bar reading a battered Michael Moorcock paperback. He was sober. When he saw me he said, 'All right, son,' and we shook hands. His light brown skin glowed under the pub lights. 'How's the family?' he said.

'Everyone's good, thanks,' I said. 'Garland, Bobby, this is Step-Light. These are friends of mine, Step.'

Everybody shook hands.

'Where you from, son?' Step-Light asked Garland, looking up at him.

'Durban, South Africa.'

'I used to sail with a big South African, years ago, in the merchant navy. Looked like you. He was a good bloke. You a sailor?'

'We're divers.'

Step-Light laughed. 'You mean you're crazy men like him,' he said, tapping me on the arm. 'I was at sea over thirty years and never got wet. No Davy Jones locker business for me!'

We talked to Step-Light about places we'd all been too, and then we left him to his book and got a table at the back of the pub.

'He's all right,' Bobby said, 'the old feller.'

'Mate, he's been everywhere at least twice,' I said.

'All right,' Garland said. 'Bobby, tell Kim what you told me.'

'You know the easiest way to bring drugs into London?' Bobby said. 'I mean big amounts, millions of pounds' worth? Straight up the river. There's no immigration or customs checks. You can arrive from pretty much anywhere in the world and you've got a hundred miles of river and just a handful of cops in boats. Before you set off a couple of divers bolt the stuff to your outside hull. Then your boat comes across the Channel and up the river. You moor up at some pre-arranged spot and then a couple of divers at this end swim up to the hull and take the stuff off.'

'So what?' I said. 'What's this got to do with Teddy?'

'Now Teddy's broke Bobby's been selling the idea to him,' Garland said.

'Teddy's been involved in smuggling before,' Bobby said. 'I told him I knew people in the stunt business who were also making big money moving cocaine. They ferry it around with all the stunt gear they move from job to job, country to country. I was just talking at first, but slowly I let him get the idea that this was something that was open for him to move into. Teddy's desperate for money just now. He said to me, "Get involved how?" I said my friends had come from Brazil to Rotterdam. They were coming to do a job in London and were flying in, but they'd stashed a load of gear on a boat that was coming here from Rotterdam. My friends were looking for somebody to take it off the boat at this end for a big payday. I told Teddy that could be me and him.'

'Why would Teddy listen to you?'

'Teddy thinks I'm his best mate,' Bobby said. 'To be honest, nobody else is talking to him. Casey's dead, thanks to him, and Rowdy's gone. Jody's disappeared. You know anything about that?'

I shook my head. 'No,' I said.

Bobby looked hard at me.

'Well, anyway,' he said, 'she's gone. Teddy reckons I'm the only friend he's got left, and that's how I behave. I honestly don't believe he thinks about the money he stole from me. If he remembers it at all it's as a laugh, ancient history. You know what he's like – he can do or say something outrageous to you, but if he laughs it off that's supposed to mean it's all over.'

'I still don't get it.'

'I've been in the dive shop ordering stock for months and hiding the gear and the invoices from Teddy. I've pushed him even further into debt than he realizes. I've got a cash buyer for all the stuff. It's worth twice what Teddy stole from me. The night before this happens, I give my guy the keys for cash. In the morning a van comes and empties the shop. The night we do it, I'm in the river with Teddy, at the spot I've told him the boat's coming to. You and Garland get in. Together we do him. Weigh him down so he'll never come up. We split the money. I'm out the country the next day, Garland too. You stay or go, it's up to you.'

'Whoa, wait a minute,' I said, and leaned forward across the table. 'You're talking about killing him? Garl, I never said anything about killing him.'

'What else are you going to do?' Bobby said. 'Do you think you can stop him any other way?'

'Garland?' I said.

'You hear about this oceanic whitetip shark in Sharm?' he said. 'Killed a German woman last week?'

'Yes, of course,' I said. 'She was killed swimming at Middle Garden, near Naama Bay.'

Bobby was sitting with his arms folded, expressionless again, not looking at either one of us.

'We've dived that reef loads of times, right?' Garland said.

'At least thirty times,' I said. 'It's a good spot for a shake-down on the way to Abu Nahas.'

'Ever see any sharks?'

'There's no sharks there, mate, you know that. Sharks have been unheard of at Middle Garden for fifteen years.'

'So how do you explain five shark attacks in one week? That's more than in the last twenty years put together.'

'They reckon somebody dumped a cargo of dead sheep in the water.'

'That's right. It's hard to imagine anything more stupid. Chumming on that scale and people wonder why there are suddenly killer sharks in the water. It's the same with Teddy. You put the meat in the water, Kim. You slept with his girl and ruined his business. Now you've got a man-eater on your hands. It doesn't matter what you want or don't want. There's only one thing you can do.'

Bobby unfolded his arms and looked at me.

'There you go,' he said. 'What you want to do is be thankful you're not on your own.'

'I know why Bobby's doing this,' I said to Garland. 'And I know why I am. Like you said, I have to. What I don't get is you.'

'You shouldn't ask a man that,' Bobby said.

'It's all right,' Garland said. 'How long did we travel together, Kim, close to ten years? Either one of us ever got in trouble in the water we knew the other would be close by. We fell out, sure, but in the end you backed me up. And that's one reason why Teddy's coming after you. That means something. I love your kids and I won't let anything happen to them.'

I believed him, because I knew him well, but I wondered if Garland had simply decided it was time to retreat, finally, and make his stand in the last of the wild places. I knew he saw himself finally making it out to the pure water. Everywhere else was lost to people like Teddy King. And I was pretty sure Garland needed money, that he would have sent everything he earned in the Baku oilfields to Tyler. He would need the money Bobby would give him.

'Won't somebody come looking for him?' I said.

'Who cares about him? Nobody, that's who. People will throw parties when they find out Teddy King's dead. Sooner or later one of his creditors is going to come looking for him, but all they'll find is an empty shop. People will believe what it looks like, that Teddy did a runner. The cops might look for him, but not for long. And we'll make sure his body won't come up.'

'Is that why you want to get him underwater?'

Bobby looked at me and he looked at Garland. He spread his hands. 'Where better?' he said. 'Where else?'

'What about you? You'll be the first person the cops look for.'

'Let them look,' he said, 'you think Bobby Ballet's my real name? You think I thought this up just now? That fucker took everything from me, and then made me work for him for nothing. I've been waiting years for a chance at him, and then you come along and manage to take everything that he cares about away from him, so that he's desperate enough to listen to me.'

Bobby reached into the pocket of his pea coat, pulled out a folded envelope and pushed it across the table to me.

'You get the money afterwards,' he said. 'This is to show you I'm serious. Garland's got one too. I asked him where you'd want to go.'

Inside the envelope was a one-way ticket to Mombasa, scheduled to leave in three days. I looked at the ticket.

'You'll have some money,' Garland said. 'You can send for Araba when you're set up over there. She'll come if she loves you. Trying to play both ends is making neither of you happy. If Araba doesn't come then maybe that's just the way things have to be. Same as it was for me. The price we pay for what we are.'

'And what's that?'

'Watermen.'

Later I called Araba on the phone she had bought for me when I got back from the Red Sea. I could see my wife, the phone and the strong hand that held it hidden by the riot of her hair, the crucifix around her neck catching the light, her head down and looking at but not seeing her flat brown planted feet. Garland was gone and I had carried on drinking. I wondered if my voice sounded thick. Araba would be studying. She would be surrounded by books about God with markers feathering the pages. Cold cups of half-drunk herbal tea forgotten as she concentrated on the meaning of passages of scripture. How to apply the lessons of compassion in her daily life. Part of her mind would be on me, worrying what I was doing. How, she would be thinking again, do I get this man to see the world as it is and not the dream he believes it to be?

'Come home,' she said, 'come home.'

Sandy was parked outside the electronic security gate.

'Everything all right?' I said.

'Tickety-boo,' he said, 'your family's safe and sound.'

≈ ≈ ≈

The day before my flight to Mombasa, and a free life on the Indian Ocean, I was awake before first light. I had come home a few days before. Araba wanted to try and work things out, and I wanted to be close by. I sat for a long time out in the yard under the cherry blossom tree that had not yet begun to flower, staring up at a half moon stamped like an icing decoration against a sky ribboned by dark clouds. Slowly the sky and the clouds were stained pink by the rising sun, and the brightness of the white moon diminished until it disappeared. I had woken from a dream where I was swimming with my children in an endless blue meadow of warm water, a place of everlasting refuge. Suzy came padding out of the house as the late-winter sun began to rise, and climbed up on my lap. She put her warm arms around my neck and kissed me. I kissed her back and ruffled my daughter's wild hair.

'Hey, Suze,' I said. 'What are you doing out of bed?'

Every morning since I had come home, either Jay or Suzy would look for me as soon as they woke up, I guess to make sure that I was still there.

'Why is the big bag packed, Daddy?' Suzy said.

'I'm going diving, Suze.'

Suzy sat up in my lap and folded her arms and pouted angrily at me.

'Dad!'

'Only for a couple of days, Suze.'

'Promise?'

'Yep.'

'Lee says your promises are a dirty word,' Suzy said.

'Mate,' I said, 'I'll be back before you're dressed,' and tickled her under the arms until she yelled.

Araba came out to the yard barefoot and sleepy, and wearing her faded red housedress that brushed the floor. She was holding two cups of coffee.

'Hey, mister,' she said, 'you two are up early.'

'Daddy's going diving, Mumma,' Suzy said, pulling a sad face.

'Only for the weekend, Suze,' Araba said.

She gave me my cup, and sat on the arm of the worn-down wooden garden chair. We drank the coffee, and watched the sun climb above the trees. I had told her that Garland, Sandy and I were driving to Sussex to spend the weekend diving.

'Is Garland staying in the country long?' Araba said.

'He's back to the oilfields next week,' I said, 'that's why we're diving. I don't know when I'll see him again, to be honest.'

Two lever-tailed magpies rose from the cherry blossom tree.

'Good morning, Mr Magpie,' Araba said, 'Good morning, Mr Magpie.'

On the other side of the garden, on Railton Road, a woman shouted, 'Fucking bastard, fucking bastard! Don't take it all, leave some for me you bastard, come back!'

Suzy hugged me tight. The soles of her feet were dirty and I brushed them off.

My phone rang. 'It's Sandy,' he said when I answered. 'I'm outside.'

'All right,' I said.

I shucked Suzy off my lap and went into the house and brought out the big dive bag. Suzy followed me into the house and back out again.

'OK,' I said, 'I've got to go.'

Araba said, 'Aren't you going to say goodbye to Jay and Lee?'

'Can you kiss them goodbye for me?' I said.

'Why, what's the matter?' Araba said.

'Nothing, I've just got to go, Sandy's waiting.'

Araba grabbed me and pulled me to her. The heat that she seemed to gather to herself as she slept was still in her when I held her. I pushed her hair off her face and stared into her honey-coloured eyes.

'What?' she said.

'Nothing,' I said. 'I love you, that's all.'

'We need to know if you're going to stay,' Araba said. 'The girls want you to. I want you to.'

'Lee always tells me not to make promises,' I said. I was thinking about Teddy King. 'You know I love you, but I can't say if I'm going to stay, any more than you can say that you'll always want me to. It's what you want now, but we haven't managed to live happily together so far. There's always been something else. For me it's still all out there.'

'What are you doing here now then?' Araba said.

'That's just it,' I said, 'there is only now.'

Araba looked hard at me. She let go of me. 'Be careful,' she said, 'and call me after the dives so I know you're safe.'

'All right,' I said, 'I'll call you.'

It was past midnight by the time Sandy drove us to the

river. We'd spent the day assembling and re-assembling kit on Sandy's floor and talking about what we were going to do. By mid-afternoon we had run out things to say. Somehow, Garland slept for a couple of hours. Sandy woke him when it was time to leave. Garland used a pay-as-you-go phone to call Bobby.

'All right,' he said to us, 'Bobby's with Teddy. They're heading for the river. Let's go.'

Sandy drove the old Volvo up Brixton Road towards Vauxhall. A black car with blacked-in windows pulled up next to us at a set of lights near the Oval. The driver had his window down, and I could see the badly drawn crown that was tattooed on his neck. A bass-heavy tune pulsed from the car and thumped against us, but it seemed to be playing at the wrong speed. When the lights changed, green marine light flooded into our car, and seemed to stay with us as we slowly approached the river. In the back, Garland, his hair tied back and tightly plaited, leaned forward and touched me on the shoulder.

'Are you all right?'

Sandy looked across at me.

'Yes, mate,' I said, 'for sure.'

Sandy parked down a slipway to a little beach near Vauxhall Bridge. We got out of the car and walked down to the dark foreshore. The river was at low tide. The muddy beach was littered with driftwood, beer cans and broken bottles, milk cartons, a yellow rubber glove, a black shoe without a heel. There was a high wall above us on our left side. Set in the wall at the high-tide mark there were three stone lion heads. The one nearest to the road was partly hidden by beach stones. As the beach went down to the water you could see that the lion head nearest the river had a mooring ring in its mouth. The middle lion's ring had broken off. Below the high-tide mark the walls were sticky and wet with green algae. Low muddy waves broke gently on the beach. The slipway and the beach were next to the Secret Intelligence Service building. It seemed crazy to be getting in there, but like Garland said, there was nothing illegal about diving, and it was a public slipway.

I looked out to the river, where Teddy King was waiting at the bottom of a line for a boat full of drugs. Bobby had said he would be with him. Bobby had said that he'd have a halogen light down there bright enough to light up a stadium. Garland and I were to swim out to the buoy that marked the line, and descend in the darkness, until we saw Bobby's light.

'Teddy will be able to see us coming,' I'd said.

'As soon as I see you two,' Bobby had said, 'I'll turn the light on Teddy. He'll be blinded, and you'll be on him before he knows what's happening.'

'Just make sure you don't put the light on us,' Garland had said, 'we want to be able to see what we're doing down there.'

'Don't worry,' Bobby had said, 'it's all organized.'

We got the kit out of the car and put it on the beach. I was in a kind of trance state. I didn't think about what I was going into the water to do. I did the next thing that needed to be done. That way I figured what was going to happen would take care of itself. We put our drysuits on over the Thinsulate undersuits we were already wearing. We kept our keys and phones and wallets in the pockets of our undersuits. Sandy helped us on with our tanks.

Garland showed me what looked like a steel hunting knife with a fixed blade maybe five inches long.

'Have you got your knife?' he said.

I carried a sharp, serrated line-cutter attached to the webbing of my buoyancy jacket.

I nodded.

'No torches?' I said.

'No torches, no light sticks. Keep hold of the line on the way down and we won't be separated. Keep going until you see Bobby's light. That'll be enough to see what we're doing. All right, come on. Hopefully we'll see you back here, Sandy. If we have to get out anywhere else we'll call.'

'All right,' Sandy said, and shook hands with us.

We waded into the black water carrying our fins. The coldness of the river took my breath away. When the freezing water was deep enough for us to float, we sat and put our fins on. Then we swam slowly on our backs to the buoy.

I could see traffic pounding over Vauxhall Bridge. I thought about Cousteau and the electric street-lights and trolley buses at Le Mourillon, where he had first dived. Visions of the countless numbers of people murdered and dumped in this river over the centuries came into my head. People who had jumped broken-hearted from the bridges and were drowned. People in over their heads, in more ways than one. I saw the ghosts of London watermen who made a living by pulling dead people out of the river and robbing them. I remembered hearing about somebody finding the torso of an unknown African boy washed up somewhere near Tower Bridge. People were lost to the river all the time, not just in the city's waters, but from the towns and villages along the Thames Valley. How many bodies were never found? How many dead people were here in the water with me?

Garland took his regulator out and spat.

'Are you ready?' he said.

'I'm cold, Garland,' I said.

'We've got to go now,' he said, 'or not at all.'

I looked at him. Like me, he wore a black hood. A black mask covered the rest of his face. The river water made moving shadows against the mask. I couldn't see the golden cast. Garland didn't need to be here, Teddy wasn't coming after him. But here he was, beside me in the freezing river.

'You're right,' I said, 'let's go.'

Garland nodded at me, and put his regulator back in his mouth. We both held up a fist with the thumb pointing up, and then turned the fist so that the thumb was pointing at the water. We gave each other the OK sign. We dumped the air from our buoyancy jackets, breathed out and slowly submerged below the surface of the river. Civilization vanished, and we headed into the dark wilderness. At first there was the barest amount of surface light penetrating the water, but too soon the darkness became complete, and I was enclosed in the cold black immensity of water.

I tried to keep my breathing steady, but my heart's thumping was loud in my ears. I kept contact with the line by circling it with the thumb and forefinger of my right hand. As I descended I could feel the line playing out through the loop

I had made. There would be a lead weight at the end of the line, somewhere down below me where Teddy was waiting, and if I pulled on the line and moved the lead, he would know that somebody was coming down.

The long black descent went on and on. I could feel Garland in the water, but I couldn't see him. Down and down I went in the freezing water. The river wasn't deep. How could it take so long to travel such a short distance? I began to feel as though I had been falling through blackness for ever, and then I finally crashed down. The river bottom was made of nothing solid, just mud and sludge, and when I hit it I began to be sucked into what felt like the accumulated muck of centuries.

Where was Bobby's light? Had we moved the shot-line after all? I put my hand up to my face but I couldn't see it. I didn't dare turn on the torch I'd brought with me. The river mud sucked at me like it was alive. Freezing water made me numb. I couldn't feel or see anything. I was being swallowed by the river. My body was sinking into the muck. Soon I would be deep enough for it to reach my mouth. Shit shit shit, where was Bobby? Where was fucking Bobby! I reached for Garland but he wasn't there. In my head I started screaming. Get me out of here! Get me out of here, Garland!

Teddy King, wearing a bright necklace of red and green chemical light sticks that illuminated the black water like fireworks in a winter sky, appeared out of the darkness and came flying at me, a massive dive knife in his hand. The light sticks lit up Teddy's face, and I could see his mad blue eyes, staring wildly and magnified behind his mask. I could hear him roaring at me through his mouthpiece. Teddy swung at me and his knife tore into my right hand, punching through the freezing numbness, and then he was on top of me, his face haloed by green and red lights. He grabbed me by the throat and pushed me further and further down into the mud of the river. He was burying me. He ripped the regulator out of my mouth. I bit down on the compulsion to open my mouth and take in the black river water. Teddy began squeezing my throat. My chest felt like it was going to cave in. Everything inside my head was red. I wanted to hold on for longer but I couldn't. There was no choice. I had to open my mouth, the same way Dug had forced me to open my mouth. The same darkness. The same freezing terror. Except that what I had wrongly believed then to be my annihilation would now be real, and this made all the difference. I began to die. Everything emptied out of me and began to go away. I saw my children. I said goodbye to them. I closed my eyes.

Suddenly, Teddy relaxed his grip on my throat. My hand found my regulator and I jammed the mouthpiece in and breathed air. I opened my eyes. In the darkness I could see that Garland had pulled Teddy King away from me and that he was fighting with him. They were up to their waists in the muck, and their heads and shoulders were framed in the lights made by Teddy's bright necklace.

Teddy slashed at Garland, and Garland tried to keep out of range and get hold of Teddy at the same time. With my good hand I felt for the small, sharp line-cutter I had brought down with me. My fingers were numb, and inside a thick glove made thicker by the river's mud, but somehow I managed to get the knife free. I pulled myself out of the sucking mud and flew to

Teddy and grabbed his air hose. Garland's big hunting knife flashed as he hacked at Teddy. Teddy kind of crumpled into the mud, but he was still stabbing at Garland. Garland tried to hold Teddy still as I sawed, one-handed, chopping at the hose with the serrated edge of the line-cutter. Teddy clawed and slashed until my knife finally bit into the hose, and great sheets of air bubbles exploded from the opening I had made. Teddy fought as the air bubbles first roared from him, and he fought even when his air diminished to a thin stream, and then slowly stopped. The only sound I could hear was the thunderous noise of my breathing. All that remained visible of Teddy was his pale, dead, hooded face in the muted glow of the light sticks around his neck. It seemed to me, although I could not be sure of anything then, that I somehow saw Dug where Teddy lay, until I leaned in and cut the string of light sticks and ripped them from Teddy's neck, and both of them were erased.

We finned away with the current, leaving Teddy buried in the muck of the river's bottom. I held Teddy's necklace ahead of me to light our way. Slowly we rose in the black water until it began to lighten. We surfaced at the Lambeth River Fire Station. Rain was falling. City lights were gold on the water. Buses and cars thundered over the bridges. I took out my regulator and gulped down air. I pulled the glove from my wounded hand, and it was full of blood. I put my hand in the river and let the water wash the blood away.

'Let's get out of here,' Garland said.

The fire station was a long grey prefabricated single-storey building. There was a pontoon bridge leading from the station to the riverside and the road. There were pilings we could climb to get up on the building and to the bridge.

'Garl, I'm stabbed, mate.'

'You'll be all right. I'll help you.'

'What about the kit?' I said.

'Dump it in the river,' Garland said.

We got out of our kit and floated it on the water. We watched the tanks and buoyancy jackets catch the current and begin to move slowly downstream. Garland tossed the hunting knife into the water.

'Put yours in too,' he said, and I did.

'What if somebody finds them?' I said.

'Good luck to them.'

I was still holding the bright lights that had been around Teddy's neck. I looked at them for a moment, and then threw them into the river. Garland and I watched the lights float on the surface of the water, and then they slowly began to sink down into the blackness. We watched until all the light was gone, and then we turned away from the river, and Garland put my wounded arm over his shoulder and helped me climb up to the station. Nobody saw us. We crossed the pontoon bridge and were on the embankment. Garland pointed across the road to a big church.

'In there,' he said.

≈ ≈ ≈

Garland and I sat together for warmth on an old bench in the garden of St Mary's church, under a stone tower that had looked to heaven for nearly seven hundred years. The tower had a huge stained glass window showing Christ standing under an irradiating sun. Below the figure was written: 'Holy Holy Holy – Lord God of Hosts. I am He that liveth & was dead. And behold I am alive for evermore, Amen.'

We were hidden from the road by two myrtle bushes and by sweet briar that grew on lattices made from the cut-away branches of a medlar tree. It was still raining, and the rain washed away the mud and the stink of the river from our dry-suits, and the blood from my hand. The rain brought out the smell of winter roses and jasmine and lilies, and the cleansing scents of lavender and sage. On the Lambeth Road side of the garden were plane trees and a high fence. I could see the lighted sign of a Novotel hotel, but unless you were a lonely traveller, unable to sleep and looking down into the garden from one of the high rooms, nobody from the outside would be able to see us. And if they could, I thought they would believe that Garland and I were a pair of homeless men taking shelter from the rain. I pressed down on the deep wound. A stream of blood spread out on my hand. I held my hand out and watched as the blood steadily dripped and was washed away by the rain.

'Where the fuck was Bobby?' I said, looking at the blood fall.

'He's gone, Kim, he's done us. Bobby used us to kill Teddy. He got Teddy down there to kill you, I reckon. Of course he didn't tell him that I'd be with you. Bobby went down there with him, just like he told us he would, but as soon as we showed he ran for it. He'll have come up downstream some-where. The only risk he took was if Teddy somehow managed to kill both of us. If he had done, all Bobby needed to say to

Teddy was that he didn't know I'd be with you. Either way, Bobby's got away free and clear. Jesus,' he said, 'we just killed a man for a couple of plane tickets.'

'Don't say that, Garl. You saved my life. I'm just sorry you didn't get the money.'

'People like us never get the money, Kim.'

'Do you think Bobby'll drop us in it?'

'No. Bobby's long gone. The only people who can say Bobby was here tonight are us, and why would we? It's the same the other way round. Bobby's not going to turn us in to the cops. He's banking on us keeping quiet.'

'You don't think the cops will be waiting for us at the airport then?'

'No.'

Garland pointed to a solid stone tomb decorated with a sculpted flame that I could just make out in the darkness.

'You know who's buried in there?'

'You know I don't.'

'William Bligh.'

'Captain Bligh? Mutiny on the *Bounty*?'

'That's him.'

I knew Bligh had been sent to the South Seas to collect breadfruit plants from the Pacific Islands and transplant them to the West Indies. Cheap food for slaves, Araba told me. To my mind Bligh was a tyrant, a monster like Teddy King. Fletcher Christian and the mutineers who found Paradise in Tahiti were the heroes of the story. After nearly a year of harsh discipline at sea, the crew of the *Bounty* spent six months in the sun of Tahiti after landing in October 1788. The stories the sailors had heard about the sexual freedom of Polynesian women turned out to be true. Many of the men took wives. The *Bounty* was off the coast of Tofoa, three weeks after leaving Tahiti, when the crew rose up in arms. Bligh was cast adrift with eighteen loyal crew members. The majority of the mutineers stayed in Tahiti until they were captured by HMS *Pandora* in 1791. In September 1789 Christian led a small band to the far southern edge of the Pacific, where he found the uninhabited island of Pitcairn. They remained undiscovered for nearly twenty years until Captain Folger of the American ship *Topaz* chanced upon the island. Folger met the one surviving mutineer, John Adams, as well as Christian's son.

Garland's hair was plastered across his face. The rain fell on the river and the streets and on the graveyard. Every so often Garland squeezed out the rain from his long plait. Even though it was very late, there was constant traffic going by on the Lambeth Road.

'You'd be one of the mutineers for sure,' Garland said.

'And you wouldn't?'

'When you think about the story I bet you think about the mutineers getting a tan on. One long beach party. All those brown girls to have sex with, like fruit on the ground. What you need to think about is Bligh navigating nearly six thousand kilometres after he was cast adrift. Can you imagine that? Forty-one days in an open boat. No food or water more or less. Navigating without charts from Tofoa to Timor. You need to value that. Not the mutineers of this world.'

'All right, Garland,' I said, 'I hear you.'

'You know what really happened on Pitcairn? Five mutineers were murdered by the Polynesians who were with them, because the sailors had taken their women. Christian was shot in the back. The natives were then killed in retribution. One mutineer was executed by his mates. One died a natural death. Another tied a rock around his neck, chained his wrists, and threw himself off the island into the sea. There's your island paradise.'

'I need to get out of here,' I said.

'All right, I'll call Sandy to come and get us.'

'What are you going to do?'

'I'm going to get on that plane. What about you, you going back to Mombasa?'

'Maybe one day,' I said, 'but not now. Maybe when the girls are grown we'll all get out there.'

'All right,' Garland said, 'good. That's what I hoped you'd say.'

'What are you going to do about your daughter?'

'All I can do is hope they come and visit when I'm settled.'

'You know Jody's having a baby?' I said.

Garland looked at me. 'No,' he said, 'I didn't.'

'But you told Jody I was going home, and you told Araba about me and Jody. That's why Araba kicked me out. You must have called her from the airport. It's all right, I understand why you did it.'

'I was hoping it would wake you up. Will you see the kid?'

'She said no,' I said. 'But things can change, you know? At least she told me.'

Garland hauled himself up. He pulled me up next to him and hugged me. He held me tight, and put his big hand on the back of my head.

'Brothers of the sea,' he said.

'Yes, mate,' I said, 'always.'

'Jesse,' he said softly, 'my daughter's name is Jesse.'

≈ ≈ ≈

My son Casey lives with his mother in Dar es Salaam. The boy comes to me in my dreams, at the place where the land meets the sea. A fair-haired imagined child, brown-skinned, in shorts forever, playing with his mother in the low tawny light of an African shoreline in late afternoon. I go to him, scared that he won't know me, just as I would not recognize my own father, nor Garland Rain his. Casey runs in and out of the surf. He comes close and turns to me. We stay like this. We come no closer to each other. I think the sun is in his eyes and he can't see me, but I can see that we look alike. In the future this is how we will recognize each other.

Sometimes in these dreams about my son – although not so often now – it's Dug and Teddy King, of course, who come out of the water at me. Not the warm Indian Ocean where my son is found. They surface from the cold black Thames, and stand dripping at the riverside in cartoon-zombie poses, hands reaching for me. Both are corroded by unknown chemicals in the river water. Their wounds are alive with eels that are feeding on them. Dug stands naked, holding a cutlass, his head haloed in a sulphurous haze. Teddy carries a huge dive knife in his hand. They are always together, and sometimes it's Dug whose size is overwhelming, and Teddy who is naked and tattooed. I know I have to fight them, and get them back under the water for another day. The fight takes hours. Garland is not there to help me. I wake up exhausted.

Each night Dug and Teddy are further diminished by the poisoned water so that I almost believe they will, in time, be reduced to nothing and I will be free of them.

Will Teddy King's body ever be found? Who knows. Maybe he'll end up drifting all the way out to the Blackwater Estuary, or he'll be washed up one morning on Canvey Island, where he was born. And if he does float up from where Garland and I left him, will anybody come asking questions? I don't know. I don't know if Garland, out somewhere with Tyler and Jesse, is haunted by Teddy King.

What I do know and can never forget is that this life I live now, the life Garland saved for me in the black water of the River Thames, could end with a phone call, or a knock at the door. Araba and I are still together. Maybe I've finally killed the wildness in me, I don't know, but like Fletcher Christian and his ill-starred band of mutineers, I live a fugitive life.

It's Sunday and I've got the day off. I'm still labouring. Three nights a week I teach swimming at the local pool. Mostly to kids Lee's age who've never learned. Sometimes I'll take a couple of tanks to the pool and let the kids have a go. Kids love diving. Lee's learning to dive. I'm not sure that she likes it too well, and mostly I think she's sticking with it because she loves me. I tell her wait until you start travelling, then you'll be happy you learned. I'm going to start teaching Jay and Suzy this summer, when Sandy's outdoor pool opens and I go to work there again. Most weekends I'm up at Stoney. Sandy has his instructor ticket now, and we turn over around half a dozen new divers a month. It makes for a long week, but I'm trying to stay on top of the bills.

I sit under the cherry tree in a blaze of spring sunlight. Showers of blossom have fallen while I have sat here. There are handfuls of blossom petals at my feet and in my lap. I have held them against my face, put them in my mouth and tasted them. I don't know that I'm doing this. Thousands of insects that will be dead tomorrow, dance in the columns of sunlight that come through the branches of the tree. Bees work in the white bell flowers of Araba's comfrey plants.

I rub the fleshy part of my right hand with my left. There is a scar there where Teddy's knife went in, about halfway between the base of my index finger and the base of my thumb. Teddy must have cut a tendon or something, because the index finger is numb all the way to the tip, and has been ever since we killed Teddy. I told Araba I did it to myself.

The big electronic gate bangs. My family are back from church. Suzy is carrying the fluffy shark I brought back for her from the Red Sea. Her hair is wild and uncontained. She runs across the yard and drops the toy shark in the dust.

'Oh sugar,' she says, 'sorry, Sharky,' and bends to pick up the shark and brushes dust from his head.

'Where is everybody?' I say.

'They're coming, Dad,' Suzy says.

A woman is singing. I can't hear the words but the melody is sad, and I feel compelled to listen. The singing is coming

HOWARD CUNNELL

from one of the top-floor flats or maybe even the roof. I look up at the building where I live – the red-brick arches and blue metal railings. There are flowers – dog daisies, poppies, stargazer lilies – in pots and boxes along the walkways. The sun hits the high windows. There's washing on the roof. If this were all underwater I could fly up the side of the building, or maybe swim in a zigzag up along the walkways, and see who is singing.

Here comes Jay. She's hot and sweaty from playing football in the church hall after the service. She storms into my arms. She climbs up on my lap even though she's getting too big. I put my hand through Jay's short black hair. I blow a raspberry on her hot neck. Jay picks up cherry blossom petals and throws them in the air.

'Dad,' she says, as the blossom falls and Araba and Lee, smiling, come into the garden, 'what have you been thinking about all this time?'

Acknowledgements

My friend Walter Shane wrote and recorded '1997 XF11'. I first heard him sing it on the beach at San Augustinillo, on the Pacific coast of Mexico, in the winter of 1999. I am grateful to Walter for allowing me to reproduce sections of the lyrics here.

Adjoa Andoh, Jeremy Cole, Dexter Dias, Rob Dinsdale, Matthew Loukes, Jeremy Reed, John Williams, Hannah Westland and Duncan White all read this book as it developed, and offered helpful criticism. Thanks also to the Leverhulme Trust, Meg Jensen and David Rogers at the Kingston Writing School and Andrew Franks and Tom Jenkins at Soul Bay Press.

Thanks to all my teachers, students and companions at Ocean Quest and Karma Divers, especially: John Bateman, Maggie Goodman, Kevin Grant, Geoff Mason-Brown, Mike Polley, Steve Northwood, Jeremy Quinn and Gordon Shaw. The late and much missed Stefano Albertario was a good friend and a wonderful diver. Nick Long, my long-time dive partner, helped fill in the gaps in my knowledge of diving technique and history. Any technical or procedural mistakes that remain are my responsibility or the responsibility of the characters who make them.

I am deeply grateful to my agent, Patrick Walsh, for his faith and skill, and to everybody at C&W especially David Llewelyn. Huge thanks also to Paul Baggaley at Picador. The careful and insightful work of my editor Kris Doyle has been invaluable.

Pierre-Joseph Proudhon wrote, 'Whoever lays his hand on me to govern me is a usurper and a tyrant, and I declare him my enemy,' in *Confessions of a Revolutionary* (1849).

The book Kim remembers in which 'death was hard to imagine when you had these blokes dancing themselves across the bay with smiles on their faces and sun in their hair,' is Tim Winton's *Breath* (2008), while Robert Stone's *Bay of Souls* (2003) is where Kim reads that, in performing the 'necessities of diving', we may become a 'different animal in a different element'. I first read about Roy Miner's 1923 coral-collecting trip to the Bahamas in Trevor Norton's *Stars Beneath the Sea* (2000).

I am happy to say a special thank you to Kieran Moroney for his practical help, and to Daniel Simpson for his wise encouragement. Throughout the four years this book took to write, Kester Aspden has been a constant source of support, and know-how.

Howard Cunnell has a Ph.D. from the University
of London, and has been a Leverhulme Fellow at the
University of Sussex. He is the editor of Jack Kerouac's
On the Road: The Original Scroll, which the *New York
Times* described as 'the living version for our time'.
A former professional scuba diving instructor,
he lives in London.